THE DEEP WELL

HarperCollins Children's Books, a division of HarperCollins
Publishers, 195 Broadway, New York, NY 10007

HarperCollins Publishers, Macken House, 39/40 Mayor
Street Upper, Dublin 1, D01 C9W8, Ireland

Quill Tree Books is an imprint of HarperCollins Publishers.

The Deep Well
Copyright © 2025 by Laura Creedle
All rights reserved. Manufactured in Harrisonburg, VA, United States of America.
No part of this book may be used or reproduced in any manner whatsoever
without written permission except in the case of brief quotations embodied
in critical articles and reviews. Without limiting the exclusive rights of any
author, contributor, or the publisher of this publication, any unauthorized use
of this publication to train generative artificial intelligence (AI) technologies
is expressly prohibited. HarperCollins also exercises their rights under
Article 4(3) of the Digital Single Market Directive 2019/790 and expressly
reserves this publication from the text and data mining exception.
harpercollins.com
Scripture quotations taken from The Holy Bible, New International
Version® NIV®. Copyright © 1973, 1978, 1984, 2011 by Biblica,
Inc. Used with permission. All rights reserved worldwide.

Library of Congress Control Number: 2024058714
ISBN 978-0-06-335913-0

Typography by Joel Tippie
25 26 27 28 29 LBC 5 4 3 2 1

FIRST EDITION

THE DEEP END

LAURA CREEDLE

Quill Tree Books

PROLOGUE

APRIL DIDN'T REMEMBER much from her time behind the wall, but she did remember the deep hole.

The deep hole dwarfed everything else. Even the fortress-like stone wall surrounding the compound—which seemed to stretch into the clouds—was nothing compared to the deep hole.

The deep hole was the Ojo de Cristo copper mine, a sprawling canyon carved into the surrounding mountains. The sides of the mine were stepped down so that at one time trucks could wind a spiral path to the bottom of the hole and back out again, laden with ore.

They were mining for secrets from the center of the earth, drilling a borehole down deeper through the earth's crust than anyone had before.

Her dad was the drilling foreman at the Ojo de Cristo borehole. While he worked, April and her mom spent most of their time in the den, watching DVDs, eating crackers, and drinking ginger ale, her mom occasionally raising her head to dry heave into a small metal pan she kept by the couch. April didn't know then, but her mother was pregnant with her sister, Jules.

Her favorite movie was *Kiki's Delivery Service*. April had watched it so many times, she began to think of it not as a movie but as an instruction manual. Her little pink bicycle with the training wheels was not a bike but a broom. Like her dad, she had important work to do, deliveries to make. Her mom smiled when April told her that she was going to make a delivery. "You can bring your dad his coffee," Mom would say, handing April an imaginary thermos.

They lived in the biggest of the workers' bungalows near Robert Steenkampf's sprawling hacienda. Mr. Steenkampf, her dad's boss, was a pale, thin-lipped old man. Everyone called him King, his crown a crisp straw cowboy hat to keep the harsh New Mexico sun off his face.

April wasn't allowed anywhere near the open-pit mine.

Of course not.

The voice was a giggle at first, like a whisper on the wind. It sounded so much like Kiki that April imagined Kiki was calling to her, begging her to be part of her delivery service. All she had to do was fly.

That day, April left Mom asleep on the couch and went out to the backyard to ride her bike around the patio. She heard the voice call her name, clear as day.

April.

She left the patio through the back gate, searching for the source of the voice.

April.

It was stronger then, coming from the direction of the open-pit mine.

Kiki, calling her to fly.

April wasn't supposed to go near the open-pit mine, but Mom was asleep. She wouldn't know.

There was a wide, dusty asphalt path from the Steenkampfs' big house that led to the drill site and around toward the open pit. It joined up with a driveway that ran through the front gate and out onto the road.

April rode her bike on the path toward the open-pit mine and the voice. As she rode down the path, Dr. Travers-Steenkampf, King Steenkampf's wife, drove by on the golf cart she used to shuttle back and forth between home and the lab. Dr. Travers-Steenkampf wore kitten heels, a white lab coat over a sleek red dress, her blond hair in a tight bun on the back of her head. April worried that King's wife would stop her from completing her mission, but Dr. Travers-Steenkampf barely shot April a glance as she guided the golf cart in a wide semicircle around the bicycle.

Her golf cart, her slingback shoes, her red lips a shade darker than her dress were etched into April's mind. She was beautiful and cool, such a contrast to her mom, heaving into a metal pan on the couch, her hair unwashed.

Dr. Travers-Steenkampf died weeks later in the accident, along with the rest of them.

Along with her dad.

The closer April got to the open-pit mine, the louder the voice became. And the voice said one thing, over and over.

Time to fly.

April didn't have to ask what the voice thought she could do, because she knew. April had magical powers, just like Kiki, and all she had to do was take that first leap.

She could fly. She knew she could.

April could ride off the edge of the open pit, and her natural flying ability, combined with the magical force of the voice, would send her rocketing around the edge of the cavern as though held by a string in the middle, flying in an ever-tightening circle up toward the crisp, blue sky.

Years later, Mom took April and her sister, Jules, on a trip to Carlsbad Caverns, and they stayed to watch the bats emerge at dusk. They flew in a tight, frantic circle, a tornado of bats gathering velocity and momentum before launching off into the night sky in search of insects. April watched the bats with a shock of recognition. This was flight as she understood it, the flight the voice from the open pit had promised her.

She wanted to fly.

She watched the golf cart turn toward the lab and disappear behind the building. April took the path toward the drilling tower and the open pit beyond. She pedaled faster, ignoring the looks of workers in hard hats and jeans, sure that if she didn't make eye contact no one would notice her. No one stopped April. Her powers strengthened the closer she got to the pit, and she could feel the magic coursing through her.

April pushed on past the drill site. The pit loomed. She could practically taste the open air, the electric crackle of the magic buoying her into the sky. Her heart pounded, but she pedaled faster, trying to gather one last burst of momentum that would launch her into the air. She closed her eyes, ready to fly over the edge . . .

And came to a dead stop. She pitched forward, her chest slamming painfully against the handlebars as her dad grabbed the seat of her bike.

He plucked April off the bike and hugged her tightly. His face was scratchy against her cheek. April didn't really remember how he looked as much as she had an impression of how strong he was.

And just like that, the voice left her. It made April sad. She wasn't going to fly after all.

Her dad ran a hand down her face, smoothing her hair.

"April!" her dad said sharply. "You know you aren't supposed to leave the yard. What are you doing here?"

"I followed the voice," she replied.

It was so obvious. Couldn't he hear the voice? Aunt Silvia did. She talked to the voice all the time.

Dad went perfectly still. He slid April to her feet and held her hand tightly. He grabbed the bike with his free hand.

"I want you to be safe," he said. "Let's go home."

Workers who had run after Dad nodded and mumbled and wandered back to work. But they'd heard what she said. They knew about the voice now.

Maybe some of them had heard it too.

April had tried to remember the look on Dad's face that day. Had there been a momentary flash of recognition? Had he heard the voice too?

It was so long ago, more than twelve years.

She couldn't remember.

She never heard the voice again after they moved away from the compound.

That was a relief.

But also a loss. She'd wanted to fly.

April wondered. Did the voice from the hole really tell her she could fly? Maybe that was her idea. Or maybe April had heard something else entirely.

There were dozens of podcasts, creepypastas, and urban legends devoted to the Bicycle Girl. To April. Blaming her for the entire disaster that followed, as though something said by an almost five-year-old could cause dozens of sun-hardened roughnecks to lose their minds.

Robert Steenkampf IV drilled a deep borehole through the earth's crust all the way to Hell and released a demon to do April's bidding.

That demon whispered in her ear. Or spoke through her or possessed her. Or killed her, threw her body into the nearby open-pit mine, and then assumed her form. Everything that happened at the compound that day—the explosion, the gunfight that broke out near the stone wall as workers tried to escape the chaos—all of that was because of April. She had unleashed something that caused everyone at the compound that day to fly into a murderous rage.

Nineteen people, dead at the end of the day.

And if you trusted the collective wisdom of the internet, April was going to bring it back from the pit on her seventeenth birthday.

She didn't go online anymore. No Instagram, no TikTok, no Snapchat. She was done with hearing how she was the living embodiment of evil on the earth. Done with hearing about the Bicycle Girl. They didn't know what actually happened. No one did.

Because April didn't even know what happened, and she was there. For all of it.

ONE

FRIDAY

APRIL WAS THIRTEEN when the movie about her life came out. *Hellhole!*

It was originally called *The Bicycle Girl*, but that name suggested an art film three thousand people would see, not the summer sleeper horror hit the studio hoped for. So the movie was subsequently retitled.

In the movie, creepy five-year-old Bicycle Girl wanted to release all the demons from Hell. There was no drill site, and no King Steenkampf, but there were teenagers. Eight of them to be exact. One of them, her imaginary older sister, Kendall, was the hero of the story. She realized early on that April was possessed by a water demon called Voidan. Kendall heard the voice. She was the only one besides Bicycle Girl who knew about the voice.

April's story was moved from New Mexico to New England. The open-pit mine was changed to a quarry lake. All the local high school students swam in the lake, and the demon killed them one by one, while she stood on the edge of the cliff laughing maniacally at each death, her eyes glowing red. The movie version of April was named July.

In the movie, her house was perched on the edge of a cliff overlooking the lake. Sometimes, she would get on her bike and ride toward the cliff, and Kendall would stop her. Even though her movie parents worried about this behavior, neither of them thought to put up a fence.

The movie ended on Kendall's seventeenth birthday. July locked Kendall into a closet, went into the kitchen, and killed both her useless parents, splattering Kendall's oversize, gleaming white birthday cake with their blood.

As Bicycle Girl began her inevitable ride toward the cliff, Kendall made a harrowing escape through the attic and out a dormer window. She stepped onto the roof in time to see July ride her bike in slow motion toward the edge of the quarry. Kendall scrambled down a convenient trellis and grabbed July the moment before her bike plunged over the edge.

April, the real April, wished that the movie had ended right there.

It hadn't.

9

Having saved July, Kendall's eyes rolled back into her head, and the voice of Voidan she'd been hearing became louder and louder until it overwhelmed her.

Kendall had always been the harbinger, the bringer of the end-times. July was just a red herring.

Kendall walked to the edge of the cliff and jumped.

The entire lake turned into a steaming volcano, spewing hot water, molten rock, and demons clawing their way to the surface from Hell. And Kendall, the most frightening demon of all.

The end.

Like a lot of movies based on urban legends, it was terrible. It was *Slender Man* bad, 15 percent on Rotten Tomatoes bad.

That didn't matter.

Right after the title credits, after a fade to black, came the words "Based on a true story."

Based on a true story doesn't mean anything other than you read something on the internet, and it gave you an idea for something else entirely, but a lot of people thought the whole story was true. You would think a water volcano spewing a steady stream of demons over a New England town and thereby bringing on the end of days would have gone viral.

It wasn't long before people online began to bombard April with questions about her plans to destroy the world. Some thought it was funny. Some people really thought she was possessed. Those people were—mean. She had no idea how mean people could be until that moment.

The movie came out in the summer. April didn't want to go back to school in the fall, but at least she had friends. She spent that summer hanging out with her then–best friends, Jessica and Emma. Most of that summer they spent in the woods across from Zach's house. There was an abandoned couch there and Zach had built a bike trail with ramps for doing tricks. The whole group—Diego, Ramsey, Emma, Jessica—spent a lot of time playing two truths and a lie. That turned out to be April's undoing. During one of these games, Emma took a video of April laughing in a slightly devious way.

Emma posted it online as "the real Bicycle Girl." People knew April had been present at the Ojo de Cristo massacre, but until then, few had connected the massacre to the movie. Thanks to Emma, the whole world learned that April was the inspiration for Bicycle Girl in the movie.

It blew up in a minor way and the conspiracy theorists found her.

Jessica had been April's best friend, but she sided with Emma. Jessica told April that she was awkward and self-absorbed and couldn't take a joke.

April was thirteen.

She realized then they weren't her friends.

Friday afternoon. There was a home football game, which meant that school would end early and there would be a pep rally.

It was a week until her seventeenth birthday and the possible end of the world.

April would have liked to put the end of the world out of her mind, but that was hard to do with all the red paint smeared on her locker. Someone had painted a very primitive, messy, seven-pointed star there.

People streamed past, craning their necks, avoiding eye contact. No one wanted to have anything to do with her this close to the apocalypse.

"Well, this is new," she said to no one in particular.

Over the years, her locker had undergone repeated assaults of graffiti in Sharpie and small, abusive notes pushed through the gills. Most of it had been reassuringly unoriginal and badly spelled, but this was next level. She'd never seen this seven-pointed star before. It had a strange, sprawled stick figure in the middle of the star attached to an arrow pointing down, suggesting free fall.

Did this have to do with the Deep Well cult?

The thought of the cult made the breath catch in her throat. She swiveled, scanned the hallway, halfway expecting to see an ominous, hooded figure holding a paintbrush, leering at her.

No one was there.

The massacre at the mine happened on April's fifth birthday. Nineteen people were killed, including her dad. King Steenkampf, the owner of the mine, disappeared amid the chaos. According to the Deep Well cultists, April opened a portal on that day, and King Steenkampf stepped through. Now they were expecting her to open the portal again on her seventeenth birthday to bring King Steenkampf back.

April never really understood why the cultists wanted him back so badly. Something about King returning to usher in a golden age. She didn't care what the cultists wanted, because no way in hell was she going out to the mine to perform some weird ritual sacrifice and a summoning. Not on her birthday. Not ever.

She imagined some of the cult members were already in town for her upcoming birthday. It was possible this star was a message for her.

She'd skulked in the Deep Well corner of Reddit years before, but she'd never seen anything like this seven-pointed star. It was probably just some dumb meme she didn't know about, unrelated to the cult. She forced a calming breath and turned back to her locker.

April had her purse and her phone. She knew better than to leave anything important in her locker. Not in a world of superglue and red paint. And worse.

"I'll just let you dry."

She wondered in a fairly uninterested way if the geography textbook inside her locker was covered in red paint. It wouldn't be the first time a textbook suffered due to her curse.

She decided to skip the full-time joy of the Copperton High School pep rally and grab her sister, Jules, from middle school, but since her car was parked in the back lot near the gym, contact with sports-related enthusiasm was unavoidable. Maybe she could crush some hopes and dreams on the way out of school. Throw a few dark, well-deserved glances in the right direction.

Outside the gym there was a huge Go Big Red banner, red paint dripping off the *G* and the *B* like bloodstains dripping down a wall.

Like paint dripping down her locker.

April stopped dead in front of the banner.

She stood a distance away, her hand on her chin in a gesture of appreciative contemplation. Thinking about whether the paint on the banner matched the paint on her locker.

Jessica sidled up next to April, a head shorter, her dark hair held in Harley Quinn pigtails with red bows that matched her cheerleading outfit. Jessica stood close to April as though her subconscious had still not made peace with the fact that they weren't friends anymore. April resisted the urge to give her shoulder a playful nudge. Old habits die hard.

"Is this your handiwork?" April asked.

Jessica grimaced.

"We didn't have keys to the supply room until the end of lunch. We didn't have time to let it dry. You know I can do better when I have the time," Jessica said, frowning.

14

"Oh, I know," April said.

She glared at Jessica, looking for a tell. Some quick, guilty cutting of the eyes or a small knowing smirk.

Nothing.

And in a way, that made April—what was the word for it?—happy. She missed Jessica. They'd been friends from first grade when they spent a lot of time in the kind of crafts that require microfine glitter. Jessica had an eye for color and when April's glitter jar turned muddy, Jessica gave her the one she'd made, green and gold and just enough black to add depth. It shouldn't have worked, but when you turned it over, it was pure Emerald City.

April still had it.

This was in the BH time—before *Hellhole!*

Emma appeared out of nowhere at Jessica's side, her shoulders squared and touching Jessica's as though they were in the initial stage of forming a phalanx to defend against invaders. April supposed that was what cheerleading was—a form of military training.

"Are you complaining about our sign?" Emma said, pert chin thrust forward.

April glanced down at Emma's hands. A telltale splotch of red paint on her right hand.

"Not at all," April replied. "I think it's delightfully creepy."

"You would," Emma said.

And there it was—the small smirk that said Emma had

painted the star on April's locker and she was not sorry about it. Not at all.

Where did the seven-pointed star come from? Certainly not from Emma's limited imagination. April vaguely remembered a video somewhere online.

"Yesss . . ." April said slowly, letting the snakelike sibilance trail off to nothing. "I would know."

April leaned into her role as the harbinger of the end-times—matte bloodred lipstick, black-and-red cowboy boots with inverted pentagrams on the sides. Cultivating a certain witchy vibe kept people at school from asking too many questions.

"Pfft," Emma said. She glared at April.

Football players slow jogged past them into the gym, wearing letter jackets in the late season heat. At the end of the line was Zach, the star running back. Old childhood friend. Emma's ex from the before time.

Zach gave the impression of not being in a hurry at all, strange considering that he was so fast on the field.

Zach glanced at Emma, the banner, and then locked eyes with April. A knowing smile played across his face as though the whole tableau—the dripping sign, Emma and Jessica, even April's own neo-goth outfit—was part of some hilarious private joke the two of them, and only the two of them, shared.

Zach hadn't paid much attention to her since seventh grade, and April imagined this surprising eye contact was all about him wanting to annoy Emma, and not about her. Still, it had been a long time since anyone had willingly made eye contact, and it was—nice.

But she couldn't just let it go unpunished.

She tilted her head and raised an eyebrow in his direction, as though to suggest that now he was damned for all time.

As Zach passed by, he gave her a small nod and a sly smile, as if to say, *I'm not afraid of you.*

She felt her face flush.

Maybe it hadn't been about Emma after all.

She watched Zach go. When she finally looked away, she realized that Emma was quietly seething in her direction. Jessica looked like she wanted to be anywhere else.

"Are you coming to the game?" Jessica asked, not looking April in the eyes. In times like these April suspected Jessica felt a little bad about how things had turned out. Sad that they were no longer friends.

April wanted to go to the game. Do something normal, for a change. Go to the kegger after the game, jump up and down in a little red-and-black skirt. She was too big and too uncoordinated to be a cheerleader, but she could have been color guard. She could have swung the hell out of a long metal pole at a football game.

If things had been different.

She decided to let Jessica off the hook with a short reply. No quip, no chaser.

"No."

Jessica breathed a sigh of relief.

No one wanted to be around the Bicycle Girl. Especially not now, not with her own personal apocalypse on the horizon.

"I already have plans," April said.

It sounded pathetic the moment she said it. They both knew what her plans were. Everyone did. April was going to hang out with her best friend, Grace. Grace was a shoo-in for class valedictorian, if she even stayed around high school that long.

An average Friday night for her revolved around helping Grace with her application essays for various college and university programs. So many essays. So many programs. Grace did not need her help with homework, but April always edited her applications to take the edge off the hungry, slightly threatening tone of her writing. The admit-me-to-your-college-or-you'll-be-sorry-later angle her essays generally took.

"Plans," Emma spat out. "Pfft."

April yawned in slow motion. She rubbed the charm she wore on the black silk cord around her neck and mumbled a few words.

She didn't actually know any magical spells, and the charm was Etsy costume satanic, but she was quite sure Emma didn't know that. April had found that mumbling a curse or laughing maniacally was a good way to end a conversation that was going nowhere.

Closure is important.

But Emma didn't move. She clung to Jessica like a barnacle, just as stony and hard to scrape off mid-voyage. April turned to walk away, mostly to spare Jessica.

April had only gotten two steps away when she heard Emma stage-whisper, "How many are you planning to kill this time?"

Jessica shushed her.

April stopped cold. Adopted a preternatural stillness, waiting.

It stung. It wasn't Emma who bothered her. She'd met a thousand Emmas on the internet. They hid in the dark and skittered away when you looked directly at them. But Jessica? At any time she could have turned to Emma and said "Not cool, Emma."

Jessica could have left Emma in the dust as thoroughly as she'd left April. They'd played this scene a dozen times and it always ended the same way.

Jessica shushing Emma. Looking trapped. Waiting for April to leave. But in this case, April didn't.

She waited long enough to be sure that this wasn't going to be the time that Jessica changed her mind.

This wasn't the time.

"All. Of. Them," April said.

She gave the appropriate dramatic pause before walking away without looking back.

TWO

WIKIPEDIA

OJO DE CRISTO MINING DISASTER [edit]

Robert "King" Steenkampf IV, CEO of Kamper Oil and Mining LLC, initially became interested in the Ojo de Cristo open pit copper mine after his wife, Dr. Ella Travers-Steenkampf, read about the history of earlier massacres at the mine site. [Main article: 1936 Ojo de Cristo mine fight] After visiting the site, King Steenkampf decided to drill a deep borehole to reach farther beneath the surface than anyone had before.

Using improved drilling techniques, engineers claimed to have reached a depth of nearly nine miles (14,484 meters), slightly deeper than the earlier Russian Kola

Superdeep Borehole (12,262 meters). However, the job site was plagued with technical setbacks and possible sabotage, which destroyed the drill before the depth could be independently verified. [citation needed]

An explosion at the site destroyed the mud lubrication system, causing the deep bore drill to seize and snap. After the destruction of the drill, a gunfight broke out at the mining compound. Nineteen people were killed in total during the event.

The motivation behind the gunfight is unknown.

According to relatives of victims, the daughter of drill site foreman, William J. Fischer, five-year-old April Fischer purportedly began to hear a voice from the borehole. [disambiguation needed]

After the massacre, Robert Steenkampf disappeared. A photo supposedly taken of him at a Kamper mine in Peru years later turned out to be a hoax. No trace of Robert Steenkampf has ever been found, leading to the speculation that he escaped through a portal opened at the site. [see The Deep Well Cult]

A 2016 horror movie entitled *Hellhole!* (known as *The Bicycle Girl* in European release), based on the story, holds little resemblance to the actual occurrences at the Ojo de Cristo mine.

APRIL HEADED TO Jules's middle school to pick her up. She was early, which meant that she arrived in the middle of Friday exodus and got stuck in the stack of mostly moms in SUVs. Jules, being Jules, saw the car from her cluster of friends near the flagpole and took her own sweet time coming over.

A shadow appeared in April's peripheral vision. A black truck slowed down and came to a stop next to her car. It was a towering high-end model, tinted windows and a row of high-lites on the top, the kind of truck that few people in the area could even begin to afford. So large, it completely blocked the drop-off loop.

Whoever was behind the dark glass could see her, but she couldn't see them. She resisted the urge to duck.

She thought of rolling down the window, of saying something snarky and Bicycle Girl. But some long-dormant animal instinct kicked in and told her to go completely still in the face of an apex predator.

Behind her, people began to honk, politely at first, like

there had been some sort of misunderstanding about the dimensions of the drop-off loop that a tiny tap on the horn could clear up.

No misunderstanding.

Whoever was in the truck was waiting for her to make a move.

April glanced back toward the flagpole, but Jules was no longer there. Her sharp stab of fear was a shock. She searched the schoolyard like a lifeguard scanning the spot where a bobbing head had just disappeared under the waves. She spied Jules's best friend, Luna, but no Jules.

Breathe.

Jules had to be around. Whoever was in the truck couldn't have grabbed Jules. There wasn't enough time. There were teachers and parents around. She tried to logic her way around the knot of panic forming in the center of her chest, but it wasn't working.

Breathe.

When April was eight, her mom spotted a suspicious man outside her elementary school and called the police. Mom had seen the man earlier on the front door security cam, pretending to be a delivery man. He had duct tape, rope, and ether in his trunk. Also, many, many guns, unfortunately all legal and registered. He wouldn't talk to the police, but April always assumed he planned to bring on the coming apocalypse sooner. Or prevent it by ending her.

He got a police escort out of town, and her mom had more security cameras installed.

He could have come back.

Breathe.

"Your truck is ridiculous overcompensation," she murmured, hoping that would make her feel superior and in control of the situation. She tried to imagine a sad beige little man at a truck dealership, asking for the maximum intimidation package. She imagined the dealer selling the sad man tens of thousands of dollars of useless and overpriced detailing.

She tried to imagine this loser and couldn't.

The truck read as ruthless and implacable, untroubled by the mild annoyance of moms in the drop-off loop.

The honks became more insistent and angry.

The truck didn't move.

Where was Jules?

April stared at the truck, unblinking. If she could have, she would have turned her head and caught the eye of one of the mothers, or the security guard who watched the foot traffic in front of the school.

Asked for help.

She couldn't.

She could never be sure that anyone in this town would help her. Not after what happened at the compound that day. Too many people had lost loved ones in the massacre.

Emma wasn't the only person in town who thought April was responsible.

The back door of the car flew open with a loud clack.

"Hey," Jules said, throwing her backpack in the back seat. "You're early."

"Pep rally," April mumbled.

April watched the truck roll slowly away, wondering if whoever was in the truck had been waiting to see which twelve-year-old girl April would pick up. Wondering if anyone else in the drop-off loop would care about a mysterious man who clearly wasn't here to pick up a kid.

No.

The man in the black truck was here for April. He must have followed her from the high school. He was her problem, and hers alone.

The last time April made it onto the radar of horror buffs and disaster tourists, Jules had been a kid. No one had noticed her.

That had just changed.

Jules jumped into the front seat.

"April, are you okay?" Jules asked.

"I'm fine." April kept her eyes trained on the black truck.

The truck disappeared behind the school and reappeared on the main street a few seconds later, like a shark circling its prey. April strained to catch the license plate number. Too far away.

"Who was that?" Jules asked, a rising note of fear in her voice.

April glanced over at her sister. Jules had followed her gaze to the black truck, tracking it as it made a slow turn on the street beside the school.

"Probably no one," April replied.

"Didn't seem like no one," Jules said.

April decided to change the subject.

Jules's dark ponytail had shifted to the side of her head, and she was wearing recently applied lip gloss that smelled like vanilla sugar. She had on a cute turquoise shirt April was sure Jules hadn't been wearing when she left the house that morning.

"I like that shirt," April said.

"It's Luna's. We traded shirts at lunch," she said.

"It looks good on you."

There was a clear space in the drop-off loop, and April pulled the car out, hoping to make it onto the street before the truck came back around.

"It's Friday. Will you take me to the football game?" Jules asked.

She leaned across the seat in a pleading posture. Close enough for April to decide that the lip gloss was cherry vanilla.

"Not this game."

Jules grunted, and leaned back in her seat, arms folded across her chest.

"You always say that."

"It's just that this week is—" April stopped mid-sentence, trying to imagine what she would say next. *This week is the apocalypse? The end of everything we know and love? This week is the worst?* It wasn't fair that Jules had to live under house arrest until after April's birthday, but there it was.

"The next home game is in two weeks. We'll go then, I promise."

"Okay," Jules said softly. "I understand."

Jules wasn't an idiot. She knew why they couldn't go. The man in the truck was only the tip of the iceberg.

April allowed herself a moment to think about a football game two weeks in the future. She would take Jules and maybe even Grace, although Grace didn't approve of football. They'd sit in the stands, cheering the game, mercifully blending into the crowd.

It had been a year since April had been to a football game. Zach had been the star player, a marvel on the field. She'd done such a good job of avoiding Zach, she imagined he was avoiding her too.

Until he locked eyes with her in the hall outside the gym.

April had always wondered what happened when you outlived your own urban legend. She imagined a life of brilliant, mundane obscurity. Years and years of being nothing to nobody, except to the people who actually knew you and, more importantly, cared about you.

"If we can't go to the game, can we at least go to the Sonic?" Jules asked brightly. "Everyone is going to Sonic."

Jules's voice was a foghorn, cutting through her thoughts. Sometimes she found Jules's in-your-face personality to be a lot, but this week she was grateful for it. Jules kept her from wallowing.

"Sure," she answered, mimicking the festive tone of voice. "Why not?

It didn't hurt to be nice to Jules, especially now. Jules rarely talked about the harsh middle school reality of life as the kid sister of the Bicycle Girl, mostly because Jules wanted to be known as anything other than the kid sister of the Bicycle Girl.

Fair.

But this week, the Bicycle Girl urban legend was going to be inescapable—for both of them.

If the man in the black truck followed them, at least they'd be at Sonic, where there would be a crowd.

Safe.

They drove the short distance to the Sonic, and April stayed in the car while Jules made for the middle school social scene by the cement picnic bench. It was cool but bright, and April rolled up the car windows to cut out the noise of Jules and her friends. She scrolled on her phone and drifted.

A crisp double rap on the driver's side window startled her awake.

A woman with soft brown shoulder-length hair and a professional-grade smile stood by her driver's side window holding an iced coffee drink. She looked vaguely familiar, but she should have been more than familiar. April thought she knew everyone who worked at Sonic. Maybe she was new, from the local college?

April rolled down the window.

"I'm sorry, I didn't order that," she said.

"Oh, I know," the woman replied.

Belatedly, April realized she wasn't wearing the uniform. And she was older than April first imagined, late twenties maybe.

"Iced vanilla caramel latte, for you." She thrust the drink toward April. "Do you remember me?"

Marianne.

It was the caramel latte that shook the memory loose. When April was fourteen, Marianne had pretended to be on a college visit, had bought her a caramel latte at the downtown coffee shop, and was—nice to her. April had been hungry for nice. In return for a caramel latte and a few sad crumbs of attention, April gave away too much information about herself and how she felt about the whole massacre thing before her spider sense went off.

When April tried to leave, Marianne had presented her a rapturous vision of how once April resurrected King to this earthly dimension, all his followers would be free from suffering and the pain of death. They would all live forever in golden harmony.

Marianne was a member of the Deep Well cult.

"How could I forget?" April shifted in her seat and looked around for the black truck. It was nowhere in sight. "What do you want, Marianne?"

"I thought we could talk," Marianne said softly. She continued to hold the coffee out, sweat dripping down the side of the cup onto her hand, a glazed smile on her face. April wondered if a spacey beatific cheeriness was Marianne's natural state of being, or if it was just something that came out when she was in the presence of the Bicycle Girl.

As she was now.

April glanced at the coffee, and back to Marianne.

"You thought wrong," she said.

In the center of the crowd of middle graders, Jules poked her head up and scowled in the direction of the car. Luna followed, and like a field of prairie dogs, the whole crowd craned their necks and looked.

Marianne leaned over, her mouth close to April's ear.

"He's alive," she whispered. "He needs your help."

A sick rush of fear hit her stomach, the smell of caramel latte filled her nose like a warning from the past. April never drank sweet coffee drinks anymore. They tasted like naivete and betrayal.

She reached out to push Marianne away and ended up

connecting with the frozen drink, slapping it out of Marianne's hand. It flew and landed a few feet away, exploding on the pavement of the parking lot.

"I think you need to get the fuck away from me," April said.

Across the row, a tall blond man opened the door of an acid-green Jeep. He leaned against the roof of the car, watching.

"Marianne?" he called anxiously.

Marianne gave him a parade float kind of wave, reassuring and vague. So Marianne had a boyfriend now.

At the same time, Jules charged toward the car. April looked at Jules and shook her head tightly. Meaning—don't come over here. A small gesture, but it was enough. Marianne followed April's line of sight and landed on Jules. She glanced back at the blond man by the green Jeep and nodded her head in Jules's direction.

April felt a cold wave of fear in the pit of her stomach.

For the second time in less than an hour, Jules had been spotted by one of the crazies who had come to town to witness the coming apocalypse. The opening of the portal. Whatever they thought was going to happen.

"We'll talk again soon," Marianne said in a patient, kindergarten-teacher voice. As though April were a child having an expected, adorable tantrum and not an almost seventeen-year-old who'd just told her to fuck off.

April grabbed her phone and held it up. "Okay, dialing 911 now."

She wasn't really going to call. When the police got involved, there was always explaining to do, and the explanations were mortifying.

Marianne turned and strode over to the green Jeep. A server named Kara turned deftly on roller skates to watch Marianne go. She'd been a senior when April was a freshman.

Marianne and the blond man got in the car and drove out of the parking lot. Marianne waved like an old friend as they drove by.

"Who was that?" Jules demanded.

"Fucking trouble," April replied.

THREE

LUNA'S MOM OFFERED to take Jules home from the Sonic. "I'd be happy to give her a ride," she said in a cheerful, apologetic mom voice that held only a hint of derision.

April got the message. Jules would be safer somewhere else—with someone else. April wasn't sure she disagreed.

"Thanks, that would be great," she replied, trying to adopt a breezy tone and failing miserably. She was still shaken from the confrontation with Marianne. Jules had picked up the empty latte cup and thrown it away, but the violent splash of latte remained, an ever-darkening outline on the cement of the parking lot, like a blood splatter at a crime scene.

Jules faced April, eyes serious.

"Are you sure you'll be okay alone?" she asked softly. "You don't mind if I go with Luna?"

"I'll be fine," April said. "Anyway, I'm going to meet up with Grace at the Coppermine, so I won't be alone."

"Okay," Jules said brightly.

April watched as Jules and Luna bounded across the parking lot to say goodbye to the group of kids clustered around the cement table.

Luna's mom nodded crisply and gave April a tight, dubious smile before turning away. April understood intuitively, at a bone-deep level, that Luna's mom had lost someone in the massacre.

None of the survivors blamed April, but no one forgave her either.

Her presence in town was a constant reminder of the horror of that day, and her upcoming birthday served to open old wounds for everyone.

April couldn't wait until her birthday was over.

The Coppermine was a small, dimly lit bar with a giant yard that backed up to the big ditch, a dry creek bed that ran through the center of Copperton. There was a coffee truck and a few rotating food trucks outside. It was chilly and people under twenty-one weren't allowed inside the bar, but there was a blazing fire in a large pit in the middle of the yard. The yard was frequented by college students and professors alike, but the inside had a distinctly sports-bar, American-beer-on-tap vibe. It was the one place in town to meet someone on a first date if you wanted a coffee and a quick escape, or the possibility of a drink by the fire if things went well.

It was also, according to Grace, the perfect place to study.

Completely unnecessary. Grace could have probably coasted for an entire semester in school without anyone even noticing, but coasting was not in her nature. Grace was an academic shark, always looking for bigger prey than their small pond of a high school allowed.

Grace had already found a picnic table near the firepit and had settled in with a coffee.

April slid into the bench across from Grace.

"Do you remember Marianne?"

"Marianne?" Grace asked.

"The girl with the caramel latte," April said.

"Oh, her?" Grace knew that story well. Of all the people who'd "accidentally" bumped into April at the downtown coffeehouse or the movie theater, Marianne had been the only one April had been taken in by. There was something archaically, suspiciously wholesome about Marianne, like she'd time traveled from a dairy farm in the 1950s to peddle the cult with missionary zeal. She should have had pamphlets.

"She was at the Sonic today," April said. "With someone else."

"Really? What did she want?"

"Oh you know, same old, same old," April replied. "She wanted me to raise King from the dead."

Grace set down her mechanical pencil and sighed.

"I guess it was inevitable," she said. "Do you ever think of going somewhere until after your birthday?"

"Go where?"

"Anywhere."

"What about Jules?"

"Jules would be thrilled to get out of town."

"And what about Mom?"

Grace was right. Jules would be thrilled to go on vacation. But their mom had been so sick lately. It was hard to imagine Mom packing up and leaving in the next day or so.

Grace looked April in the eye. It was the kind of stern, no-nonsense look April imagined Grace leveling at her future postdocs when their work wasn't yielding results. There was no winning a staring contest with Grace.

April caved and looked away, searched for a distraction and a way to change the subject.

Her eyes found Zach.

He was working the counter at CHAR, a food truck dedicated to covering all foods in roasted green chiles.

"Did you see that Zach's here?" April asked. "It's Friday. Shouldn't he be getting ready for the game?" April hoped that she sounded only mildly curious.

Grace looked toward CHAR as Zach stepped down from the side door of the truck with a tray of food that he deposited on a nearby table. He saw them, turned, and gave a half salute that managed to convey embarrassment and amusement in equal measure. Like all Zach's physical gestures, the emotionally freighted half salute had an easy cool that drew the attention of everyone in the yard.

April felt a tiny leftover rush of endorphins from the eye contact they'd shared earlier outside the gym.

Maybe his wave was for Grace. You ignored Grace, future valedictorian, at your peril.

"He probably wants to keep his brain," Grace whispered. "It's a decent brain, you know?"

"Decent brain" was high praise from Grace. Very few people in the school came close to decent brain status in Grace's opinion.

"What do you mean?" April asked.

"You know—CTE," Grace replied.

April imagined this was a medical term. Grace's mom was head of the ER at the local hospital, and Grace had inherited a lot of arcane medical knowledge.

"CTE?"

"Zach was knocked unconscious during a game."

April was shocked. She didn't go to games for the obvious reasons, but she wasn't aware of how fully she'd pulled back from everybody and everything at school.

"Knocked unconscious?" April said. "When did this happen?"

"A few weeks ago," Grace said looking mildly disappointed.

"How could you not know? Everyone's been talking about it. . . ."

April's phone rang with the *Halloween*-themed ringtone she'd pegged to her aunt Silvia. The slasher movie sound made her jump, and she cursed her own dark humor. Across the picnic table, Grace shivered involuntarily and pulled her jacket closer. She knew what that ringtone meant.

"Come out today," Aunt Silvia said when April picked up.

Aunt Silvia lived in a hunting cabin overlooking the Ojo de Cristo mining compound. Aunt Silvia had been a cook at the compound and King Steenkampf had given her his hunting cabin after she made the best Texas chili in the whole state of New Mexico. Or his favorite chocolate cake. Aunt Silvia never told the same story about the cabin or King Steenkampf twice.

When the cabin was built in the 1870s, it had overlooked what must have been a beautiful mountain view, but now it presided over the desolate wasteland of the mining compound. In the 1930s the whole mountain was dynamited and ground up for copper. Somehow, the cabin remained untouched.

After the massacre, April's mom received a generous settlement from the Steenkampf estate. Mom had wanted Aunt Silvia to move into the big adobe house in the center of town. There was more than enough room. But Aunt Silvia chose to stay.

Grace had been out to the cabin with April before. The place was creepy—even to someone as rational as Grace. Last time they were there, Grace walked too close to Aunt Silvia's compost pile, disturbing a nest of rats who scattered in a frantic explosion in all directions. One ran over the tip of her shoe.

Grace hated rats.

"It's pretty late," April said. "I don't think I can come."

April thought of the strange, merciless, blank quality of the black truck and shuddered. The drop-off loop was one thing, but Aunt Silvia's cabin was in the middle of nowhere.

"I'm *un-gry*," Silvia said, her voice digitizing into near nonsense. Her cabin was in the mountains, and the cell reception out there was terrible.

Hungry? April had groceries delivered to the cabin two days ago. Which meant this was an excuse to get April to visit. She understood—Aunt Silvia was lonely. But now was not a great time.

"You should have plenty of food," April said.

She used to deliver the groceries herself, until a couple of months ago when two guys in an old Toyota with California license plates followed her to Aunt Silvia's cabin. April had sprinted through the underbrush, hoping to lose them, but they stuck close, phones held out to record the elusive sight of the Bicycle Girl running away. Like Bigfoot. Hoping for all the views. They'd almost caught up with April when she hit the clearing in front of the cabin.

When they made it through the clearing, Aunt Silvia was standing on the porch in a tattered white dress, cradling an ancient shotgun. She'd fired it overhead and they'd taken off, running back to their car, back to California with a story to tell. So much for views.

They were so scared, they hadn't even managed to get a photo of Aunt Silvia.

"No more in-person deliveries," April's mom had said after that episode. "If Silvia wants to see you, she can get an Uber."

April and her mother always argued about Aunt Silvia. But April was forced to admit that her mother was right, for a change. She didn't need to go anywhere near the compound. At least not until after her seventeenth birthday.

"Just come . . ." Aunt Silvia said. "*Screed* tell you something."

"I don't think I can come right now," April said. "Things are too weird."

Aunt Silvia of all people knew weird. She'd chased off more than a couple of would-be horror influencers and urban explorers.

"I know," Aunt Silvia said softly. ". . . is important. One last time . . . Please."

April had a hard time hearing over the static, but the way Aunt Silvia said "one last time" struck a chord in her. Her mother had been sick for a long time with diabetes and fibro-myalgia. And it had gotten worse lately. In contrast to her sister, Aunt Silvia had always seemed like the poster child for living off the grid. She had muscles from chopping wood and tending her small garden that would put the average middle-aged gym rat to shame. But lately she'd seemed different. She wasn't sick or frail the way Mom was, but she was off some-how. That worried April.

She sighed and looked at the sun lowering over CHAR. She decided she could run out to the cabin with a sandwich and be back before it was completely dark. If she saw anyone trailing her up the mountain, she would abort the mission. Turn around and head home.

April put the phone down, riffled through her purse for a credit card, and slapped it onto the picnic table in front of Grace.

"Do you mind going to CHAR and ordering me a dirty bird sandwich and a side of green chili cheese fries to go?" she asked. April didn't want Zach to think that because he'd granted her a tiny wave, she would use the desperate excuse of buying a sandwich as a reason to bask in the glory of his presence.

"You're not really going out to your aunt Silvia's, are you?" Grace whispered.

"I'm just going to drop off the sandwich and leave. Every-one is going to be at the football game anyway."

Grace opened her mouth to say something and thought

better of it. She picked up the bank card and headed toward CHAR.

Aunt Silvia's voice rose from the phone face down on the picnic table, and April picked it up.

"You're not listening to me," Aunt Silvia complained.

"I was making your food order."

"Did you hear me?" she asked.

"Yes," April replied.

April wasn't really listening. She was watching Zach sprint back to CHAR with an easy grace, watching the college girls drinking beer at a nearby table watch Zach.

"*Ng* the truth . . . *afore* . . . too late." Breaking up again.

The connection dropped. Either that, or Aunt Silvia had hung up.

The temperature seemed to have fallen five degrees and April shivered.

Learn the truth, before it's too late. Did Aunt Silvia really say that?

No. She couldn't have.

April closed her eyes, phone in hand.

Aunt Silvia was one of the few known survivors of the massacre. For years, April had begged Aunt Silvia to tell her the truth about what happened at the compound. Aunt Silvia always said she didn't know what happened that day. She was just the cook.

Now Aunt Silvia had decided to tell her the truth.

Aunt Silvia had been there for the explosion that had killed her father. She had to know the true story of what happened to him and the other men who died that day.

What happened to King Steenkampf.

Whatever the truth was.

Did April really want to know exactly how her dad had died? The thought of him held a heavy weight of uncertainty, like a boulder in the center of her chest. When she was little, she refused to even believe that he was dead.

In April's disjointed memory of that day, she was at the compound, and then she was at a motel with her mother. There was a Coke machine in the hall at the motel, a tiny pool out back, but they didn't have swimsuits. Her mom let her swim in shorts and a T-shirt, and let her push the button on the Coke machine for a fizzy orange drink.

Her head was empty then. The voice—gone.

April didn't remember anything important, just the disaster vacation afterward, the sympathy ice cream and the house tours, the sense that her dad had simply vanished from their lives so cleanly it was as though he'd never been there in the first place. They never even had a funeral. The roughnecks who died were from out of town, but some of the workers who died were local and some of the families blamed her dad for the massacre. Mom had been afraid to have a public funeral.

Now her mom acted like it had never happened. Usually

when April brought that day up, her mom changed the subject.

When her mom did talk about the compound, she told April that her dad knew something was terribly wrong at the drill site in the days leading up to the massacre. Nothing supernatural according to Mom, just unexplained equipment failure and a sour mood that spread through the drill team. These were wildcatters who'd followed her dad from a successful drill off the coast of Mississippi to an abandoned copper mine in New Mexico with no hope of a strike. No one really knew what they were looking for.

Not even her dad.

Supposedly, Dad had hustled Mom and April away before the explosion and the subsequent gunfight, but something about Mom's story didn't quite add up. Her father never made the official list of the dead following the massacre. In the Wikipedia pages, in all the urban legends he only rated mention as foreman of the site. Father of the Bicycle Girl.

Aunt Silvia had been the cook for the whole camp. When April and Mom left the compound, she'd stayed behind. And if Aunt Silvia had been there for the explosion and the gunfight, she had to know what really happened that day.

She would know what happened to April's dad.

"Are you okay?" Grace asked.

The sound of Grace's voice startled April out of her thoughts.

"I'm fine."

"You don't look fine. What did Silvia say?"

April debated not telling Grace, but that would only launch a game of twenty questions. Grace would figure it out eventually. She always did.

"Aunt Silvia says she wants to tell me what happened."

"At the compound?" Grace lowered her voice. "You mean, the day of the massacre?"

"I think so."

"Why now, of all times?" Grace frowned furiously. She bit her lower lip, a sign that she was restraining herself from a full-on diatribe. "Going out there is a spectacularly bad idea. What about your birthday?"

"I know."

"Do you, though?" Grace lowered her voice. "What about Marianne?"

"I can handle Marianne," April said, with more assurance than she felt. Marianne, she could handle, but Marianne wasn't alone.

"You're going to go anyway," Grace said, barely containing her disgust.

April couldn't explain it to Grace. She wasn't sure she fully understood herself. If there was a chance she could find out the truth about what happened to her dad, she had to go.

Before it's too late. That was what Aunt Silvia had said.

Zach held out a white paper bag and headed their way. Her order was ready.

"Do you want me to go with you?" Grace asked.

Grace leaned close to the table, arms wrapped tightly around herself, chin-length dark hair covering her face. She looked cold, the kind of cold you can't shake off just by going inside. She didn't want to go back to the cabin. But she was willing to, for April's sake.

"No. I'll text you when I get back."

Grace brightened with palpable relief.

"If you don't text me, I'm going to come looking for you."

Zach stepped up to the table and handed April the paper bag.

"You're leaving?" he asked, seeming truly surprised. "You just got here."

Did he actually care if she left?

"Duty calls," April said.

Zach raised an eyebrow. April had no official duties other than ushering in the impending apocalypse. But Zach smiled like he got the joke, and headed back to CHAR.

Second smile in one day, after years of nothing.

That smile opened up an unexpected tug of hopefulness in the center of April's chest. She reminded herself that Zach smiled at everyone like that. Good customer service.

"April?" Grace called after her.

She turned.

"Be careful, okay?"

"Always," April replied.

She'd spent a lifetime looking over her shoulder. That wasn't going to change now.

FOUR

AUNT SILVIA'S CABIN was only a thirty-minute drive away from the center of Copperton, but it felt like driving to another world. The temperature dropped as April piloted her car steadily upward, past the national forest and through the mountain pass.

April crested the mountain pass, and the compound came into view. Her ears popped uncomfortably, and a familiar feeling settled in the pit of her stomach.

The compound was surrounded by a huge and forbidding stone wall, with a padlocked iron gate. It was topped by a swirl of barbed wire but viewed from above, it was dwarfed in scale by the open-pit mine, that single deep circle, stair-stepped down, a perfect conical bowl.

She hated seeing the compound. That feeling of unease never went away.

Aunt Silvia hadn't always been this much of a recluse. When Jules was still a baby, they'd pull up to the wide spot in the road where the deer trail to Aunt Silvia's house began. Mom would honk the horn and Aunt Silvia would come strolling through the underbrush, all smiles. They had picnics. Sometimes Aunt Silvia would stay over for the weekend.

All that changed after *Hellhole!* came out.

Horror movie buffs and paranormal investigators drove for miles to try and catch a glimpse of the mine. Aunt Silvia became obsessed with chasing people away. Like it was her job.

Sometimes she claimed that King Steenkampf had given her the cabin so she could stand guard.

Aunt Silvia wasn't the only one who had changed. April's mom had always been tolerant of Aunt Silvia's eccentricities, but after the movie's release, she didn't want to go out to the cabin anymore. April and her mom would drive out a few times a month to deliver groceries, sometimes less, Mom standing on the porch looking strained, or waiting in the car if her fibromyalgia was bad.

And then her mom stopped going out to the cabin altogether.

Mom had groceries delivered, but April felt bad. Aunt

Silvia was alone. When April got her driver's license a year ago, she started bringing Aunt Silvia groceries.

She didn't know what happened between Mom and Aunt Silvia. It was more than just her mother's declining health. Maybe if Aunt Silvia was in the mood for the truth, she would tell April what caused such a rift between the two of them.

April parked her car by the side of the road and trekked through the underbrush along a deer trail. A small creature skittered away, and that noise was followed by a silence so deep and unnatural it made April nostalgic for the rats in Silvia's compost pile. At least they were alive.

Aunt Silvia lived in the border between the forest and the mine, a landscape as hostile and alien as the surface of the moon.

The mine destroyed all life.

April glanced toward the sky and quickened her pace. The horizon was rapidly turning a deep bluish purple to the southeast. It was near the end of monsoon season, and the area was due rain. She needed to get back over the mountain before the rain hit.

Aunt Silvia's cabin was very old, a jumble of adobe and colonial Spanish carved wood. The four ornate columns on the front porch were intricate and strange and didn't match the rustic rest of the building. They came to points like obelisks. There were no windows on the front of the house, and the door was heavy carved wood, a crescent moon with a face in the middle panel, thirteen rays of light emanating in all directions. The collective internet would have called it a witch house, if Aunt Silvia ever let anyone close enough to photograph it.

She didn't.

Every so often, a historical preservation society from Santa Fe sent a representative to their house, hoping her mom could convince Aunt Silvia to sell the cabin.

"Good luck with that," Mom always said.

The front porch, the scrub surrounding the house, the carved columns were all covered with a thick layer of dust that regularly blew off the mine, a pale greenish tint from the copper.

Aunt Silvia had cut out the moon panel and hinged it on the backside to make a face-height window. Every time April saw the rough cut Silvia had made in the hundred-and-fifty-year-old, one-of-a-kind door, she imagined the historical society clutching their collective pearls.

April stamped on the steps to announce her presence and knocked on the door.

The pale moon swung open and revealed a pair of eyes so much like her mom's that for an instant, April thought it was her.

"Aunt Silvia," she said. "You startled me."

Aunt Silvia stayed with her face in the window, unblinking. She wasn't used to the normal rhythms of conversation,

51

and sometimes would simply stare for seconds at a time, as though trying to figure out if April was real or not.

Whenever Aunt Silvia called, April always came in the hope she'd find the aunt she remembered from childhood. The Silvia who drew detailed pictures of birds and flowers. The aunt who made chocolate cake and laughed in the sunshine.

Lately April worried that Aunt Silvia's eccentricity had ripened into something else.

But April wasn't here for chocolate cake and sunshine. She wanted to know the truth about the day of the massacre, and she expected that truth to be dark.

"Did you bring me anything?" Aunt Silvia asked finally.

April held up the to-go bag.

The door swung open. Aunt Silvia stepped out onto the porch. Barefoot, her long dark hair loose, wearing jeans that were practically all holes. April brought her new clothes all the time. It didn't matter.

She handed Aunt Silvia the bag and they sat together on the edge of the porch.

"Where are the folding chairs I brought you?" April asked. She'd bought Aunt Silvia a pair of good camping chairs a few months ago.

"Coyotes got 'em," Aunt Silvia said.

Coyotes got 'em was Aunt Silvia's answer to all disappearances. Coyotes were a good reason why she no longer had a chicken coop. Coyotes stealing camping chairs made less sense.

"Was someone out here?" April asked.

Not for the first time, she wondered if Aunt Silvia was truly safe. Aunt Silvia had her ancient shotgun, but what good would that really be if she faced a home invasion? If the cultists showed up for April's seventeenth birthday en masse?

"No one but me and the ghosts." Aunt Silvia quirked a strange smile as though the idea of living among ghosts was funny, but it really wasn't. Not out here.

"So why did you want to see me?" April asked.

Aunt Silvia ignored the question. She ruffled through the bag and shoved a handful of fries in her mouth.

April should have known better than to rush her. Aunt Silvia dug her heels in at direct questions.

"Green chili cheese fries," Aunt Silvia murmured contentedly.

"You're welcome," April said, and she meant it. Her mom was on an all-natural, anti-inflammatory diet, and that extended to the groceries she ordered for the family and for Aunt Silvia. April had quickly learned that if there was anything she could bond with Aunt Silvia over, it was food. Aunt Silvia loved the meals April brought her from local food trucks, the kind of high-end fast food that hadn't existed when Silvia last lived in Copperton.

"You know, we could go out to dinner sometime," April said hopefully. She'd tried to talk her into coming down to Copperton before. It never worked, but she kept trying.

Silvia munched on a fry.

"Number seven special," she said. "With a margarita. Tia's Roadhouse. Is it still there?"

"I think so."

April had no idea. But she wasn't going to tell Aunt Silvia that if she could lure her out with the possibility of a margarita and a number seven special.

Silvia laughed.

"Why should I leave when you'll bring me what I want?"

She unwrapped the chicken sandwich and dug in.

"What did you want to tell me?" April asked, trying to keep a note of impatience out of her voice. Trying and failing. The sun was going down, and she hadn't left a cozy fire and the relative safety of the Coppermine bar just to bring her aunt Silvia a chicken sandwich.

She wanted the truth.

Aunt Silvia looked at April, still chewing. Taking her time. April felt jittery anticipation well up inside her. She desperately wanted to know what had happened the day of the massacre—what had happened to her father. It wasn't logical, she knew that.

Hope never is.

Aunt Silvia put the sandwich down and gazed reverently

at the open-pit mine below. April followed her gaze to the mine. She stood and craned her head to get a better look. The idea that there was a portal to another dimension was laughable back in Copperton. But out here, looking over the wasteland of the abandoned mine, April felt a gravitational pull. She tried not to look toward the mine, but it was like trying not to look at the sun. The mine, that giant hole, was the center of this world. Out here, she always felt that if she stood too suddenly, she might fall and keep falling, as though something were pulling her inexorably toward the open pit.

Or maybe I would fly . . . she thought.

Strange thought.

It didn't feel like her own.

"You feel it, don't you?" Aunt Silvia murmured. "So do I."

The last rays of sunlight cleared the gap in the western side of the mountains, hit deep on the curved steps of the mine, and turned them a brilliant copper-gold. It was wrenchingly beautiful, so lovely that April couldn't look away.

Time to fly.

Time to fly.

It had been over a decade since April had heard the voice inside her head, but it had never really left her. That lovely, relentless desire to be free, beckoning her. Buried under years of myth and movie, the cartoon simplification of her urban legend.

It was still there. After all this time.

The sun slid behind the tree line and the sides of the mine went dark. April shook her head, and the image was gone and, with it, the burning desire to fly.

"I almost forgot," Aunt Silvia said, her expression suddenly cheerful. "I have something for you. Call it an early birthday present."

April flinched, almost a hypnic jerk, like coming out of a sleep with the sense of having fallen. Staring at the mine had put her into a trancelike state, before Silvia's voice brought her back around.

Aunt Silvia stood, balled the rest of her sandwich up, threw it in the paper bag, and wiped her hands on her jeans.

She rushed inside the house before April could formulate a question.

Aunt Silvia left the door open, and April got a rare glimpse into the gloom of the main room. Cardboard filing boxes and random furniture, a canvas on an easel in a ray of light from a single window. Aunt Silvia was an artist, and a good one. Two years ago she'd done a simple line sketch of April while they talked. April had it framed.

Aunt Silvia returned with a shaggy bundle of paper and notebooks held together with twine. She set the bundle next to April.

A distant but unmistakable wail came from the direction of the mine. It was a panicked noise, the sound of someone

56

in flight, telling you to run. A sick thrill of fear hit the pit of April's stomach. She shot to her feet and craned her head to look out over the open-pit mine. A small blur of movement near the pit, too far away to make out. And then it was gone so quickly April wondered if she had imagined it.

"What was that?" she asked.

"Coyotes," Aunt Silvia answered.

"It didn't sound like coyotes."

Aunt Silvia smiled, the same closed-mouth half smile her mom would make when April asked her a difficult question. The look she reserved for easy answers. Close to a lie, but not quite.

Sound traveled strangely out here, echoing across the artificial canyon of the open-pit mine. April tried to calm her breathing. Coyotes. Had to be.

Time to leave. It would be dark soon, and the rain clouds to the south were closing in.

April reached down and picked up the bundle of papers. It was surprisingly heavy, tied tight like a stack of newspapers from an old movie.

"What is all this?"

"He's alive," Aunt Silvia said. "The proof is in there."

The same thing Marianne had said.

April took a step back and stared at her aunt, feeling a brief swell of revulsion that passed almost as quickly as it came, like driving past roadkill and only smelling the rot a half mile down the road. The last thing April had expected from Aunt Silvia was cult dogma. A plea for April to use her magical Bicycle Girl powers to bring King Steenkampf back to life.

"Are you really asking me to bring King back from the dead?" April said bitterly.

"I'm not talking about King," Aunt Silvia said. "I'm talking about your father."

Father. The word seemed to echo across the artificial canyon below, resonating with the rocks and stones. The string cut into her fingers, and she tightened her grasp, pulling the string closer to her palm.

"You think my dad is alive?" she said.

Aunt Silvia nodded.

April searched her emotions for anger or denial, something to temper the sudden anxious excitement she felt. Searched, but didn't find. Out here, overlooking the mine, everything felt possible.

He is alive.

"How do I find him?" April asked.

"It's all in there," Aunt Silvia said, gesturing toward the bundle of papers in April's hand.

April gripped the string tightly, feeling a surge of frustration.

"Why don't you just tell me what I need to know?" April demanded.

Aunt Silvia looked out over the open-pit mine, eyes unfocused.

"There's so much you need to know," Aunt Silvia said. "And it's better that you find out for yourself."

"Where do I start?" April said. "I don't even know what I'm looking for."

"You'll know when you find it," she said.

Aunt Silvia picked up the paper bag, went into her house, and closed the door behind her.

FIVE

THE THICK BUNDLE of papers had a silent weight in the darkened car. On closer inspection, April noticed the edges of spiral-bound notebooks, interspersed with what looked like old newspaper clippings and sheets of sketch paper.

She tried to imagine what was in Aunt Silvia's assembled drawings and journals that could tell her, finally, where her dad was. She tried to tamp down the swell of hopefulness she felt.

Aunt Silvia had a lot of strange and dark ideas. A few months ago, April brought Aunt Silvia a set of art pens and a new sketch pad. Aunt Silvia had returned the sketch pad the next week with a series of drawings of the open-pit mine. They were good.

But the pictures gave April the shivers every time she looked at them. The shading was done in a fine-point cross-hatch, but if you looked closely, there were dozens of small human figures nested in every detail and shadow. Splayed, broken bodies at the base of cliffs; tiny, skinny gingerbread men cartwheeling over the edge of the open pit.

Scenes from a massacre.

But there were more than pictures in the pile: There were notebooks and documents.

If Aunt Silvia was right, there was proof that her father hadn't been part of that massacre.

Her anxiety lifted slightly as she drove through the mountain pass, but the uneasy feeling she had anytime she was near the compound wasn't entirely gone.

And then, things got worse.

There was an access road into the national forest just over the crest of the hill. No one ever used it. It was really there for firefighters. April rounded the curve, and the access road came into view. There was a dark truck parked on the road, lights off. She couldn't see inside the truck. Too dark.

A distant bolt of lightning lit up the sky right before her car passed the truck. It was the truck that had been at the drop-off loop.

April sped up as she passed the truck. She looked in her rearview mirror to see the truck pull onto the road behind her, lights on.

"Fuck!" she whispered.

Her heart sped, a sick, sour taste of adrenaline and fear like old coffee in the back of her throat. And anger. It made her angry to be afraid. Maybe it was nothing. She'd had a hundred false alarms, the sudden feeling of being watched that turned out to be her imagination.

Or not.

What if it was the man who'd tried to abduct April when she was eight?

Or someone just like him, ready to leave April in a ditch somewhere, just in case there really was a portal to Hell?

Better safe than sorry.

What if he was back?

April headed toward home, toward downtown. The black truck kept an even distance in the long drive down the mountain, never getting too close or straying too far. But there was nowhere else for him to go. Maybe it was just a coincidence that he was behind her.

Once she hit the edge of town, she turned off the highway onto Cedar Ridge, hoping that the truck would simply speed past on the way to I-10. The truck slowed, then made the turn behind her.

The small seed of anxiety in April's chest blossomed into a full-blown panic.

She slowed on the main road and made a sharp turn onto a neighborhood street in front of an oncoming car she hadn't seen because she was watching the truck in the rearview mirror. The driver of the oncoming car laid on the horn, and the black truck kept going, unable to make the turn. April's hands tightened on the wheel as she pulled her car back to the right to correct the overturn, her breath coming in short, jagged spurts.

She was driving too fast in a neighborhood, at risk of running into a parked car or worse. Fat, solitary raindrops were falling now, making the dry streets greasy slick.

She spotted an empty driveway on a cross street and turned, planning on that old trick of pulling into a driveway and killing the lights. It wasn't the best idea, because her powder blue car was very recognizable. But then again, so was the truck. If she told the police that she was being followed by someone in a brand-new black extended cab with tinted windows, they would find him. There weren't many trucks like that around.

April was about to turn into the driveway when a set of high beams appeared in her rearview mirror, nearly blinding her. Close now. She'd tried to shake whoever was following her once, but they weren't going to let that happen again. The neighborhood was empty; there was no one to help her.

Her phone was in her purse and her purse was in the footwell of the passenger side. She couldn't reach it.

Copperton was a sleepy town, but there would be someone around at the college. It was Friday night, and all she had to do was drive around until she found a frat party or a busy parking lot.

Somewhere with witnesses.

She turned onto University Avenue and drove back up the hillside toward the mountains and the small college. The truck followed, but now that she was back on a broad street the truck eased up a bit. Police cars routinely drove up and down the street from the center of town toward campus.

She had to run into one eventually. April would blare her horn, flash her lights, anything to get their attention.

She passed a gas station. It was empty except for a small woman at the register, mostly obscured by a display of lottery tickets and five-hour energy drinks. The woman was staring at her phone. April willed her to look up, but even if she did, what would she see? A car with a black truck close behind. Nothing weird about that. April was alone.

The sun had just gone down and only a few sprinkles of rain had fallen, but the streets were so empty it could have been midnight. Everyone was at the football game or inside for a long night of monsoon rain.

And then she saw him.

Zach, riding toward her on a bicycle so small, it could have been the same bike he used for trick riding in middle school. He should have looked ridiculous on the tiny bike, but he stood on the pedals and coasted downhill, hair blowing in the breeze behind him, oblivious of the drops of rain. April had never seen anyone more beautiful in her life.

She pulled the car across the empty oncoming lane and into the driveway of a funeral home, blocking his path.

"Whoa!" he said. He stopped the bike quickly, sending it in a skittering arc on the sidewalk. Small frown of annoyance.

April rolled down her window, trying to sound much cooler than she felt.

"Need a ride? It looks like it's about to start pouring."

Zach held his hand out, as though testing the air for the temperature of her desperation.

"No thanks. I'm good," he said.

The word "please" stuck in her throat.

It's not what you think. Please help me.

The truck sped past them. The tight band around her chest loosened. Too soon, as it turned out. The truck pulled a U-turn and came to stop half a block up the road, idling throatily.

Zach followed her eyes to the truck and back again.

"Who is that?" he asked.

"Just one of my fans, I guess," April said, trying to keep her voice light. Trying and failing.

Her voice cracked with fear. She hated that she was afraid. Hated that she needed help. April resolved that someday she would be just like Aunt Silvia, with a wild look in her eye and a shotgun in her lap.

She wouldn't be afraid of anyone. People would learn to be afraid of her.

Zach's eyes flashed with recognition, and he looked back

at April, putting the pieces together. Bicycle Girl, and crazed stalker.

"Want me to have a talk with him?"

"No!" she said too loudly.

She wanted to say that some of her fans traveled in packs. Some of her fans had guns. Zach thought he could handle anything, but he didn't know the depths of the world.

April pulled the handle to pop the trunk lid.

"Just—get in," she whispered hoarsely.

Zach appeared to contemplate this for a long second. Too long. Maybe he was thinking that this drama was her mess and not his.

April was afraid.

She didn't know what she'd do if he left her here.

But then again, she did. She'd just keep running.

Maybe Zach saw the fear in her face, or maybe he just hated a bully. He threw a backward glance and glowered at the guy in the truck.

Zach wedged his tiny bike into the back of the car and opened the passenger door to find the bundle of papers from Aunt Silvia in the passenger seat.

"Just put those in the back seat," April said. "Carefully."

The papers were important.

Zach picked up the bundle, and a stray paper fluttered to the passenger side floor. But he wasn't looking at it. He was watching the black pickup truck speed past with an angry roar of engine noise.

"Do you know him?" Zach asked.

"Never seen him before."

She closed her eyes and leaned her head momentarily against the steering wheel. It was raining in earnest now, and she shivered from the damp cold, or adrenaline. She waited for the inevitable barrage of awkward questions she didn't want to answer.

Do you recognize the truck?

Are you going to call the police?

Does this happen often?

Are you really going to open a portal to Hell?

"You okay?" Zach asked softly.

April nodded, her hair brushing the steering wheel.

"Do you think he's gone?"

"Maybe," Zach said. "I'll watch while you drive."

Zach yawned and settled into his seat. Normally, April would have attempted to fill the emptiness with conversation, but they were both silent, watching the roads as she drove. The silence was comfortable because it contained no questions. The four-year gap since the last time they hung out vanished.

She drove past the turnoff for the main street toward her house, winding along the park road toward the lower big ditch.

"You know how to get to my house?" he asked.

"I remember."

He smiled, a sly, closed-mouth smile, and she remembered

half a dozen nearly forgotten things. How much fun it had been to sit on that broken-down abandoned couch hidden in the trees near his house. They'd built a bunch of impromptu dirt-pack ramps for bike tricks in the empty lot at the end of his street. All of this before the movie came out.

The last time April had felt normal.

She hit a red light before the turn to his neighborhood.

They looked around for the truck, but it was nowhere in sight.

"It feels like he's gone," Zach said.

April exhaled. She felt as though she'd been tethered to the black truck and the line had snapped. She didn't trust that feeling. Maybe less the warm feeling of calm spreading over her limbs. Though it was probably an illusion, she felt safe around Zach.

Zach reached down to the footwell of the car and picked up the paper that had fluttered loose and studied it.

The overhead streetlight showed a photocopy of a government document, something to do with the mine. It looked pretty dense, but someone had taken a yellow marker and highlighted lines with the words *gold* and *silver*.

Strange. She wondered what a very old mining report had to do with her dad. He'd been foreman of the mine, but they hadn't been looking for precious metals. Copper mining had stopped long before the borehole project. She didn't know anything about gold or silver.

"Digging for gold?" Zach asked.

"Hardly."

Lightning flashed nearby, followed almost immediately by the crack of thunder. After studying the paper for a few seconds longer Zach reached into the back seat and set the paper on top of the bundle.

"So what is all that stuff?" he asked.

"Some papers that my aunt gave me," she replied.

She felt strangely protective of the papers. She had a sudden irrational feeling that if she didn't keep the papers to herself, her chance to find her dad might evaporate.

"Just a bunch of drawings and notebooks," she added. "Nothing important."

"Your aunt who lives near the mine?" he asked.

April nodded.

"I'm surprised you remembered," she said.

Not many people knew about Aunt Silvia, even among people in the town. April had admitted she had a hermit aunt who lived in a cabin overlooking the mine during a game of two truths and a lie years ago.

"She was there that day, wasn't she?" Zach asked.

That day. When anyone in town mentioned the massacre, it was always "that day," as if saying what really happened out loud would bring bad luck to the whole area.

"Aunt Silvia?" she said evenly. "I think so."

Zach turned his head back toward the mountain.

"My uncle was up there that day."

A sudden squall of rain cut the heavy silence in the car. A lot of people were there that day. A few people had survived. She hoped that Zach's uncle was among them. She should have known, but she couldn't remember him talking about his uncle. Maybe she didn't want to know, back then.

"He was killed?"

"Well, he didn't come back, so I guess so," he said.

April felt a sudden rush of shame. She'd lost her father to the massacre and later when the movie came out, she'd lost so much more. It was easy to forget half the town had also lost someone that day.

"I'm sorry," she said.

"Why are you sorry?" he replied. "It wasn't your fault."

"Not everyone agrees with you on that."

Zach shrugged.

"You know, sometimes it doesn't feel like he's really gone," he said. "It feels like he could just walk through the door."

She turned her head to look at him. The streetlight through the rain on the windshield gave the illusion that his face was melting, dark streaks running down his high cheekbones, the broad planes of his face. She had the sudden urge to tell him what Aunt Silvia had said about the bundle of papers in the back seat.

She felt the urge to confess to something.

He turned and smiled at her and the moment was over.

"I know that sounds weird," he said.

"No, I feel the same way about my dad," she replied.

He'd never felt dead.

And maybe he wasn't.

April turned onto the street next to the big ditch and guided the car onto the ancient wooden bridge. It was supposedly haunted, but more than anything, it felt borderline unsafe, especially in the rain.

"Do you ever worry that this bridge will fall into the ditch?" she asked.

"Can't happen soon enough," Zach muttered.

April looked over, surprised, but didn't say anything. Maybe the bridge was haunted after all. Wasn't her business.

Zach lived in one of the old manufactured homes along the ditch. His house wasn't hard to spot. He lived next door to a man with a junk pile disguised as yard art. There were more old-timey windmills and rusting Pepsi signs in his yard than she remembered.

"I see Mr. Wallace is still around," April said.

Zach quirked an eyebrow.

"You remember?" he said.

"Of course I do," April said softly. Her voice hung in the close air of the car, mournful. She remembered everything about the middle school days they'd spent hanging around the lot across the street. The strange glittering thrill she'd felt when he smiled or did a dumb trick on his bike and looked her way. She searched for a dry quip to salvage the moment, but her usual Bicycle Girl snark eluded her.

He put his hand on the car door, ready to dash out in the rain and grab his bike. He turned back and caught her eye.

"Hey, April, thanks for not asking," he said.

"Asking what?"

"Why I'm not at the game tonight," he said. "You're the first person not to ask how I'm doing."

She remembered what Grace had told her about Zach being knocked unconscious. He was out of the game and the team probably wasn't doing so well without their star running back. She wished she'd paid more attention.

"I'm not a fan of awkward questions," she said.

"Good to know," he said, his sly smile returning.

He nodded appreciatively before bolting from the car and retrieving his bike from the trunk. April thought about the way he'd said her name, like it was a gift. She watched him run the bike across his already flooded yard, then leave it on the tiny porch. She drove home, watching for the black truck the whole way.

SIX

BY THE TIME April made it home and pulled under the portico and out of the rain, warm percussive sheets of water streamed off the edge of the tile roof. She turned in her seat and looked at the street behind her, wondering if she'd be able to see that black truck through the rain.

There was a streetlight very near the front of the house and she waited until a car drove by, headlights piercing the gloom. Dark sedan. Not a truck.

She reached for her purse and dug for her phone. A shower of messages from Grace and Jules had arrived sometime after she crested the mountain, and one from Mom wondering where she was. Not good.

I made it home, she texted Grace.

I'll be over in the morning, Grace texted back.

Terse and to the point. April knew Grace planned to lecture her about going to Aunt Silvia's. She also knew that lecture would stop the minute April showed her the papers. Grace, more than anything, loved a research project, and April needed help if she was going to read through everything before her birthday.

She grabbed her purse and the bundle of papers and went in through the side door.

Jules was in the living room, sprawled on the couch, playing *Red Dead Redemption II* on an older system like a true chaos goblin. April was strangely relieved to see her. The chase down the side of the mountain left her with the kind of free-floating anxiety that too easily attached itself to Jules.

"Where have you been?"

Jules paused the game and lunged across the room to give April an aggressive, awkward hug. Normally, April didn't keep Jules apprised of her movements, but nothing was normal right now.

"I'm sorry, I should have told you. I went out to—"

"Aunt Silvia's, I know."

Jules pulled out of the hug and gave April an oversize eye roll. "When you didn't answer my texts, I had to ask Grace where you were." Jules looked down toward the bundle of papers.

"What's that?" she asked.

"Some papers that Aunt Silvia wanted me to go through," April answered.

She tried to make it sound like Aunt Silvia had given her three years of records of back taxes, dull as dishwater. Just holding the bundle of papers gave April a strange, hopeful feeling she couldn't quite explain to herself. It was too early to share that with Jules.

Her low-key tone of voice must have worked because Jules went back to her game.

"Mom wants to talk to you," she said.

"Did you tell her I was at Aunt Silvia's?" April asked.

"No. But I think she figured it out," Jules said without looking away from the game.

April sighed. She was dying to open the bundle and find the truth, but she had to talk to Mom first.

April hesitated in the wide arched doorway, wanting to look away from the game but unable to, drawn into the loveliness of the open starlight sky and computer-generated fire.

In the game Jules firebombed a group of men sitting around a campfire.

"How do you know those aren't the good guys?" April asked.

"Um, because they're bandits," Jules replied.

Another NPC tried to put out the flames, stomping at them ineffectually with pointed-toe cowboy boots. It didn't work. The realistic screams of burning cowboys echoed in

April's ears. A flaming man ran away from the fire and collapsed, CGI characters imitating tortured death throes.

Run.

Cowboys crawling away from the catastrophe, muscle and bone, flesh moving in pointless, random motion. Insides liquefied from the blast . . .

April looked away, the panicked yell she'd heard at Aunt Silvia's cabin still ringing in her ears, morphing into the screams of CGI cowboys. There was something there, something at the edge of her memory.

She shook it off.

"How many bandits are you planning on killing today?" April asked.

Jules looked up.

"All. Of. Them."

Jules turned her attention back to the screen. Her character got back on his CGI horse and rode away from the screaming.

April listened in relief as the yelling receded in the distance, drowned out by pounding horse hooves.

April left Jules to her game. She deposited the bundle of papers on her desk and went upstairs to Mom's room.

Mom was in bed, listening to an audiobook. With her eyes closed, dark hair loose around her face, she looked younger.

Mom turned off the audiobook when April entered. The lights were low, almost like candlelight, which was how her mom liked it. The shades were up on the windows. The storm had tapered off, and the mountain beyond was dotted with diffuse light from houses, flickering like candles in the slow rain. Mom's room had a panoramic view of the mountains and desert to the west. It was pretty at night, even when it was raining. April dropped onto the upholstered chaise by the bedside.

"How are you doing?" she asked.

Her mom hated to be asked this. She would rather talk about anything other than her fibromyalgia, but sometimes that was all they had to talk about.

"I'm fine. No brain fog right now, so that's good," she said crisply. "So you went to see Aunt Silvia?"

"She called me," April replied. No point in trying to lie.

Mom sighed deeply. She did this a lot. Fibromyalgia fatigue, worry about Jules, frustration with Aunt Silvia: It all blended together into a general weariness.

"What did she want?" Mom asked.

"A chicken sandwich."

Her mother peered at her skeptically.

"A chicken sandwich? Really?" Mom sighed. Again. "I thought we'd agreed you wouldn't go out there. Not right now."

"Sorry," April said.

Mom twisted her mouth into that disapproving line she reserved for all talk of Aunt Silvia. April had a snapshot memory from the before time, waiting on the front porch with Mom for Aunt Silvia. Because she was the cook at the compound, Aunt Silvia had a stash of mango ice cream she kept hidden in the big freezer. Mom and Aunt Silvia would sit on the front porch, laughing and eating ice cream, gossiping about all the people in the compound. They were sisters, but once, they'd been the best of friends too.

"Mom, how did Aunt Silvia end up at the compound, anyway?" she asked.

"Your dad offered her the job," Mom said. "He thought she'd keep me company. Of course, King adored her."

"Really?" April was surprised. She had vague memories of King Steenkampf as beyond old, sun wizened, and gaunt. Silvia was the younger of the sisters.

"Not like that," Mom said, making a face. "He loved her cooking. That's all."

April leaned her forehead on the side of her mother's bed. Carefully, because sometimes even small movements caused her mother pain. Her mom reached down and smoothed April's hair. And for an instant, she remembered what it was like when her mom was well and in charge.

"April, promise me you won't go back out there," Mom said. "At least until after your birthday."

April nodded.

She didn't need to go back out there.

She had the papers.

SEVEN

AUNT SILVIA HAD tied a bow with rough twine around the bundle. April tugged on the end of the string and it came free. There were spiral-bound notebooks and a dark blue leather blank book she'd given Aunt Silvia the previous summer. Several oversize pieces of sketch pad paper, lab notebooks, and two bound books of computer printouts.

She flipped through the pile of notebooks and found a slim hardbound book entitled *Supergravity and Akimov's Torsion Fields*, by G. Scripps Gardiner. She opened the book and started to read. She'd got as far as "The Einstein–Carton–Sciama–Kibble torsion theory of gravitation . . ." followed by a bunch of equations on the first page when the words swam away from her. It reminded her that she was behind in physics and needed to bring her grade up.

It wasn't going to help her find her dad.

Near the bottom of the pile was a stack of weathered sketch paper. April set the top of the pile aside until she reached the sketch paper. It wasn't one sheet but several taped together, yellowed, coffee stained at the edges, and ragged. April carefully unfolded the sheets and smoothed them flat on her desk.

It was a map of the compound, drawn in topographical detail. Numbers strewn across the landscape. The open-pit mine filled the center of the map, the edge rimmed by mountains to the back and right side of the mine.

The map was covered with small, tidy numbers, some clustered around the bore house, others around the pump, five near the edge of the pit. Two at the big house.

April stared at the map, the topographical loveliness of it. Aunt Silvia had a gift for rendering something so deep and three-dimensional on paper. It felt like if she leaned over, April would fall and keep falling, cartwheeling down like one of Aunt Silvia's gingerbread men.

In the corner of the map was a numbered list of names. Nineteen names, matching nineteen numbers on the map. At the top of the list was a guide to the abbreviations by all the names. GS: Gunshot. Exp: Explosion. F: Fall. P: Poison.

It was a map of the exact location and manner of death of everyone who died the day of the massacre.

A death map.

April knew that nineteen people had died that day, but the number had always been an abstraction for her. There could have been three or three hundred victims, and it would have landed in the same place in her psyche. Her father was the only victim who mattered to her.

But the map brought home the enormity of what happened the day of the massacre. Nearly two dozen people had died horribly, violently.

Somehow, Aunt Silvia had managed to account for every death at the compound.

April ran her finger down the list of the dead, checking and rechecking. Her father's name wasn't there.

Neither was King Steenkampf's.

If they hadn't died in the massacre, where were they?

She felt a sudden strange thrill of hopefulness, as though she'd found an ancient lottery ticket to an unclaimed prize.

For years after the massacre, she'd lain awake in bed at night, waiting for the sound of the front door opening, her dad's heavy boots on the floor.

No. It wasn't possible. Her father had been gone for too long.

She stared at the map, committing contours to memory, searching for hidden numbers in the topographical lines. They had to be there.

She turned the map over.

On the backside, in Aunt Silvia's neat print was a list of names.

April Fischer—left.
Olivia Fischer—left. Her mom.
Silvia Martin—left. Aunt Silvia.

Someone else also left before the massacre.

Dan Turnbridge—left.

And at the very bottom:

David Hernandez—?
Robert (King) Steenkampf—?
William J. Fischer—?

Her dad, a question mark.

April stared at the map for a very long time. Her mom had told her that Dad had died in the explosion. April had long suspected that wasn't the truth.

Now she knew.

The bundle of papers held daunting piles of lab notebooks, mining reports, old newspaper clippings, and geophysics reports that went over her head, but there were also years and years of Aunt Silvia's notebooks. There were recent notebooks but also ones that seemed to go all the way back to her time at the compound. Aunt Silvia had skipped writing for a few years after the massacre, but three years later, she'd picked it back up.

April decided to start with that journal. If she was going to find the history of what happened at the compound, it would be there.

She pawed through Aunt Silvia's drawings of desert rats, red-tailed hawks, and coyotes; recipes; and notes in a red spiral-bound notebook.

A fourth of the way in, she found something that stopped her cold.

I went into the compound today, Aunt Silvia had written. *I hoped to find some sign of where the portal might be, but the mine is so vast and so desolate, I couldn't find anything. I know April will remember someday.*

Oh god. Aunt Silvia believed in the portal.

Aunt Silvia, whom April had always loved and trusted, was a Deep Well cultist. How could it be that Aunt Silvia was aligned with a group of people who had tormented April for years?

And yet, it was right there, in Aunt Silvia's notebook.

Not only did Aunt Silvia believe in the portal, she was convinced that April had all the answers, just like all the cultists who were gathering in town expecting April to perform some dark and hidden rite to summon King Steenkampf. Such a secretive ritual that April had no idea what it was.

No.

Aunt Silvia would never betray her.

She wasn't like all the other cultists.

She certainly wasn't like Marianne.

April continued to read Aunt Silvia's journal, looking for more about the portal and King Steenkampf. She was relieved to find that when Aunt Silvia mentioned King Steenkampf, it was with none of the cultists' messianic, dear-leader ridiculousness. He was her boss, but they were on friendly terms. She found a typical entry.

King asked for chicken-fried steak tonight. He said he was tired of drinking his dinner through a straw. I told him his doctors wouldn't approve and he said, "Let's just keep it a secret, then." Hopefully it won't matter soon.

Hopefully it won't matter soon—that was odd. Was King Steenkampf ill?

It was hard to make sense of.

April put her head down on her desk and closed her eyes for a moment. It had been an insanely long day, of being hunted by the man in the black truck, of Aunt Silvia and chicken sandwiches.

And of Zach.

She smiled, thinking of the moment he'd told her that the massacre had nothing to do with her.

Maybe he was right.

She'd left the compound on her fifth birthday. How could a five-year-old know anything important?

And yet . . .

I know April will remember someday.

Aunt Silvia's words.

Aunt Silvia thought there was a secret locked in April's memories, something that would help to bring her dad back. April remembered so little of that day, it was hard to imagine what that could be.

She picked up the scruffy red spiral-bound notebook and kept reading.

EIGHT

SATURDAY

GRACE APPEARED ON the doorbell cam early the next morning. She held a box of something April could only assume were donuts from Breakfast Taco. Locals knew to go to the small anonymous house on the outskirts of town for the best donuts in this part of the state. The only hint that the house served anything was an ancient hand-printed sign in the front yard that said Breakfast Taco. That, and the line around the block on Saturday and Sunday mornings.

Jules beat April down the long hallway, elbows out. She threw open the door and gave Grace a big hug. Grace was not a big hugger, but from Jules she accepted it, donut box held to one side. The other hand patted awkwardly at Jules's back, until Jules finally released her.

April stood at the edge of the door.

"You went to Breakfast Taco for donuts?" she asked.

"They're not for you," Grace said pointedly. "They're for Jules."

Grace was annoyed with her for going out to Aunt Silvia's when there were dangerous people in town. April had expected this. And truthfully Grace had been right.

"I need milk," Jules said. She grabbed the box from Grace and hurried down the hall toward the kitchen.

Grace stepped through the doorway.

"You scared her, you know?" Grace said when Jules was out of earshot. "When the rain started, and you still weren't home, she texted me and—"

"I know," April said quickly.

The hissing sound of the espresso machine came from the kitchen. Jules was making coffee for them.

"And you scared me."

"I had a good reason to go out there." April lowered her voice. Jules was in the kitchen, but that didn't mean she wasn't eavesdropping. "Aunt Silvia gave me a bunch of papers."

Grace raised an eyebrow.

"Papers? What kind of papers did Aunt Silvia give you?" she whispered.

April lowered her voice to a bare whisper. "Journals, mining reports, lab notebooks—there's a lot."

Grace's eyes widened. "Lab notebooks?"

"I made coffee!" Jules yelled down the hall and they both

startled. They followed Jules back into the kitchen. The box of donuts sat open on the long butcher-block island. Slightly irregular, zero fucks given to decoration or donut adornment of any kind. Jules had made a cup of coffee with a lopsided foam tree. She didn't drink coffee yet but liked to make it, if for no other reason than to practice foam art.

April grabbed a donut and bit in. Warm, sugary heaven.

Grace ate a quick donut, passed on coffee, and insisted on washing her hands with a surgical thoroughness before she touched any of the papers.

"We really should wear gloves if we're going through old documents," she groused.

"Documents?" Jules asked. She straightened, looking far more interested in the papers than April liked. "Are these the papers you brought home from Aunt Silvia's last night? What are they?"

"Mostly mining reports," Grace answered breezily. "Aunt Silvia thought they might be of historical value, and she asked April to sort through them, with the idea that someone in the geology department of the college might be interested in having them. Do you want to help us?"

Jules's eyes had glazed over before Grace got to the end of her first sentence, and April marveled at how thoroughly Grace had quashed Jules's curiosity. It wasn't a lie, exactly. But it wasn't the truth either.

"No, I think I'm going to go play a game," Jules said.

Jules dropped the uneaten half of a second donut in the box and bounded from the room before Grace could ask her again.

"Brilliant," April said, once Jules had left the room.

"You're welcome," Grace replied.

"The papers are in my room," she said. "I'll go get them. Meet me in the dining room."

April took the bundle of papers to the dining room. She set the papers on the long, rough-hewn table. Like so much of the furniture in her house, the table seemed to have come from a different time, suitable for a family of fifteen. They almost never went into the dining room, April and Jules at least, preferring to eat at the big kitchen table.

April carefully unfolded the death map and smoothed it out on the table. She didn't say anything. She wanted Grace to come to her own conclusions.

Grace stood by silently, staring at the map. April understood the silence. The map had the same effect on her even though she'd seen it before. It was so finely detailed, as if Aunt Silvia had drawn it from an aerial photograph. April trusted every square centimeter of it.

Grace ran her hand over the numbers on the map, matched them to the key in the upper right corner.

"It's a map of where everyone died?" Grace asked.

"I think so," April replied.

Grace ran a hand down the legend, and leaned over, studying the names.

"Your dad isn't listed here," Grace said. "Neither is King Steenkampf."

"That's because their names are on the other side," April said.

April turned the map over and pointed to the question mark beside her dad's name.

"What do you think the question mark means?" Grace asked.

"I think it means neither of them died at the compound," April said.

"Hmmm . . ."

Grace pulled out her phone and sat in the nearest chair. She typed something into her phone, scrolled, typed some more, scrolled. She was definitely taking her time.

"I thought your dad died in the explosion," Grace said.

April looked up from the letters.

"That's what Mom has always told me."

"But you don't believe that?" Grace said.

April shrugged.

"I used to. Now, I don't think so."

Grace typed in a new site on her phone.

"What are you looking at?" April asked.

"Forensic pathology," Grace said.

"That explains everything," April replied somewhat impatiently. Grace tended to answer all questions in a way that only led to more questions.

April watched as Grace chewed her lip, a sign that she was thinking.

"Did you know that after a suicide bombing, a certain percentage of the injuries are people who are hit with flying bone fragments?"

"From the suicide bomber?" April asked.

"Uh-huh," Grace said. "The point is, soft tissue can liquefy in an explosion, but even if you are at the center of the blast, there should be bone fragments."

April dropped heavily into a chair, her stomach roiling at the mention of liquefying soft tissue. Bone fragments. She'd always been told that her dad had died in the explosion, but she never wanted to think about what that meant.

"Only people in the immediate blast zone die instantly," Grace said. "If you're within a certain range, your organs burst. If your aunt Silvia had come across the scene after the explosion, she wouldn't have been able to recognize the people closest to the blast."

Grace turned the map over to the front side and studied it. She traced a circle around a group of numbers clustered by what must have been the center of the explosion, a little distance from the bore house.

"Look at this," she said. "Most people in this circle probably wouldn't have died instantly. A certain number would have died of shrapnel injuries or head wounds, which could have taken minutes or even hours. But there is no number directly inside the blast zone."

April tried to ignore the feverish glow in Grace's eyes as

she imagined all the anatomically possible modes of expiring and calculated the lengths of time it would take to actually die from each one.

But even more disturbing than Grace's enthusiasm was the thought of Aunt Silvia, threading her way through the carnage, taking notes. Perhaps even drawing preliminary sketches in preparation for making the full death map. Why had she been obsessed with keeping track of every death? Did she suspect, even then, that King and April's dad wouldn't be among the dead?

"Maybe that's what the question marks are for," April said. "Maybe the question marks were for people who were so mangled Aunt Silvia couldn't recognize them."

She didn't want it to be true. Her dad, obliterated in an instant.

"Do you understand what I'm telling you?" Grace sharply set her phone down on the table. "Even if your father had been at the very center of the blast, pieces of his bones would have been embedded in other victims, even the surrounding ground. The FBI went all over the place and no bone fragments like that were ever reported. Your dad didn't die in the explosion."

April felt a sudden surge of excitement. She'd expected Grace to bring her back to earth, not to provide further evidence that her father wasn't dead.

"So if Dad didn't die in the explosion, where is he?" April said.

"You tell me," Grace said.

April sighed deeply. She would have to tell Grace sooner or later. Better to get it over with now.

"Aunt Silvia thinks the portal is real. She thinks both Dad and King Steenkampf went through the portal."

April couldn't look her in the eye. Grace, of all people, knew how much the cultists had made April's life hell.

Grace lifted an eyebrow, but at least she didn't laugh.

"Portal?" she said. "You mean, she thinks they traveled to another dimension?"

"I know it sounds crazy," April said, "but Aunt Silvia isn't a cultist. She's not obsessed with King Steenkampf. She was at the compound the day of the massacre, and she really believes in this."

"That's Aunt Silvia," Grace said. "What do you think?"

April closed her eyes for a moment. She had a fleeting image of a flash of light, a loud noise. She didn't know what it meant, or if it even had anything to do with the portal.

April tried to grab hold of that flash of light, to assign meaning to it, but the image dissipated, leaving her frustrated.

"I don't know what to think," April said. "I've tried to remember, but I can't."

"That's not surprising," Grace said. "Whatever happened the day of the massacre, it had to be traumatic."

"Maybe there really is a portal," April said, "but I know you must think that's impossible."

"I didn't say that," Grace said evenly. "I don't know what happened."

April was grateful that Grace's empirical mindset could extend this far. She'd expected Grace to reject the idea of a portal out of hand.

April glanced down at the pile of papers on the table: the lab books, notebooks, and letters. It seemed improbable that in the random stack of mining reports and reminiscences she'd find something that would not only jog her memory but would also help her figure out how to bend time and space. But she had to try. To bring her dad back.

"Aunt Silvia said I'd find the answer somewhere in all— this." April swept her hand over the table, gesturing at the piles of notebooks and the death map. So much to get through in a week.

"Maybe it would help if we figured out exactly what happened that day," Grace said.

April stood by her side and leaned over the map. She watched as Grace traced her finger down the names in the corner.

"Dr. Travers-Steenkampf is number one on the map," Grace said. "She must have been the first to die. And then number two, also at the house, is Gardener. No first name listed."

"Wait a minute," April interjected. "Are you saying that the deaths are in chronological order?"

She didn't know why this hadn't occurred to her earlier. April had assumed it was just easier to put numbers rather than names on the death map. She didn't imagine the numbers meant anything special to Aunt Silvia.

"I think so," Grace said. "So if you ignore the first two deaths, the next one is here, in the open-pit mine."

Grace pointed at the number in the pit, and back to the list of names. *F* for *fall* was written next to Tyler Landry's name.

"Number three, Tyler Landry."

"It's strange that he was the only person there to die of a fall," April said.

Grace looked up from the map.

"It is," she said. "And four people died next to the spot where he fell. That seems strange, doesn't it?"

An image from the movie came into her mind. Four teenagers under the demonic influence of Voidan tossing a boy over the edge of a cliff. That idea had to come from somewhere. The filmmakers claimed the Deep Well cultists believed a human sacrifice was necessary to open the portal. In all her time researching the cult online, she'd never heard mention of such a thing.

But that didn't mean it wasn't true. You wouldn't talk about human sacrifice on a Reddit thread.

"Do you think Tyler Landry was—a sacrifice?"

April shuddered involuntarily. It was easy enough to dismiss the idea of human sacrifice when it came from a movie as goofy as *Hellhole!*, but the possibility that a real person had been sacrificed on the day of the massacre filled her with horror.

"I don't think we can rule it out," Grace said. "The other possibility is that Tyler Landry fell accidentally, and people came running. But that doesn't make sense of the gunfight. What if people at the bore house saw the group by the pit sacrifice Tyler Landry and then opened fire?"

Grace's matter-of-fact tone brought April back from a dark place. This was all forensics to Grace, and that brought April a strange comfort.

"So deaths number four through eleven are over here, by the lubrication pump."

Grace circled her finger around a wide area on the map. Aunt Silvia had drawn a dotted outline of a rectangle to suggest where the pump had been. Scattered around the rectangle were the numbers. April looked up the names. All had died in the explosion, except for one.

"Number four, Roger Jones," April said. "He died of a gunshot wound, not the explosion. That's weird."

"Yeah, I'm not sure what that means," Grace said. "And then the rest of the deaths were from gunshot wounds. From gunfire back and forth from roughly here"—Grace pointed at the area around the bore house—"to the edge of the pit where Tyler Landry died."

April looked back at the map. If the four people who were shot by the pit had sacrificed Landry, they got what they deserved.

"Everybody had a gun," April said.

Something about that teased the corner of her mind. She wasn't surprised to find that so many people in the compound had guns, and she should have been.

Grace looked at her quizzically. "Why would so many people carry a gun at work?"

April shook her head. She felt like she knew the answer to that, but couldn't quite put her finger on it. She stared at the map, feeling that there was something she was missing.

Grace turned to the stack of notebooks.

"Maybe there's something in here that will make sense of things," she said.

They settled into reading. April decided to leave the science stuff to Grace and focus on making her way through Aunt Silvia's journals. She was afraid to skip anything in the journals for fear she would miss something important, but there was so much to read. So many recipes and observations about the garden.

Hours later, they were still reading.

Grace pushed away from the table and yawned.

"I have to go soon," Grace said apologetically. "And I have regionals tomorrow so I can't come over. . . ."

"Of course," April said.

Grace played the cello. Like everything she did, she took it seriously. Regionals led to all-state, and all-state would pad her already generous CV.

Grace pointed to the book, *Supergravity and Akimov's Torsion Fields.*

"Can I take this with me?" she asked.

"Sure."

April tried to return to reading after Grace left, but couldn't focus. She couldn't stop thinking about all the guns.

It was almost as if someone had planned for there to be a massacre.

NINE

SUNDAY

THE PATIO STONES *were triangles and squares. Some were dark brown, some pale beige shot through with red, and some almost pink. She played a game of getting from one side of the patio to the other by only touching the pink stones. Mom told her not to go over to the house, not to bother the doctor, but she wasn't ever there. A man worked on the yard, cutting and trimming. The gardener.*

April worried that he would yell at her for playing on the patio, but he didn't. He looked down and smiled. She thought he would go back to work, but he stood there smiling until his smile turned dark and scary.

"Open the door," he said.

"What door?" she asked.

"Time to fly."

He tilted his head and went back to cutting bushes with something that looked like a giant pair of scissors.

She hopped from the middle of the patio, hoping to make it around to the edge and back again using only pink stones, but the pink stones led in one direction—to the front door. She was trying to avoid the house, in case Dr. Travers-Steenkampf was there, and she would get mad and tell Mom she was "unattended." That was a bad word—unattended.

She tried to stay away from the door, but she couldn't because of the pink stones.

The double doors to the house were open, thick, carved doors thrown wide. The house was dark, like a mouth ready to swallow anyone who came near. April didn't want to go into the house.

He put a hand on her shoulder. She didn't turn around because she didn't want to see the man with the giant scissors again. But it wasn't the man with the scissors. It was King.

"I think we're going to sit this one out, sugar," King said.

He smiled down at her.

And then he was gone, and she was inside the house, wandering through the wide, tiled corridor, the open main room with a fireplace that stretched to the sky. April kept walking until she got to the dining room.

Dr. Travers-Steenkampf was there. She was seated in the tall chair at the top of a long table, head down on the table. April knew it was her because of her yellow hair in a tight bun on the back of her head. Dr. Travers-Steenkampf wasn't moving, so maybe she was dead, or maybe she wasn't dead, but there was a pool of something that looked sticky under her resting face. April didn't want to touch her. She didn't want to come any closer and find out. She walked around to the other side of the table. Dr. Travers-Steenkampf's tongue was out of her mouth, and it looked big and dry. Her eyes were half closed, and her face was a funny color.

April didn't think she was alive. But then, as she watched, Dr. Travers-Steenkampf sucked her thick, dry tongue back into her slack mouth. Her eyes flew open, and she looked at April, though she also still looked dead. Her limp hand came off her lap, and she reached out and grabbed April's shirt and pulled.

"Why did you let him kill me?" she screamed.

April awoke with a start.

The room was still her room, the same outlined shapes in the dark, the slim neck of a guitar on a stand in the corner, armchair piled with a shapeless mass of clothing. But something was different. A strange musty scent like moldy books filled the room. April had a dim sense of wrongness, and as her eyes adjusted, she realized with horror that the lowest drawer of the dresser was open and a ragged outline of papers showed, just a slim pale band against the dark dresser. It was the bundle of notebooks and papers from Aunt Silvia, gathered together after Grace had gone home.

April knew she'd hidden that bundle under a layer of T-shirts.

She knew she hadn't left the drawer open.

April didn't want to move, but she willed herself to get out of bed. She crept over to the dresser, poked the edge of the bundle back down, and slammed the drawer. It squeaked closed.

She leaped back in bed and kept her eyes trained on the dresser. She didn't want to take her eyes off it. As long as she watched, the bundle would stay in the drawer and out of her dreams. They were so real.

The air was thick with silence. April felt like she wasn't alone. She stayed perfectly still, watching the drawer for any sign of movement for what felt like hours before she finally fell asleep.

In the first light of morning, April realized that the bundle of papers hadn't moved by itself. Her mom wasn't likely to have gotten up in the middle of the night to riffle through the dresser. That left only one possible explanation.

Jules.

April opened the dresser drawer slowly. The bundle was still there on top of a stack of T-shirts.

She picked up the bundle and turned it over. Everything looked exactly as it had when she put it away for the night, stacked in the same order, tied up with the same twine. If anything, it looked too neatly tied.

This was Jules's handiwork, no doubt about it. Jules was a master of prying open locked drawers, shuffling through stacks of mail for urgent notices from school, and returning the mail to almost exactly the same position as before.

She couldn't be sure if Jules had taken something, but she couldn't be sure she hadn't either.

"Jules?" she yelled.

Jules didn't answer. She didn't come running like she usually did when April called her name.

April found Jules standing at the long butcher-block island, eating a bowl of muesli.

"You were in my room last night." It wasn't a question.

Jules looked up in surprise, her face so guileless April momentarily entertained the idea that the bundle of papers had thrust itself out of her chest of drawers on its own.

"But I wasn't!" she protested.

"Wasn't what?" Mom stood in the doorway, wearing a soft knit wrap dress and slippers, a look just slightly more formal than pajamas.

"Trying to steal my red lipstick," April said, fixing Jules with a this-isn't-over look.

"You're too young to wear red," Mom said.

For once, Jules didn't argue.

April headed for the espresso machine and made a cup.

"Mom, can I go to Luna's house?" Jules asked. She launched her half-eaten bowl of cereal at the sink, eager to escape.

103

"I can take Jules to Luna's house," April said.

"I don't need a ride," Jules said.

"Could you? That would be wonderful," Mom answered.

"I don't need a ride," Jules reiterated.

They both ignored Jules.

"Hello, am I even here?" Jules said, twisting her face into a mask of grievance. "I said I don't need a ride. I can walk."

"I don't want you walking alone," Mom said. "Not right now."

Jules glowered but relented. "Not right now" was a coded reminder of danger. Jules had seen the black truck in the drop-off loop. Like everyone else since Emma basically doxed her in middle school, the guy in the truck knew where she lived. He probably knew that April had a younger sister.

The thought of the man in the black truck trailing Jules through the streets sent a cold shiver down April's spine. She wished there was somewhere—anywhere she could send Jules until her birthday was over. Somewhere safe.

April put on a high-necked Victorian-style dress, oversize dark sunglasses, and floppy sun hat that, in combination with the glasses, obscured a full 80 percent of her face. She went to the car to wait for Jules, ignoring the two men in the ancient Honda Accord across the street, who raised phones when she appeared. She could feel the waves of frustration coming from the car, as they took videos of her hat.

Oddly, the presence of these two horror chasers reassured her. If the man in the black truck showed up, they'd post him on TikTok three minutes from now. He was creepy enough.

Jules ran out the front door, one arm through her jacket, trailing her tiny fake fur purse that looked for all the world like a dead hamster. She called it Booshie. Watching her run across the yard like that, April remembered that Jules was twelve. Everything that was happening around them had to be weighing on her.

Jules threw open the door and fastened her seat belt.

"Let's go," Jules said cheerily.

She couldn't blame Jules for being thrilled to escape the house. After the man had shown up at April's elementary school, Mom had installed a state-of-the-art security system—multiple cameras and an alarm that went straight to the local police. The house felt safe in the way that prison feels safe. No easy way in, no easy way out. Not with the parade of disaster tourists driving by.

April backed the car down the driveway and took off toward Luna's house.

They settled into silence. April tried to figure out the best way to ask Jules about coming into her room in the middle of the night. The more she thought about it, the creepier it felt, and the more unlike Jules. Jules could be sneaky, but she'd never come into April's room while she was asleep before. Jules was a heavy sleeper, and April wasn't. The idea that Jules would be up at three in the morning, prowling silently around the house struck April as unlikely.

"Did you come into my room last night?"

"God!" Jules huffed. "I told you I didn't!"

At the long traffic light on the highway, April turned in her seat to stare at Jules for a full ten seconds, long enough to make Jules squirm.

"You know I can read minds, don't you?" April said.

Jules shot a look April was used to seeing from her more gullible classmates. Guarded curiosity, mixed with fear. When Jules was in fifth grade, someone at a sleepover told her that April was the Bicycle Girl, and that April could read minds. Jules halfway believed it.

April regretted pulling her whole Bicycle Girl routine on Jules. Jules had reason to be scared of the entire world right now. April didn't need to add to that.

"You're being so creepy," Jules said.

"Sorry," April said.

Jules wrapped her arms around her chest, chewed on a thumbnail.

"What do you and Grace think you're going to find out anyway?" Jules asked. "Are you trying to debunk the portal before your birthday? Before the weird cultists arrive?"

"But what if they're right about the portal?" April said absently.

Jules frowned and chewed furiously on her thumbnail.

April regretted saying anything.

"Trust me," April said. "I know things seem crazy right now, but I know what I'm doing."

They rode in silence. April worried that Jules was going to chew her thumbnail down to the quick. She was glad that Jules was going to spend the day playing video games and painting fingernails with Luna. She needed to get away.

She pulled to a stop at a red light, and Jules took her thumb out of her mouth and turned in her seat.

"Okay, technically, I didn't go into your room, but I stood at the doorway," she said quickly. "Your door was open, which was weird, and you were—moaning."

April studied Jules's face.

"You didn't open the drawer and pull out the bundle of papers?" April asked.

"No." Jules looked confused.

April didn't always know when Jules was lying, but she usually knew when Jules was telling the truth. As she was now. Jules hadn't snuck into her room.

"You talk in your sleep," Jules said.

"No, I don't," April said, laughing. She'd never once talked in her sleep.

"You did last night."

"What did I say?"

"'I didn't kill you,'" Jules answered, looking away.

A wave of nausea washed over April as the dream came back to her: Dr. Travers-Steenkampf's head in a pool of sticky liquid, her tongue, dry and swollen, protruding between cracked lips. Blaming her. She hadn't killed anyone, but whatever had happened at the compound that day, it was something April had set in motion.

And if she'd done it before . . . ?

She pulled into the driveway of Luna's house and put the car in park.

Jules turned in her seat and faced April.

"Are you okay?" Jules asked.

"I'm fine," April answered reflexively.

She wasn't fine and Jules wasn't an idiot.

"Once we get past your birthday, everything will be better," Jules said in a small voice. "I have a plan. You'll see."

"Better," April murmured absently.

She tried to shake the image of Dr. Travers-Steenkampf, dead on the dining room table. If April was going to undo what she had done, to bring her dad and, yes, King Steenkampf back, she'd have to unearth her memories of that day and make sense of—everything.

"Text me when you're ready to come home, and I'll get you," April said.

Jules bolted from the car and ran to Luna's front door, tiny furry purse swinging behind her.

TEN

WIKIPEDIA

1936 OJO DE CRISTO MINE FIGHT

On October 10, 1936, eleven men were killed and eight injured when a fight broke out at the edge of the Ojo de Cristo mine. According to eyewitness accounts, the fight started when John Coraghessan pushed foreman, Lowell Herbert, into the open-pit mine, killing him instantly. John Coraghessan claimed that the bosses were "stealing all the gold." The mine was slated to be decommissioned due to depressed copper prices, and tensions were already running high at the site. Subsequently, fighting broke out between hired security guards and disgruntled workers.

At trial, John Coraghessan pleaded not guilty, swearing a voice from the open pit told him to look for hidden gold. He was found guilty of first-degree murder and was executed in 1940.

Spencer County records from the period show that in 1933 the Ojo de Cristo mine shipped 2 million tons of copper, 200,000 ounces of silver, and 10,000 ounces of gold. Between 1934 and 1936, the mine shipped equivalent amounts of copper and silver, but no gold. There is no evidence that Lowell Herbert was in any way responsible for the disappearance of the gold, worth roughly seven million in today's dollars.

The gold has never been recovered.

APRIL STARED AT the image of the big house on the map.

Dr. Ella Travers-Steenkampf, number one—the first person to die.

The one person who died in the main house.

P for *poison*.

Number one, in the dining room with the poison. Like a perverse game of Clue, but real. The dream had not just been a dream, it had been a memory. She'd seen Dr. Travers-

Steenkampf, dead on the dining room table, swollen tongue protruding from between her lips.

Almost everyone else in the compound had died from the explosion or from gunshot wounds. Dr. Travers-Steenkampf was the only one to have died of poisoning.

And yet, April had seen Dr. Travers-Steenkampf, or more accurately her corpse. She remembered it now. Aunt Silvia must have seen her too, or she wouldn't have been able to place her on the map.

How had that happened? Who poisoned her? Or had she killed herself?

No. Not Dr. Travers-Steenkampf.

It didn't make any sense.

April was sure of one thing. She had been there, in the big house. When had Dr. Travers-Steenkampf died?

It had to be before the explosion. Before she and Mom made their way out of the compound and ended up at the motel with the swimming pool and the Coke machine.

The timeline didn't make any sense.

Sometime between the moment April had seen Dr. Travers-Steenkampf dead on the dining room table and the moment Mom had ushered her out of the compound, Dad and King Steenkampf had disappeared off the face of the earth.

If only she could remember.

April settled in to skim through years of old mining reports. She learned that the mine not only produced copper but silver and gold as well. The mine had been closed and reopened half a dozen times over the twentieth century.

It was hard to tell what any of this had to do with the portal. The bundle of papers Aunt Silvia had given her seemed thrown together with little sense of organization.

She sighed and put her head down on the table.

A flash of light, a loud noise, and then—gone.

That image had flitted across her mind, and now, when she thought about it, she felt a tight grab of emotion in the center of her chest, something almost gleeful, like the whisper of a voice telling her . . .

Telling her—what?

Nothing.

Whatever it was, it was gone.

She glanced at the unfolded map spread out on the table. The death map was an attractive nuisance, horrifying and beautiful in equal measure. There was something about the map she was missing, a bigger piece of the puzzle.

She turned it over and studied the names on the back of the map.

> *April Fischer—left.*
> *Olivia Fischer—left.*
> *Silvia Martin—left.*

They weren't the only ones who escaped that day.

Dan Turnbridge—left.
David Hernandez—?
Robert (King) Steenkampf—?
William J. Fischer—?

April googled Dan Turnbridge. There were several Dan Turnbridges, none of them from Copperton. There were two from Louisiana and one from Mississippi who were possible candidates, but she couldn't narrow it down.

And then she remembered.

Zach said his uncle had died in the massacre.

Zach's last name was Hernandez.

David Hernandez. There was a question mark by his name. Just like by her dad's. She didn't know why it hadn't occurred to her earlier. David Hernandez had to be Zach's uncle.

She needed to talk to Zach.

There was a college football game, and Zach would almost certainly be working a late lunch rush at the Coppermine. Maybe it was a mistake to go to the Coppermine during a football game, but the clock was ticking. She couldn't wait until school on Monday to see him.

April went to her room, put on some makeup, and changed into black jeans and her favorite shirt, which was black with lace insets. She drove to the Coppermine bar, the carefully folded death map on the passenger seat beside her. She kept checking her rearview mirror for the black truck.

The parking lot was more full than usual—even for a game day. April couldn't help but wonder how many people were in from out of town for her birthday. There had to be a few in the yard would recognize her on sight, maybe even a Deep Well cultist.

She scanned the yard, looking for anyone suspicious, but it wasn't like they'd be wearing signs.

Zach was working the front at CHAR. He saw her and nodded through the window and went back to work.

April stood awkwardly in the middle of a yard filled with older people in crimson and white, watching a game on a big screen under the eaves. She was dressed all in black, emanating a black and uncertain mood in all directions. People stared. That was nothing new, but she didn't usually wade into the middle of an open space as though on display, and certainly not six days before her birthday. She'd hoped that the football crowd would provide safety and anonymity.

It had been a mistake to come.

She wanted to leave, but it was too late to back away slowly. Zach had seen her.

He strode out of the food truck with an order of green chili cheese fries, looking extra shiny in the Sunday afternoon sun.

It did not improve April's mood.

He deposited cheese fries on a table, made a random chummy remark to a middle-aged man about the game on TV, before ambling toward her as slowly and deliberately as someone tall and known for his speed on the field could manage.

"April?" he said in a voice that was sandpaper to her already frayed nerves. It was deep and customer-service friendly but also interrogating the idea of customer-service friendliness. She half expected him to say "May I take your order?" and smirk.

"Hey," she said. "I didn't realize you were so busy. I can come back later."

Game watchers at a nearby table whispered and laughed.

When April glanced over, a guy in an American flag button-down shirt held his phone out and looked at her. She imagined he was comparing the viral video of April entering her house with the real thing. Had to be the stupidest video ever.

He met her eyes and murmured, "Oooh, spooky!"

"Don't mind them," Zach said in a cheery voice, slightly too loud. "They're idiots."

The guy dressed in the flag shirt looked Zach up and down and decided to ignore the comment.

In a way, Zach reminded her of Grace. He had a certain gravitational stillness borne out of being exactly the person he seemed to be. It was pleasantly intimidating, without being overbearing.

April searched for some of the frosty Bicycle Girl remove that had seen her through most of high school, but it failed her.

"What's in your hand?" he asked.

"It's—something my aunt Silvia drew," she said.

His eyes flashed, and he leaned toward her, an intense look of interest on his face. She felt a glow of happiness spread across her, followed almost immediately by an icy slap of self-annoyance. Her rationale for showing him the map was paper-thin. She'd driven here with the death map just to see him again, outside of school.

"And you wanted to show it to me?" he asked.

"I just thought, since you asked about the papers . . ." She trailed off.

Had he really asked about the papers? She couldn't remember. The way he smelled, his sly smile when she'd said she wasn't a fan of awkward questions—this is what she remembered from the drive home in the rain. The conversation, not so much.

A man went to the window at CHAR. Zach waved to him.

The man at CHAR's counter shifted from foot to foot and glanced over impatiently. Zach ignored him.

"You're so busy. I'll come back later," she said, both of them knowing that she wouldn't.

People were waiting to order dirty bird sandwiches, cheering at a near touchdown.

"Give me a couple of minutes, okay?" he said. "You can wait over there."

He nodded toward an empty table near the back fence, far away from the screens and the game watchers. Zach went back to work.

April sat at the table. She took out her phone and stared at the blank screen just as Lara from the coffee truck came over with a warm gingerbread cookie and a coffee.

"From Zach," she said.

"Oh." April was too surprised to remember to thank her. It had been a while since anyone bought her a coffee, or at least one she'd actually drunk. April thought of Marianne, standing in the parking lot of the Sonic, sweat from the side of her to-go cup dripping down her arm.

April took a sip of the coffee, but her stomach was sick and sour, threatening to turn. What if his uncle had a different last name? David Hernandez could have been anyone.

Zach probably wasn't going to thank her if he found out that his uncle had been shot or died in the explosion.

Mom had told her that Dad died instantly and painlessly in the explosion. Of course, Grace had thoroughly and gruesomely debunked that idea.

If Zach's uncle died in the explosion, she'd sell that fantasy of instant death. She knew from experience that it was easier to take.

Ten minutes later, Zach rounded the corner of the CHAR truck and headed her way.

"Sorry about that," he said.

"No worries. Thanks for the coffee and the cookie."

"What did you want to show me?"

He nodded in a way that made her think he was still on limited time. The crowd had settled, but the line at the open bar window for beer was as long as it had been when she arrived. It snaked past the wide opening to the gravel parking lot and the college guy at the door checking IDs.

She spread the map out on the picnic table, weighting the corners against the cool fall breeze with salt and pepper shakers.

"Wow—it's the mining compound, isn't it?" Zach said.

He leaned over and studied the map intensely.

She understood his awe. It was a very detailed and technical drawing that somehow managed to capture the massive scale of the thing.

"What are the numbers for?" he asked. He was already tracing his hand down the names in the corner, making the connection.

"Um—it's a map of where everyone died," she said.

Zach leaned over the map, fingers tracing the scatter plot of death.

"So many gun deaths," Zach said, staring at the map. "Where did all the guns come from?"

"Steenkampf collected guns," April replied. "I think he handed them out."

The answer to the question that had puzzled her yesterday popped into her mind, unbidden. Why so many guns? Because King wanted them there.

"How do you know that?" Zach asked.

"He let me fire one."

Seeing the map again had shaken loose her memories. They tumbled out randomly now, but never the one thing she wanted to remember.

There was a firing range at the back of the main house, and she remembered Mr. Steenkampf clamping a set of oversize hearing protectors on her head, holding her hands steady as she squeezed off a shot with a pistol. The gun was pretty. Pink pearlized handle and very small.

April had the feeling he'd bought it just for her.

Zach looked up from the map and studied her face.

"You were five when you left the compound," he said. "Are you sure?"

"It was a very small pistol," April replied.

"And your mom was okay with that?"

Mom would never have let her fire a gun, and certainly not at five. April was sure King Steenkampf hadn't asked her.

"I don't think she knew."

"Wow," Zach said softly. "That's so fucked-up, April."

"Just part of being the Bicycle Girl," she said. She tried for a breezy tone of voice but failed to keep the bitterness out.

"I never thought of you as the Bicycle Girl," he said.

She bristled, thinking of all the times Emma had made a joke about her being the Bicycle Girl, when they all used to hang out together in the field across from his house. He never said anything terrible, but he never stopped Emma either. Usually he just got back on his bike or board and did another cool trick on one of his homemade ramps. He literally skated on empathy back then.

"You did when we were thirteen."

Zach looked down and grimaced.

"Yeah, I was kind of an asshole back then," he said. "But, then again, I was thirteen."

"Fair," she said.

She remembered herself at thirteen. How she'd made fun of Mr. Wallace's yard trash, and the general junkiness of Zach's neighborhood. She'd probably been just as much of an asshole.

Zach turned his attention back to the map. He leaned over and read through the list of names in the upper right-hand corner of the map.

"Is your uncle there?" April asked.

He shook his head.

"I don't understand? He died there. This map is wrong."

"What's your uncle's first name?"

"David," Zach murmured.

She knew before he told her. His uncle was a question mark, one of the three men in limbo, fate unknown.

She turned the map over.

David Hernandez—?
Robert (King) Steenkampf—?
William J. Fischer—?

He leaned over the paper, staring at the names at the bottom.

She waited. It was a lot to absorb.

Zach straightened.

"I don't get it," he said. "Why is there a question mark by my uncle's name?"

"It means they never found his body," April said.

"But what about the explosion?" he said. "My uncle was supposed to have died in . . ."

Zach stopped mid-sentence, his eyes trained on something in the distance. April followed his gaze to the parking lot, past the now much shorter line of people at the beer window.

The black truck drove slowly past the opening in the wooden fence. The tinted windows on the truck were closed, but she could feel whoever was inside the cab scanning the parking lot, looking for her.

"Isn't that the same truck that followed you the other night?" he said.

She nodded, her mouth too dry to speak. The sick, sour taste of fear and adrenaline mingled with coffee in her mouth, her heart racing. He knew what her car looked like.

Zach stepped in front of her, blocking the truck from view. More importantly, hiding her from the man in the truck. Her heartbeat slowed, marginally.

At least she wasn't alone—this time.

"What's your number?" Zach asked quickly.

She rattled off her phone number and he texted her. She felt the phone ping in her pocket.

"There's a gap in the fence behind CHAR," he said. "Go and wait for me to text. When he comes in, I'll text you so you can get out of here."

"How will you know who he is?" she asked.

Zach looked grim.

"I'll do my best," he said. "But text me and let me know that you got away. If I don't hear from you in a couple of minutes, I'll come out."

She nodded.

She took the time to fold the map carefully. It was history and proof.

Zach put a hand on her arm, and she turned back.

His dark eyes were warm and filled with concern. An unfamiliar feeling flooded her.

"I want to know more," he said. "Can I come by your house tomorrow after school?"

"Of course," she said.

Zach walked alongside her to the edge of CHAR and then kept going.

"Wish me luck," she said, turning to thread her way behind the food trucks.

"Luck," he said.

April crept behind the truck until she found a place where two sections of the wooden fence overlapped, leaving a small

122

space between. She squeezed through and walked along the wall toward the parking lot.

She hid behind the fence and waited for Zach to text.

Across the big ditch, two kids playing in a small backyard looked up and stared. April wondered if they recognized her as the Bicycle Girl. Probably too young, but it gave her an exposed feeling anyway.

Two guys came in at the same time, Zach texted. **I think I know which one is the guy in the truck.**

April's pulse ratcheted up. The man who had chased her down the mountain, who showed up outside Jules's school was here. And if he didn't find her in the yard, what would he do?

Where is he? she texted.

Heading in from the parking lot—stay hidden.

She pulled her back against the fence and held the phone tight to her chest. It was on silent, but even the small vibration of an incoming text felt like too much noise.

She tried to still her racing heart. If the man in the black truck found her, she'd scream. She was standing only a few yards away from a couple of dozen people watching the game. Someone would come. They were yelling at a ball game, drinking beer, and half the people in the crowd would probably cheer if someone dragged her off, but . . .

No. That wasn't fair. Zach was here. Zach would help her, and if he came running, people in the yard would follow.

The thought gave her courage.

Zach sent a grainy picture of a stocky man in his late thirties. He was wearing dark glasses and a baseball cap.

This is the guy. He went into the bar, Zach texted. **Go now!**

She turned the corner and walked toward the row of cars parked on the gravel.

Her car was toward the end of the row. The black truck that had followed her down the mountain was parked three cars away. It was a massive truck with an extended cab, and the truck bed stuck out in the parking row. No mistaking it.

She stopped behind the truck, heart pounding.

A sticker on the bumper read *John 8:44*.

The sound of someone laughing startled her out of a reverie.

April shot a glance behind her toward the open door in the fence. She watched as a couple of college students made their way in through the double doors, wallets out, digging for driver's licenses for the guy carding by the door.

She had to trust that the guy Zach had seen searching the yard was the man who had chased her.

She ran to her car, then peeled out of the parking lot with a spray of gravel.

When she made it home safely to her driveway, security cameras surrounding the house in all directions, she pulled out her phone and typed in *John 8:44*.

A Bible verse popped up immediately.

You belong to your father, the devil, and you want to carry out your father's desires. He was a murderer from the beginning, not holding to the truth, for there is no truth in him. When he lies, he speaks his native language, for he is a liar and the father of lies.

The words on the screen blurred. April realized her hand was shaking. She scanned the street behind her, the side yard, feeling suddenly exposed.

Even at her darkest moments, after the movie came out, April knew that for most people the whole Bicycle Girl thing was a big joke.

But not to everyone. After the movie came out, she and her mother and Jules had been shopping for school supplies at a store near the highway, when a woman came up and screamed "Spawn of Satan!" at April, over and over. It took one overwhelmed security guard and eventually two long-suffering policemen to drag the woman away.

You belong to your father, the devil, and you want to carry out your father's desires.

April knew it was just a Bible verse, but it felt like a personal attack. Like the woman in the office supply store, the man in the black truck was a true believer.

And now, April was absolutely certain that he wanted her dead.

ELEVEN

MOM HADN'T COME down to dinner, and April and Jules made grilled cheese sandwiches to go with store-bought tomato basil soup. After a dinner at the kitchen table, Jules lounged in the living room watching a rom-com on Netflix, and April sprawled on a nearby couch. She tried to focus on the story, but she couldn't shake the uneasy feeling of being watched.

She knew that feeling wasn't entirely rational. The house had a half dozen security cameras, dead bolt locks, and barred lower floor windows. No one could so much as peer into a window without setting off alerts. The house felt safe—for now—but it also felt like a prison. They were all marking time until after April's birthday. Waiting for some future when they would be safe to leave the house again.

Knowing that the man in the black truck could be lying in wait just out of range of the security cams made April feel restless and trapped.

She abandoned the rom-com and went to a room at the back of the house.

The office room was full of things Mom had gotten out of storage after the massacre, and it felt more like a museum than a part of the house.

There was a box of her parents' wedding photos and memorabilia on the bookshelf. It was one of the few reminders of her father in the house. The box was white satin brocade–covered, easy to find.

She opened it on the desk and set aside the white lace garter and dried bouquet of roses. Laid neatly on top of a stack of pictures was her parents' marriage license, signed by them both. Mom's handwriting was a hurried scrawl.

Dad's signature. Big *W*, big *F*, the rest evenly spaced and unhurried. Underneath, his name in block print.

"Whatcha doing?"

April turned. Jules leaned in the doorway eating a mango bar.

"Looking at Mom and Dad's wedding photos," April replied.

"Why?"

"No particular reason," she said.

April pulled a group of photos off the stack. One of the first was her mom and dad right after their wedding, Dad in a guayabera shirt, barefoot on the beach, Mom in an off-the-shoulder lace dress, looking regal and serious. They'd gotten married on a casino beach in Mississippi, just a few miles from the offshore rig where he was a foreman.

He looked younger than April remembered, more relaxed than she'd ever seen him. All her memories of Dad were from the compound. He'd been a stern presence, but it was possible he'd been worried about everything going on around him. She wished she'd known this barefoot, laughing version of Dad.

"Can I see?" Jules stuck the last of the mango bar in her mouth and wiped her hands on her jeans.

April held out a stack.

Jules stared at the top picture.

"Dad was hot," Jules said.

"I guess he was," April replied.

Jules held the photo next to April's face and squinted.

"You look like Dad," she said.

April supposed that was true. People often remarked how much Jules looked like Mom. Mom and Jules both had heart-shaped faces, arched eyebrows, bow-shaped lips. April had high cheekbones, straight brows and lips, a square jaw, like her father. It was a face of serious angles and moods, occasionally given to what Grace called her "resting murder face."

"What was Dad like?"

Jules had asked her this before, and April always gave an

easy answer: He was big. He was tough but sweet. She didn't get to see him as much as she liked.

Answers from the five-year-old April had been the last time she'd seen her father. She didn't know him, not really.

If Aunt Silvia was right, Dad had gone through a portal to another dimension more than ten years ago. Ten years was a long time, if time even functioned in the same way in this alternate dimension. What would he be like if he came back?

He'd be the only father Jules would ever know.

That alone was worth the risk.

"He liked to laugh," April said. Remembering how he used to pretend to be asleep on the couch, and she would try to run by him quickly so he couldn't grab her and tickle her. Which he always did.

She picked up the next picture from the wedding, a group of guys on the beach. Friends of Dad's or people he worked with, most likely some combination of the two. April wondered where they would be now if they'd stayed in Mississippi. How many members of the wedding party had followed him to New Mexico and death?

It was an accident. Dad didn't mean for any one of them to die.

Dad was in the center of the picture on the sand, left arm holding a champagne bottle, wrapped around the shoulder of one of his friends. Another friend on the other side. Some of the wedding photos seemed professionally done, probably at an earlier time, but this one was a Polaroid. Someone must have brought their camera to the wedding.

She turned the picture over absently. The date of the wedding was written on the back in black Sharpie, along with names of the people in the picture. Hector—Bill—Dan.

Dan.

The name was familiar.

"I don't see what's so special about this picture," Jules said.

"It's just—Dad looks so happy here," April said.

Dad, his pants legs rolled up, wet at the bottom as though he'd splashed around in the ocean. Drinking champagne, laughing. She wished that she'd gone to the ocean with Dad, just once.

"Do you ever wish you'd gotten to meet him?" April asked.

"Um—yeah!" Jules said with as much eye-rolling sarcasm as she could muster. Which was a lot. "It's not really fair that you got to be with Dad, and I didn't even get to meet him, is it?"

"Sorry," April said.

"Not like there's anything we can do about it now," Jules said.

Not exactly true, April thought.

Jules chucked the stick from the mango bar in the trash and left to play video games.

April set the Polaroid of Dad on the beach with his friends to the side. Whatever else it might be, it was just a great picture. She decided she would put the picture in with the bundle of papers Aunt Silvia had given her. It was a reminder of why she was doing all this.

She carefully restacked the photos underneath the marriage license, the garter, and the dried bouquet, and put the white brocade box back on the shelf. She had hoped that seeing a picture of Dad would trigger a memory of the last moment she'd ever seen his face. The moment before he disappeared.

Instead, it simply reminded her of everything she'd lost.

April went to her room and found the pile of papers. She unfolded the map and laid it out on her bed next to the Polaroid of Dad and his friends on the beach.

There was no one named Dan on the front side. She turned the map over and immediately realized why the name had stuck with her.

April Fischer—left.
Olivia Fischer—left.
Silvia Martin—left.
Dan Turnbridge—left.

Someone named Dan had left the compound before the massacre. Was this the same Dan who'd stood on the beach with her dad on the day of the wedding?

TWELVE

MONDAY

PEOPLE HURLED THEMSELVES *into the open-pit mine, so many that the walls of the first step ran red with blood. April knew that it was all her fault, just as she knew she was the only one who could stop the carnage.*

All she had to do was fly.

She didn't want to.

Then Jules lined up at the edge of the pit alongside the others, glassy-eyed, under the same strange lemming compulsion to throw herself in. April would never reach Jules in time. She was too far away. All April could do was throw herself into the pit, and hope that she hit the ground in time to wake Jules from her trance. As she took off at a dead run toward the cliff and launched herself into the open air, she turned her head to see Jules fall headfirst into the mine. . . .

April woke as a choked sob escaped her throat.

It was a dream. She knew it was a dream, but that didn't stop her from getting out of bed and padding down the hall to her sister's room. She stood over Jules and watched her sleep. *Too quietly*, April thought. She resisted an urge to shake Jules awake and annoy her. Asleep, Jules looked too small and vulnerable for her liking.

Eventually April went back to her room and fell into a dark and dreamless sleep.

School was rough. April wore dark glasses and a baseball cap to class, strictly forbidden by the dress code, but none of her teachers called her on it. April was unsure whether this was a kindness given her current situation, or whether they were afraid of her.

Probably a little of column A, a little of column B. Surely the administration had noticed the morning traffic had increased as disaster tourists and general gawkers tried to get a picture of her on her way into school. They probably appreciated her attempts at anonymity.

And anonymity was hard to find. Someone had taken a video of her coming home. April cringed at the sight of herself, in the dark clothes she'd worn three days ago looking worse for the wear at the end of the day. April scanned to the left and the right of the door, looking beyond paranoid, friendless, and creepy. Did she really look like that?

Who had taken the video? Was it Emma or some nameless disaster tourist who'd camped outside her house one day?

Or maybe it was the man in the black truck.

April shuddered at the thought.

Someone had taken the video, but others had run with it. April scrolled through the same shot of herself over and over, different darkening filters to background horror tracks. There was yet another horror video with that slightly British-sounding computer-generated voice explaining in lurid, overwrought detail how April was planning on ending the world in six days.

Well, five now.

Grace had a different lunch period and April didn't see her until after school. They met in the hallway by the back parking lot, Grace ready to link arms with her, preparing to fend off waiting zealots. They lingered in the hall before making the dive to their cars.

"How was regionals?" April asked.

Grace swatted away the question like regionals was a swarm of gnats she'd accidentally walked through, and only briefly at that. April assumed that meant regionals had gone well.

"Fine. I'm having trouble with the book. My dad suggested I read *The Road to Reality* to get a background on quantum mechanics—"

"You mean the torsion field book?" April interrupted Grace before she went any further into quantum mechanics. Any dip into quantum mechanics with Grace was already too far. "You don't have to—"

"I really want to help here," Grace said abruptly and a bit angrily.

April didn't take it personally. Grace was angry at torsion fields, not her.

People swarming by on the way out of school cut a wide semicircle around them. Whether it was April's Bicycle Girl vibe or Grace's entirely self-directed angry energy was hard to tell.

"I can't come over today," Grace said. "I have my internship. I could get out of it, but I don't want to leave a bad impression."

"Of course not," April said softly. "It's fine."

April tried to imagine the professor at the college who was guiding Grace's research internship. The only impression Grace ever made was that she was intense, focused, and totally incapable of giving up on any project. She imagined said college professor advising Grace not to work quite so hard. But she also knew that Grace's self-image didn't match the reality of being Grace.

April pushed through the doors and out into the sunshine of the parking lot.

"It's okay, anyway. Zach's coming over later to research," April said.

135

Trying to sound causal. Her heart fluttered a bit at the thought of Zach.

"Zach?" Grace exclaimed too loudly. Heads turned.

April leaned close to Grace's ear.

"His uncle is on the death map," she whispered.

"Gunshot?" Grace said. "Explosion?"

"Question mark," April said softly.

Grace raised an eyebrow. "Interesting," she said.

"Isn't it?" April replied.

April saw the car first. The acid-green Jeep, shining like a beetle in the sun. A blond man in sunglasses, hands gripping the steering wheel at the ten and two positions, and her heart sped, though whether from fear or anger, it was hard to tell. Probably both.

Marianne.

She was here.

Marianne threaded through cars, appearing directly in front of them. Her soft brown hair was loose today, and she was wearing jeans and sneakers, as though trying to blend in with the high school crowd. Somehow it made her seem older.

"April," Marianne said.

Grace nudged her, and April gave her a small nod.

"Grace," she said. "This is Marianne. *The* Marianne."

Marianne gave a tiny wave. She would have done better to offer Grace a handshake. "Hi," she said sheepishly.

"Marianne," Grace said, "I wouldn't have thought you were allowed within fifty yards of a school zone."

Marianne laughed nervously.

"April, could we possibly go somewhere and talk?" she said.

"Yes, let's," Grace said acidly. "I know a place where they make a great caramel latte."

"Who's your boyfriend?" April asked quickly.

She couldn't believe she was trying to spare Marianne from Grace. Marianne, of all people.

Marianne shot a glance over her shoulder, toward the man in the green Jeep. He was casting about nervously, as though looking for someone. April realized he hadn't turned the car off.

Did he imagine she was going to call the police? It was a thought.

Maybe he was nervous about the crowd around them. No one was close to them, but April had a dim sense that people nearby were paying attention. And for once, she was grateful for the relentless scrutiny of her peers. There would be no ether-soaked rag, no quick shove into the passenger seat of the car. . . .

"Oh, Jonathan?" Marianne said. "It was awfully sweet of him to drive me all this way."

April got the impression that Jonathan was used to doing Marianne favors. She wondered how far "all this way" was.

"April, I have to go," Grace said. "Do you want me to walk you to your car?"

Marianne turned toward April, eyes pleading. "We don't have to go anywhere," Marianne said. "I just want to talk to you for a minute."

"What about?" April asked.

Marianne looked around the parking lot and lowered her voice.

"About the ritual," she said.

Any annoyance she might have felt toward Marianne evaporated in a rush of excitement. It was possible Marianne knew something useful. April was convinced her dad had gone through a portal to another dimension, but she had no idea how to bring him back. She remembered the bang, the flash of light when he disappeared, but little else.

"You can go ahead," April said to Grace. "I'll be okay."

"Are you sure?" Grace asked. The sharp edge to her voice made April realize she was in for quite a lecture about safety later.

April looked around the parking lot at the dozens of people milling around. Grace followed her gaze, then shrugged.

"Fine," she said. "I'll text you later."

Grace gave Marianne a parting glare that would have peeled the top layer of skin off a normal person. April assumed Marianne was not a normal person. She watched Grace get in her car and pull into the line of leaving cars before she spoke.

"What did you want to tell me?" she asked.

"I just wanted to tell you to be careful," Marianne said. "There are dangerous people around."

And there it was again. Eyebrows knit in concern, the soft, almost maternal worry. It touched a buried wellspring of annoyance in April.

"Okay, good to know," she said sharply. "Thanks for the warning. I wouldn't have figured that out on my own."

She turned to walk toward her car.

"April, wait!"

There was such an edge of desperation to Marianne's voice, April turned back reflexively, a move she instantly regretted. How many times was she going to fall for Marianne's manipulations?

"I'm not like the others," Marianne said.

"The other members of the Deep Well cult?" April said.

Marianne nodded.

This was interesting. Marianne had never talked about the cult. Like a good salesperson, she'd stuck to the golden-promise-of-the-future pitch.

"We don't call ourselves that, but—"

"So you admit you're a cult member," April said quickly.

"I was," Marianne said.

Was. Past tense. April waited for her to explain. The parking lot was emptying out now, but there was still a line of cars waiting to leave the parking lot. No one was going anywhere in a big hurry.

"So how are you different from the others?" April asked.

Marianne took a step forward and lowered her voice.

"There are those who believe that the portal can't be opened without a certain amount of . . . upheaval."

Marianne hesitated on the word *upheaval*, and April suddenly remembered her dream. Dozens of people lined up on the edge of the open-pit mine, eyes glazed, faces rapt with religious fervor or abject terror, or some combination of the two. Swan diving headfirst into the open pit.

Waiting for her to save them.

"You mean a human sacrifice?"

Marianne flinched.

"I don't believe in the sacrifice," Marianne said. "I don't believe the king would want us to bring him back—that way."

That way.

So the movie *Hellhole!* had that much right—the sacrifice was real. Grace had suggested that Tyler Landry had been sacrificed on the day of the massacre, but April hadn't wanted to believe it. Now she knew it was true.

"How *do* you plan to bring King back?" April asked.

Marianne began talking in a soothing voice, all caramel sweetness, but April had trouble following. She had the same dizzy feeling she'd had on Aunt Silvia's porch when she'd looked down into the vast expanse of the open-pit mine and heard the voice calling to her.

"And it wouldn't take long at all. I know all the words, and we could be out there long before dark. I'm not sure how we'd get in," Marianne continued. "But we could leave right now, just you and me and Jonathan."

"What?"

The mention of Jonathan brought her back to reality. Marianne was suggesting they drive out to the compound.

The three of them.

"We're hours before sunset, so if we went out there now—" Marianne began.

"No," April said sharply. The idea of being out at the compound at dusk with Marianne and Jonathan made her shudder. Night fell early in the shadow of the mountain.

"Not now. Not ever."

If that discouraged Marianne in any way, she gave no sign.

"We'll be at the Morgan if you change your mind."

So Marianne was staying at the Morgan, the historic deco hotel, blocks from her house. Terrific.

There would be other cultists there soon, no doubt.

Marianne turned and walked back to the green Jeep, and Jonathan.

Out to the compound. The reality of the situation hit April fully for the first time. There was no way she was going anywhere with Marianne, and especially not Marianne and her twitchy boyfriend/chauffeur, Jonathan.

But if she was going to open the portal and bring her dad

back, it would have to be at the compound. And it would have to be before her birthday.

The longer she waited, the more likely it was that the cultists would choose a sacrifice.

She would have to go behind the wall, to the open-pit mine, for the first time since the day of the massacre. The thought sank to the pit of her stomach like a stone in still water. Not for the first time this week, April wished that the whole thing was over and done with. She did not want to go anywhere near the compound.

It was unavoidable.

THIRTEEN

WHEN APRIL PULLED into the driveway, Mom's car was missing.

Before she got out of the car, April pulled up the security app on her phone. Only two things showed up on the app: Mom leaving at one thirty to get Jules from school for a dentist appointment and later a UPS delivery man with a package. The delivery driver's hat was pulled over his face, and she couldn't see his features on the video. He could have been anyone.

Was he the man in the black truck? Posing as a delivery driver would be the best way to get close to her house. And what was in the package he left behind?

April checked the camera that faced toward the street. At

the same time the delivery man showed up, a brown UPS truck had been visible on the camera.

Just a delivery.

She scanned the street looking for the black truck. Nowhere in sight.

She gathered up her purse and water bottle, went in through the side door, and quickly locked the door behind her.

The house was empty and silent.

She checked the front door and the door to the pool in the backyard. Both were double locked.

April was as tired as she could ever remember being, and the last thing she wanted to do was to jump into reading endless journal entries about different types of hawks and mining reports from the 1930s.

She would have to go back to the compound. That much was clear. Her conversation with Marianne brought that awkward truth home to her. There would be no getting her dad back without finding the portal within the compound.

A brilliant flash of light, a loud noise. This memory returned when she closed her eyes. It felt important—cataclysmic, even. She had no idea what it meant. She stretched out on her bed and closed her eyes.

It was more than she could think about.

She woke to the sound of Jules's excited voice echoing down the hall.

"I could make you coffee," she said. "And I think we have some donuts around here somewhere."

Luna was too young to drink coffee, and April doubted Luna's mom would let them anywhere near the house right now. It had to be someone else.

April started to drift back to sleep, but the sound of the milk steamer on the espresso machine brought her back around with a start.

Zach.

She'd forgotten she'd invited Zach over to look at the papers. She leaped up and gave a cursory glance at the mirror. There wasn't time for anything else.

She could hear Jules chattering away, now and then a murmur of assent or a low question from Zach. She made her way down the hall to the kitchen.

Zach and Jules were sitting at the butcher-block island. Jules had microwaved the remaining donuts, based on the sugary smell. She'd made Zach a cappuccino.

"Jules told me you were asleep," Zach said.

A small twist of his lips, a smile almost. He nodded in her direction, as though noting her makeup gone astray or her bedroom hair. She felt herself blush.

"I haven't been sleeping well," she said. It was true. Ever since Aunt Silvia tossed the bundle of papers at her, she'd barely slept without an endless parade of disturbing, half-remembered dreams.

Zach's face grew serious.

"Me neither. Not since you told me about the—"

April cleared her throat and Zach got the message—not in front of Jules.

Jules also got the message. Her face twisted in annoyance.

Zach craned his neck and looked through the kitchen window toward the pool. It was overfull from recent rain and a little cloudy. The pool maintenance people would have to treat it after the rains ended, and by then it would be too cold to swim.

"How come you've never had a pool party?" he asked.

He'd forgotten that she was a pariah now. She'd never held a pool party for fear it would just be her and Grace. And Jules.

"Right?" Jules said indignantly. "We should definitely have a pool party, don't you think, April?"

"Would you have come?" she asked Zach.

He smiled.

"I would."

Present tense. She noted that.

"So it's settled," Jules said happily. "We'll have a party."

Just you, me, Grace, and Zach, April thought. No way Luna or any of Jules's other friends would be allowed to come to a party here. Not now. And her friends? Aside from Grace, she really didn't have any.

She didn't say anything. Why burst Jules's bubble?

"Do you want to get to work?" she asked Zach.

"What are you guys doing?" Jules asked.

"Homework assignment," Zach said unconvincingly.

Jules shrugged and reached for a donut. It was better coming from Zach. If April had told her that they were doing homework together, Jules would have given out a savage eye roll. It didn't hurt that Jules knew exactly who Zach was—everyone did.

"I'll be right back," April said.

She went to her room for the bundle of papers. When she returned, Jules was back at her video game in the living room, half-eaten donut beside her. Zach stood nearby, watching her play.

"Come on," she said.

He followed her into the dining room.

April spread the map out on the table. Everything else she stacked in neat piles.

Zach leaned over the map, studying it greedily. She realized he'd only seen it for a few seconds before the man in the black truck had appeared.

The man in the black truck.

"Thanks for yesterday," she said. "I don't know what I would have done if you hadn't been there."

He looked up from the map and smiled slyly.

"If I hadn't been there, you wouldn't have been there," he said. "So technically, I owed you that one."

She felt heat creep up her cheeks. She'd come to the Coppermine bar, looking for him, ostensibly to show him the map. She hated the thought that she was that transparent.

She hated that she needed rescuing.

"That's the second time you've saved me from him," she said. "I won't ask again."

He looked away.

"I'm just sorry I didn't get the license plate number," he said.

"I didn't either," she said. "And I walked right by his truck."

She remembered the Bible verse and pulled it up on her phone.

"He did have this on a bumper sticker. 'John 8:44.'"

She handed Zach her phone.

"'You belong to your father, the devil, and you want to carry out your father's desires,'" he read out loud. "'He was a murderer from the beginning, not holding to the truth, for there is no truth in him'—April, this guy is serious! Don't you think you should call someone about him?"

"Like the police?" April said. "They won't do anything. When I was eight, some guy showed up at our school with guns and duct tape and rope in his trunk; but since he hadn't broken any laws, they let him go."

"Fuck," Zach murmured. "I had no idea."

He frowned, and when his eyes met hers, they were filled with surprise and something approaching regret. She realized that he'd probably made a Bicycle Girl joke or two, or at least listened to one, and now felt bad. She didn't blame him for not knowing about the kidnapping attempt or just how terrible things had been for her. They'd known each other so well back then, but, in the way of thirteen-year-olds, not at all.

She shrugged. "Hopefully it will all be over soon."

"If you need anything," he said haltingly. "I mean, I don't have a car, but as fast as I can get over here on bike . . ."

"Thanks," she said quickly.

A hard lump formed in her throat, and she swallowed past it and clenched her teeth together to keep her lips from quivering.

Mercifully, he turned his attention back to the map.

"I couldn't stop thinking about this," he said. "I knew about the massacre, but seeing it all laid out like that, with the numbers?"

"I know. A death toll is just a number until you think about exactly how everyone died."

She shuddered, as Dr. Travers-Steenkampf's face from the dream came back to her, unbidden. He looked up from the map and she realized she'd made a small whimpering noise.

"You okay?"

"Fine," she said.

He eyed her dubiously.

"It's just, I'm starting to remember things from that day. I was there and I saw—a body."

She looked away, unwilling to fill in the blanks.

"You sure you want to do this?" he asked softly.

She nodded.

"I don't think I could stop if I wanted to," she said.

Her memories were unspooling in random order, useless. If April was going to undo what she had done, to bring her dad and Zach's uncle and, yes, King Steenkampf back, she'd have to piece together her memories and make sense of—everything.

"What else do you remember?" he asked.

"I remember a flash of light and a loud noise," she said. "I feel like it has something to do with the portal, but I don't remember anything else about it."

He studied her face.

"You think you saw the portal open?"

"Maybe," she admitted.

Zach leafed through the notebooks, the letters, and the mining reports.

"So what is all this stuff?" he asked.

She collapsed into a chair with a sigh. There had to be a reason Aunt Silvia gave her such a huge amount to go through, but just facing the mountainous pile of notebooks and lab reports was daunting.

"Papers my aunt collected," she said. "Journals mostly. Mining reports. Dr. Travers-Steenkampf's lab research."

"What was she researching?" he asked.

"Some sort of energy field, I guess?" she said. "I imagine it had something to do with the portal. There was a book about torsion fields and geophysics, but I couldn't make sense of it, so I let Grace take it."

Zach quirked an eyebrow.

"Torsion fields? I guess if anyone can make sense of research into an obscure energy field, it would be Grace."

Zach picked up a blue notebook and started reading. He went back and forth between his phone and the book, looking things up. She'd had to do that herself, with some of the denser material. In the end, she'd given up on the geophysics, leaving that for Grace.

She remembered something Marianne had said: *I know all the words.*

Marianne made it sound like there was a ritual to open the portal, unrelated to the sacrifice. Or it could have been a trick, Marianne's way of convincing April to come out to the compound with her. For all April knew, Marianne was lying about having left the cult.

Parts of Aunt Silvia's journals were written in verse. April had skimmed that part, but maybe there were incantations hidden in the journals.

She thought about what Grace would say about all this. Why would a geophysical phenomenon require a magic spell?

Still, she had to look.

Twenty minutes later, Zach looked up.

"Can I ask you a question?" he said.

"Sure." She closed the notebook she was reading, glad to be out of Aunt Silvia's claustrophobic world, if only for a moment.

"Your dad was foreman on the drill site, right?" Zach asked. "What did he do before he came to the mine?"

"He was an oil rigger," April answered. Mom had told stories of his work first in Louisiana and then off the coast of Mississippi. It had always seemed like a strange jump, to go from drilling for oil in the Gulf to a New Mexico mine.

"So why did he come to Ojo de Cristo?" Zach asked. "There's no oil here and the copper mine shut down years ago."

"King Steenkampf wanted to drill the deepest hole in the history of the world," April said. "Dad wanted to be part of that."

"No," Zach said. "That can't be true. The deepest hole in the world is called the Kola Superdeep Borehole. It was done in Russia during the Soviet Union era. I don't think it's possible to drill any deeper than that."

Zach took out his phone, pulled up something on Wikipedia, and handed the phone to April. She looked at the picture of the tall building that housed the drilling rig at the Kola Superdeep Borehole. It was similar enough to the rig at the compound to trigger a memory of standing next to Dad by the edge of the borehole housing, the hum of the drill rig working away.

Dad had told her that they were drilling to the center of the earth.

It was the kind of story you tell a child, and it had captured her imagination. Her father had been like an astronaut to her, or an explorer, a man devoted to expanding the limits of human knowledge. A hero.

His story wasn't true.

Why had he agreed to work for King Steenkampf?

"I don't know why he was there," April said finally.

"I think this is your dad's notebook," Zach said.

He pushed it across the table. April had seen the cloth-bound dull blue notebook before, but she'd lumped it in with Dr. Travers-Steenkampf's lab notebooks.

She had no idea that her dad had left a book behind. She regarded it reverently. There weren't many things of Dad's left in the house. The wedding pictures, a few CDs they had no way to play, books. This notebook felt like history.

She turned to the first page. The book was graph paper, and the notes were written in thick block print, lined up in the squares of the grid pattern.

She recognized his printing.

She leafed through the pages. He'd written notes for himself, most of them in frustratingly opaque engineering language.

What she did understand painted a dark picture. The project had been plagued with equipment failures and setbacks. Normally reliable workers, men who'd followed her dad from a Gulf Coast oil rig into the desert, left suddenly without notice.

I'm not sure I trust the Turn, her dad wrote.

The turn. Was it possible that Steenkampf had made her dad change directions while drilling? Maybe King Steenkampf hadn't been satisfied with the results and wanted to drill at a different location.

Toward the end of the notebook her dad's printing became darker and a bit more irregular, as though he had simultaneously written his notes faster and pressed harder.

The hydraulic system for the mud agitator is on the point of failure—again. I told Roger to keep an eye on it. Going to talk to Bob about beefing up security. I think someone is deliberately tampering with it.

She looked up from the notebook.

"Mud agitator?" she said.

"Mud is what they call the lubrication system on deep well drilling sites," he said. "I looked it up."

Zach handed her his phone.

She looked at a drill site schematic and a picture of a mud agitator. She read far down enough to realize that if someone shut down the mud agitator, the drill would have frozen up and the project would have come to a grinding halt.

"My dad thought someone was trying to sabotage the drill site," April said.

"It seems like," Zach replied.

April shuddered. She'd grown up believing that the explosion at the mine was a terrible accident. But what if it wasn't?

The name *Roger* stuck with her. She looked at the death map and found Roger Jones, number four, gunshot. The man her dad had put in charge of watching the mud lubrication system had died next to it, after Tyler Landry, but before the explosion.

"Look at number four on the map," April said. "Grace thinks that the deaths are in chronological order."

"Makes sense," Zach said. "Maybe Roger Jones was trying to stop someone from sabotaging the lubrication system, and they shot him."

April turned the page to the next entry in her dad's notebook. It was mostly abbreviations and numbers, nothing she could understand, but after each entry was a series of question marks, some of them drawn over and over, as though her father had sat pondering the answers, retracing the question marks absently.

These numbers can't be right, Dad had written at the bottom of the page.

I need to have a long talk with Ella before I get back to Bob with this. I don't want him leaping to conclusions.

Ella—Dr. Travers-Steenkampf.

She looked up at Zach.

"So my dad was working with Dr. Travers-Steenkampf?" she said. "The drill project had to do with her research?"

"I think so," he said. "But I don't know exactly what they were doing."

The answer had to be in Dr. Travers-Steenkampf's lab notes. Or in the book about torsion fields.

"Maybe Grace will be able to tell us," she said.

Zach bit his lip.

"Your mother was there, right?" he said. "Wouldn't she know what your dad was doing?"

"I suppose she would," April said reluctantly.

"You could ask her," he said.

"I could do that," April replied, knowing that she wouldn't. Mom shut down any and all conversation about the mine, the massacre, or anything Aunt Silvia–adjacent.

But Zach was right. Mom had to know a lot more than she was telling.

FOURTEEN

DINNER WAS A vegetable medley, brown rice, and a chicken breast. Jules had her giant bottle of Valentina sauce on the table and was liberally and, to April's mind, passive-aggressively dousing her chicken in it.

"April, are you okay?" Mom asked. "You look tired."

April guessed her mom would know what tired looked like. It was the first thing that popped into her mind, but she didn't say it. Her mom always looked tired. Except today, she looked better. Probably better than April.

"I'm fine."

Mom sucked in her lower lip and looked over at Jules, who had her head down and was dragging vegetables through a dark orange puddle on her plate.

April stabbed her chicken breast and began sawing away, stalling on eating. She wasn't hungry.

"April, I'm worried about you," Mom said. "You don't seem like yourself."

Of course she wasn't herself. How could she ever be herself with Dad trapped in another dimension? They'd all been living in a state of suspended animation. And one thing was clear from Aunt Silvia's journals. Mom had lied to her.

"Are you sure you're . . . ?" Mom began.

April dropped her knife on the plate with a clatter. Jules looked up, startled.

"How did Dad die?" April asked.

April hadn't planned on talking to Mom in front of Jules, but she was tired: tired of non-answers, tired of feeling hunted.

Mom put her fork down.

"Did Aunt Silvia say something to you?" she asked.

"No," April said. "What do you think she would have told me?"

Mom shot a look at Jules and back to April. Her message was clear—*Can we talk about this later?*

The look wasn't lost on Jules.

"Hey!" she said. "He was my father too."

"He died in the explosion," Mom said in a tone meant to put the matter to rest.

"Did they find his body?" April asked.

April knew they hadn't. He'd gone through the portal with King Steenkampf. She was sure of that now. Why was her mother lying?

"No," her mom replied.

April wanted to push.

"Bones? DNA sample?" she said.

Mom pursed her mouth into a thin line.

"What was Dad even doing there?" April said. "He was an oil rigger."

"He was an engineer," Mom said. "Drilling is drilling."

April didn't know much, but even the little reading she'd done told her that wasn't true. You wouldn't go from an oil rig to a copper mine.

"No, it's not, Mom."

"April!" Mom said sharply. "This isn't going to help anyone."

Their mostly untouched dinners sat cooling in the deepening silence between them. Jules shot April a look. Their mom had gotten up today. She'd shopped and cooked dinner, even cleaned house a bit while they were at school. One day out of her pretty severe fibromyalgia flare-up, and April was pushing boundaries and asking difficult questions.

"I'm sorry," April said. "I'm not hungry."

She took her plate to the kitchen, covered it in plastic wrap, and stuck it in the fridge.

* * *

Zach had said that the Kola Superdeep Borehole was the farthest anyone had ever drilled into the earth. While there wasn't a lot written about the borehole at Ojo de Cristo, there was a lot online about Kola.

Like her dad's drill site, Kola was plagued with difficulties and setbacks. The drill broke and they had to change directions of drilling several times. That might have been why her dad had written that he didn't trust the turn. Maybe he felt they weren't drilling in the right direction.

At the Kola Superdeep Borehole, people began to hear a strange voice coming from under the ground.

The voice. She'd heard it at the compound too.

So had others.

Was it the same voice?

April spent hours going down a rabbit hole on deep bore mining, but in the end she didn't feel like she knew any more than she did at the start.

She was hungry and remembered the untouched dinner in the fridge. It felt late. She crept down the darkened hall toward the kitchen, past the living room where Jules had apparently fallen asleep in front of a video game, her virtual horse reflexively whinnying and pawing the ground in mock impatience.

She made her way in the darkness between the glow of the video game on the TV, the light of the kitchen, her hand on the smooth adobe wall.

She opened the fridge door in the dark. The kitchen light went on suddenly, blindingly.

"What are you doing?" Jules said from behind her.

"I was hungry," April said.

"Oh."

April turned. Jules stood in the doorway of the kitchen, a peevish look on her face. It was the same look she'd had as a baby anytime she woke up in the car seat. Angry, like they'd tricked her into falling asleep and she'd missed all the fun. April felt a weird rush of tenderness for Jules, and for the baby she'd been. She'd missed out on so much.

She'd missed out on Dad.

"Midnight snack," April said. "You want to join me?"

Jules looked at her phone.

"It's only 11:37," she said.

"Okay, literal girl," April said.

April reheated dinner, while Jules toasted a piece of nine-grain bread and slathered it with cashew butter and honey that April didn't even know they had. Jules was a master of turning health food into junk food.

"Are you okay?" Jules asked between mouthfuls.

"I'm fine," April said.

"Maybe you should stay home from school," Jules said.

Staying home from school was Jules's go-to answer for everything from a bad mood to cramps.

"Me?" April said. "What about you? Maybe *you* should stay home from school."

It would be safer. April thought about the man in the black truck. He'd shown up at Jules's school.

Jules rolled her eyes.

The microwave dinged. The kitchen had a somber look in the soft hanging lights over the butcher-block island. Out of the corner of her eye, April saw movement along the baseboard, a gray form that skittered behind the Viking stove and disappeared. Did they have mice now? Terrific.

April opened the microwave and removed the plate. The chicken breast had shrunk into a steaming hunk of rubber, the broccoli had turned a greenish gray and smelled . . . sulfuric and slightly rotten, like her room. As if the smell of the bundle of papers had reached out from her room and all the way to the kitchen, permeating the microwave. She stared at the plate in front of her. As she watched, something moved out from under the rice, a tiny crawling bug or fruit fly, desperately trying to escape the heat, liquefied innards cooking from within, a last-ditch crawl toward oblivion.

How many of the people at the compound died like this, mortally wounded, crawling toward hope of rescue, crawling away from the scene of the catastrophe? Or just crawling, muscles and bones moving, pointlessly, aimlessly, without thought . . .

April dropped the food in the garbage, set the plate on the counter with a clatter, and leaned back against the fridge door with her eyes closed.

She stayed there, feeling the cool of the stainless steel against her back. When April opened her eyes, Jules stood at arm's distance, peering at her. Jules held out the remaining corner of her honey cashew bread, like a kid at a petting zoo attempting to feed a goat she's been told is mostly tame.

April leaned over and took a bite. Very sweet, very sticky.

"I can make you one," Jules said hopefully.

April wasn't even sure she was still hungry anymore, but she nodded anyway. She recognized the look on Jules's face. Their mom's pain was too simultaneously all-encompassing and too amorphous to grab hold of. There was nothing April could do to help Mom, but still, she brought her sandwiches and cups of tea to feel the comfort of doing something.

The same impulse prompted Jules to make April coffee, or to toast bread in the hope of making things better.

"April," Jules said in a small voice, "how do you really think Dad died?"

"He's not dead," April answered, without thinking.

Jules's eyes widened.

"What? Why do you say that? Where is he?" Jules's voice rose and April worried she'd wake their mom.

It was too late to lie to Jules. She should have kept her mouth shut.

"I have something to tell you, but you have to promise not to tell anyone—okay, Jules?" April said.

Jules nodded seriously.

163

"I think Dad went through a portal at the compound," April whispered. "I think I can get him back."

Jules made a small bleating noise and dropped her hand, the remains of the bread with cashew butter falling to the floor. She took a step away. "That's crazy," Jules whispered hoarsely, almost as if she was talking to herself.

"I know it sounds improbable, but, trust me, it's all in the papers."

"The papers?" Jules said blankly.

Jules knew about the papers—she had to. She'd been in April's room and had untied the bundle and riffled through the papers. Unless it was someone else.

Nothing made sense anymore.

"The papers Aunt Silvia gave me," April said.

"Okay," Jules said slowly. "Maybe we should talk to Mom about this?"

"No!" April blurted out, louder than she meant to. "It's just, you know how Mom is about Aunt Silvia."

Jules took another step back.

April couldn't blame her, not really.

She was unraveling. They all were. Mom was sicker than she had been, as though all the lies she'd told about their dad weighed on her soul and her health.

April glanced down at her phone: 11:58. In two minutes, it would be Tuesday.

Just four days to piece together this puzzle.

"Don't tell Mom, okay?" April said. "You know she's been sick."

"I won't tell her," Jules said. "But don't do anything weird, okay?"

"You have to trust me," April said.

Jules set her mouth in a thin line of determination. April realized she had no idea what Jules was thinking.

"You have to trust me too," she said.

FIFTEEN

TUESDAY

WHEN SHE WOKE up Tuesday morning, April went to the bathroom to brush her teeth and do something with her hair. She was startled by her own reflection.

She didn't recognize herself.

Her hair hung limply against her scalp. There were dark circles under her eyes, and her skin had an unfamiliar greenish undertone. April stared at her face, smoothly blank and disturbingly unfamiliar. She'd had another terrible night, and what little sleep she'd gotten had been haunted by fitful, half-remembered dreams of people cartwheeling into the open-pit mine. Cultists sacrificing themselves on her behalf.

Four days left until her birthday.

"Hello, Bicycle Girl," she said to her reflection.

She expected the girl in the mirror to smile back, but she didn't.

"Time to fly," April whispered.

Trying it on.

It wasn't funny anymore.

She was getting close to the truth. Maybe she really was the Bicycle Girl.

And if she really was the Bicycle Girl, it was up to her to figure out how to open the portal before the cultists put their crazy ideas of human sacrifice into motion.

In the kitchen Jules was waiting at the butcher-block island with a cup of coffee for her. It was sweet, but also a sign that everything normal in their world had shifted slightly off-kilter.

"God, you look terrible," Jules said.

"Thanks a lot."

"I didn't mean it like that," Jules said. "So is Zach your boyfriend now?"

The sudden shift took April by surprise.

"No, of course not," she spluttered.

"I think you like Zach," Jules said, giggling.

"Everybody likes Zach," April said. She realized as she said it that it was true, and not just in an *all the girls and half the boys have a crush on him* way. People genuinely liked Zach because he was a good guy, and he was also the star running back.

What must that be like?

"I think he likes you too," Jules said.

April felt a sudden rush of warmth. She wondered if Zach would have even noticed her if she hadn't shown up to his work with the death map and a mystery about his uncle.

For better or worse, she was the Bicycle Girl. At least there was one good thing about it.

At lunch period, April went out to the courtyard. As she stood under the eaves, trying to look as inconspicuous as possible, her phone buzzed with an incoming text.

Meet me in the library. We need to talk, Grace texted.

It struck her as strange that Grace was skipping a class to meet with her. Maybe she'd found something in her research that was more important than keeping her perfect attendance record.

Be right there.

The library was mostly empty. The librarian made hopeful eye contact, imagining April was there for a book.

"I'm looking for Grace," she began in a performative stage whisper. "We were supposed to study. . . ."

"She's in the back," the librarian answered.

April thanked the librarian and walked through the shelves to the small carpeted room with a table and six plastic chairs. One sad erasable whiteboard with what looked like repeated and not quite successful attempts to remove a permanent marker mistake.

Grace sat at the table studying *Supergravity and Akimov's Torsion Fields*.

"What did you want to show me?" April asked.

"I found something I think you should see."

Grace leafed through the book until she found the right page. She turned the book around to face April.

She leaned over the table. Spidery cursive notes were scrawled in pen in the margins.

Akimov and Gennedy—not enough power to open the torsion field. Iron core + copper-rich earth? Gordon suggests Ojo de Cristo site would work.

She looked up from the book.

"It's got to be King's writing, don't you think?" Grace said. "He did end up buying the Ojo de Cristo mine, after all."

"So when he says *torsion field*, what does that mean?" April asked.

"Well, it's complicated," Grace said. "From what I understand, King Steenkampf felt that if he drilled deep enough, he would find enough heat energy to power a torsion field, and given the conductive nature of an untapped vein of copper he could—"

"You're right," April said impatiently. "It's complicated. Can you give me the short answer?"

"Steenkampf thought he could use energy from a deep borehole to open a portal to another dimension. Like a giant battery. I think it's why they were drilling."

April felt the air leave her lungs and she slumped in the

chair. She looked over at the faded whiteboard, and the ghost words written in permanent marker. *What is* was clearly visible; the rest was just a shadow.

What is true . . .

What is real . . .

This was what she'd been hoping to find. What she'd been hoping Grace would find.

"I'm not sure Dr. Travers-Steenkampf was fully on board with the idea of a portal, but she *was* there to study the energy field," Grace said. "It appears she worked pretty closely with your dad. She mentions him in her notes."

Her dad had known why he was drilling. He'd talked about the torsion field in his notes. Did he know about the portal? A dozen different thoughts crowded in her mind, all leading to the same place. The portal had opened once, and it had taken her dad away from her.

But if a portal had opened once, it could open again and bring him back.

"There's something else I wanted to show you," Grace said.

Grace frowned as she leafed through the pages of the book, looking for the right spot. She found a section with another burst of the same spidery handwriting in the margins.

April is a very special girl. I used a torsion field energy detector on her—lit up like a Christmas tree. Believe she's the key to everything.

April stared at the page, her name in that shaky cursive,

as though the person writing had been very old or very ill. Or both.

King Steenkampf.

Very special girl.

It triggered a memory.

It was his name for her—*my special girl.* King had brought her to the patio on a bright late summer day. Someone gave her half a cherry Popsicle, and she ate the Popsicle as they talked, her fist closed around the wooden stick, licking the sweet, red drops off the side of her hand.

They asked her about the voice. There was another man there too, but his face was a blur. She remembered him being there, but not anything about him.

Maybe it was her dad?

No.

She wasn't supposed to tell her dad about any of this.

Her mom either.

They wanted to know the things the voice had said to her, because she was a very special girl, and the voice talked to her. The others heard the voice, but not like she did. They didn't know the words.

And the voice, it had told her how . . .

"April?" Grace said.

At the sound of Grace's voice, the scene vanished, like a wisp of smoke in the night air. The voice had told her something important, but she had no idea what.

And now it was gone.

"Maybe we should stop this," Grace said.

She frowned and took the book from April's hands. Grace closed the book and stuck it in her backpack, and April felt a territorial stab of resentment. The book belonged to her, not to Grace. Even if she couldn't read or understand it.

"Why?" April demanded. "You've found evidence for the portal. That's good."

"I have a bad feeling about this," Grace said.

"A bad feeling?" It surprised her, Grace wasn't one to give much credence to intuition.

"Maybe there is a reason you can't remember that day," she said. "A lot of traumatic things happened at the compound. Do you really want to unearth the truth?"

"I can't stop now," April replied.

April could only remember the flash of light, the loud noise before Dad and King vanished. But she knew in her heart that Dad and King were together somewhere, trapped. If there was even a remote chance of bringing them back, she had to take it.

Grace sighed. Of all people, she understood a research obsession.

"I'll keep looking for answers," she said.

SIXTEEN

WIKIPEDIA
THE DEEP WELL CULT

The Deep Well is a millenarian cult formed in the five years following the massacre at the Ojo de Cristo mine. [see Ojo de Cristo mine disaster] The Deep Well cult is thought to have been started by two men who left the compound the day of the massacre.[citation needed]

Members of the cult believe that mine owner, Robert Steenkampf IV, chose to drill at the Ojo de Cristo site after being advised of the location's unusual metaphysical energy readings.[citation needed] They believe that Robert "King" Steenkampf drilled deep enough to reach an energy field that allowed him to open an interdimensional portal. King Steenkampf disappeared the day of the massacre.

King's disappearance is thought by the cultists to indicate he successfully created the portal and traveled through it to a higher plane.

According to the cultists, before the massacre at the compound, April Fischer, five-year-old daughter of the foreman, William Fischer, heard a voice from the other side, asking to come through the portal. King Steenkampf believed that April Fischer was the necessary conduit to open the portal.

A series of notes supposedly written by King Steenkampf surfaced on the Reddit thread r/truewell in 2018. In the notes, the members of the inner circle are mentioned by code names: the cook, the gardener, the girl, the king. According to the notes, King predicted his ascension and the subsequent return of April Fischer, the girl, to the compound on her seventeenth birthday. King prophesied that April would reopen the portal and release him from an alternate dimension. Proponents of the Deep Well cult believe that on his return, King Steenkampf will reveal the secrets of health and eternal life to his followers.

In Marjorie T. Gortner's 2022 book, *Death Cults*, she disputes the authenticity of the King notes, claiming that the notes contain information that could only have been known by someone who witnessed all the events at the compound on the day of the massacre. "Since King Steenkampf was supposedly transported to another dimension, it seems highly unlikely that he would have paused to update his journal for posterity before leaving this earthly plane. I've read the King notes, and I consider them to be a forgery."

JULES WAS IN the kitchen, scrolling on her phone distractedly, dipping carrots into hummus. April grabbed a can of lemon sparkling water from the fridge and sat on a stool across from Jules.

Jules didn't look up from her phone, and that was fine. Sometimes April liked to hang out near Jules—no conversation necessary, like cats basking in a single ray of sunlight.

It was better than being alone.

She felt jealous of Jules's uncomplicated phone time.

Normally, April kept away from her phone. The internet was Alice's trip down the rabbit hole, a fall into the dark, promising a quick and painful landing but somehow stretching into an eternity of bookshelves and mirrored surfaces. She could watch herself plummet into despair from a variety of flattering angles.

No, thank you.

But now, her phone burned a curiosity hole in her pocket. Marianne had mentioned the words she needed to say. And April had remembered a day on the patio in the bright sunshine, Aunt Silvia and King talking about the words the voice wanted her to say.

She didn't remember what the words were, but Marianne knew, and if she knew, so did the members of the Deep Well cult.

A while back, April found a thread that went by the unassuming name of r/truewell. She'd found it by accident. She was on another thread, pretty much useless. She'd gone to the site under the name of Abrilpescadora, followed by her birth year. Spanish for "April Fischer." Stupid, but she'd been fourteen. She'd been looking for the truth about what had happened to her father.

A woman private-messaged April and suggested a more factually based thread—r/truewell. She also suggested that April drop the name.

April took an anonymous username and went on r/truewell. The moderator went by TH3D33PW311. Oddly, TH3D33PW311 didn't show up in the thread very often. But there were others who had been consistent on the site for years.

April was convinced that there were people on the site who were actual cultists and not simply disaster tourists.

176

Not everyone of course. But the number of members on the forum was very small. The moderator had a habit of banning people who got too nosy.

People on the site knew things that weren't common knowledge.

Aunt Silvia had managed to fly under the radar everywhere else. She wasn't mentioned on the Wikipedia page or on any of the multitude of conspiracy sites devoted to plumbing the depth of "what actually happened that fateful day."

Somehow, it never occurred to most conspiracy theorists that an industrial site miles from anywhere would have a cook.

To horror buffs who patrolled the compound, Aunt Silvia was known as the wild woman with the gun. People had seen her, and half the internet thought she was a ghost of some long dead and discontented settler. Few put the wild woman with the gun and Aunt Silvia together, but on r/truewell, Aunt Silvia was known as "the cook," as important to the mythology as "the gardener."

The gardener was on the death map. Number two, on the patio. No one in April's life knew about the gardener except for Aunt Silvia.

April was absolutely sure someone on r/truewell had been in the compound before the massacre.

She was convinced that the words the others had asked her about on the patio all those years ago had to do with opening the portal. The voice had spoken to her, had told her what to do.

It was a long shot to believe that the other man who'd been on the patio that day alongside King Steenkampf was on r/truewell, but if he was anywhere on the internet, he was there. Maybe someone here would be able to tell April what she couldn't remember.

Going back on the thread wasn't without risks, but her username was anonymous, and she hadn't been on for a while. At worst, the regulars would assume she'd just wandered into the thread, and they would shut her down. It might be hard to get any useful information without revealing herself, but it was worth taking the chance.

Four more days.

And true to form, most people on the site were talking about ride-sharing out to Copperton, as though they were all going to Burning Man or something. It would have been funny, if it weren't four days before her birthday. Too little time to figure out how to get her dad back before the horde descended.

But it was easy enough to pretend to be one of them. She decided to jump in and ask for a rideshare.

Is anyone leaving on Thursday? she typed.

She didn't expect anyone to answer right away.

The response was instantaneous.

She's here, TH3D33PW311 wrote.

A wave of nausea hit her. How did TH3D33PW311 know she was here?

It's her!!! April? It's you, isn't it? realamy7070 asked.

Then a deluge of comments from people April had never seen on the site before.

April?

She's come back to us.

Omg!!!! Does this mean it's happening?

It's time. Are we all going?

Happy Birthday!!! realamy7070 sent.

Happy Birthday!

Happy Birthday!

Happy Birthday!

April stared at her phone as birthday wishes continued to roll at a frenetic pace. It was *Hellhole!* all over again, the same feeling of being sucked down into a dark hole she couldn't climb out of. But these people were different. They believed. And they were coming. Most of them would be in Copperton by the end of the week.

She's gone, realamy7070 said.

No, she's not, TH3D33PW311 entered. **She's still here. I can feel her presence.**

Are you sure? realamy7070 said.

Yes.

"Fuck," April whispered under her breath. She looked around the room reflexively, as though someone was here, watching her. How did TH3D33PW311 know it was her? She'd been so careful to cover her tracks. Did they have her IP address?

Jules looked up from her phone.

Time to fly, TH3D33PW311 posted.

April threw the phone face down on the butcher-block island so violently, she worried that she'd cracked the screen.

The voice in her ear all those years ago, the bell-like laughing voice she'd called Kiki, though even her five-year-old self had known it wasn't Kiki. It was something darker, something that wanted her. . . .

Something that had wanted her to fly.

Or did "Time to fly" mean it was time for someone else to fly in her place?

Time to fly.

Time to fly.

Time to fly.

April shut her eyes and wished that it would all go away.

"What's wrong?" Jules said.

April opened her eyes.

"Just something I didn't want to see," April said.

She didn't want Jules to see it either.

"Oh, was it that video someone took of you in front of the house?" Jules said.

"That's the one." April picked up her phone before Jules could look at the screen.

"So stupid," Jules said. "I can't believe anyone thinks you're going to end the world."

"They don't," April said. "If anyone *really* believed I was going to end the entire world, they'd make sure I couldn't go out to the compound and . . ."

April trailed off mid-sentence. The look on Jules's face stopped her. It was the kind of dark joke she made all the time, but it landed differently now with all that was happening.

Maybe Jules was thinking about the man in the black truck.

He seemed serious enough.

And then there were the cultists, hell-bent on sacrificing someone, just to bring King Steenkampf back.

How did TH3D33PW311 know it was her? It had to be her phone. Logical enough, but she had a horrible feeling that she was being watched from all angles.

April picked up the phone, took a screenshot and sent it to Grace.

So you poked the bear again, Grace texted back.

I should have known better.

You know the drill, Grace texted. **Get offline for a while, and they'll lose interest.**

Even through text, Grace's no-nonsense voice calmed April down. Grace had talked her off this particular ledge before. But there was no getting offline, no waiting the cultists out this time.

They'd be here in a matter of days.

If you wanted to leave town before your birthday, I'd go with you, Grace texted.

April was touched. For Grace to walk away from not only school but all her extracurricular activities for almost an entire week was a huge sacrifice. She hadn't really told Grace about the man in the black truck, but Grace did know about Marianne and Jonathan. People were keeping tabs on April. She didn't love the idea of the two of them driving out into miles of open desert where anything could happen.

Thanks, she texted. **I'm probably safer here, hiding in plain sight.**

"Is that Grace?" Jules said. "Tell her I said hi."

Jules says hi, she texted.

Jules.

She was the other reason April couldn't leave. She couldn't leave Jules and Mom behind.

Even if she could, she didn't want to lose the chance to bring Dad back.

SEVENTEEN

THERE WERE FEET *sticking out from under the bushes because the gardener was dead. She didn't like looking at those feet.*

"I think we're going to sit this one out, sugar," King said.

"Why?" she asked.

"Eh, there's someone else who will do it for you," he said, chuckling.

And then suddenly, Jules was there.

No.

Not Jules.

Never Jules.

The two of them were standing on the edge of the pit together. Only it wasn't the pit, it was the porch of Aunt Silvia's house, and April knew she could fly. April turned to tell Jules, but she wasn't there anymore. She'd fallen into a dark hole.

"April!"

Jules's voice from the well was frantic. April couldn't see her.

"April!" Jules said.

"April, wake up!"

April opened her eyes. She stared up at Jules. Why was she so upset? Jules held her phone out, casting an unearthly bluish glow over the bed.

"What's going on?" April mumbled.

"There's someone outside," Jules whispered urgently.

April shot up in bed, and leaned against the headboard, suddenly wide awake.

"Did you look at the security cams?" she asked.

"I don't have the app," Jules replied.

April grabbed her phone off the nightstand and flipped impatiently back and forth from each camera, but there was no one there. Jules hovered close by, craning her head to look at the image on the phone.

"Go to the recording," she said.

"Where did you see them?"

"Out front," Jules whispered.

April rolled back the recording of the front camera. There was nothing there. And suddenly, there was a gray shadow at the very edge of the camera. It was there and it was gone the next instant. Just a shadow in the streetlight. Barely a human shape.

"There!" Jules said. "Do you see?"

184

"The fuck?" April said.

Was the man in the black truck outside her house? Had he finally come for her?

"We should call the police," Jules whispered.

"Not yet," April said. "Not until we see who is out there."

They huddled together on April's bed, staring at her phone, waiting, breaths held.

Jules shivered in her nightgown, little more than a thin, long T-shirt. She pulled the covers around her and leaned closer to April.

Finally, a figure in a hoodie walked within camera range. A woman's face and a few strands of hair emerged from beneath the hood.

April recognized her.

"It's Marianne," she said in a huff, a combination of relief and annoyance.

She pushed the speaker on her app.

"Marianne, what are you doing here?"

Marianne quickly walked to the porch and pulled back her hood. She stared into the camera, her eyes looking black and soulless in the night vision.

The intercom crackled with movement or maybe a sigh.

"April, thank god you're here!" she said. "I need to talk to you."

Marianne cast a quick glance over her shoulder. Her voice, even distorted over the intercom, quivered with fear.

Her fear could have been real, but more likely it was another ploy.

Marianne turned back, and for an instant, her eyes flashed white, like a deer caught in a wildlife camera. For a second, April would have sworn there was a shadow over her shoulder.

"Marianne, it's really late," she said into the intercom. "Can we talk tomorrow?"

She didn't want to risk waking Mom up. If she saw Marianne on the security app, she'd almost certainly call the police.

"There's someone with her," Jules whispered.

"It's probably just her boyfriend, Jonathan," April said. "You know, the guy she was with at the Sonic?"

Jules's eyes widened, glowing white in the reflected light of the phone.

"How do you know his name?" Jules asked.

"I saw Marianne yesterday," April said. "He was with her."

"I thought you were going to stay away from her," Jules hissed.

"Hello, do you think I went looking for her?" April said.

She turned the camera around to show Jules the video of Marianne, standing on the front porch, shivering. She was persistent if nothing else. But April couldn't stop thinking about something Marianne had said to her.

I know all the words.

Marianne had been part of the cult in the past, and April was more convinced than ever that Marianne knew how to open the portal. April had struck out on r/truewell, and she wasn't going back on the site.

Marianne might be her only hope.

She had to take a chance.

April pushed the intercom again.

"Meet me at the end of the driveway," April said. "Five minutes."

Marianne looked up at the camera and nodded. She hurried off the front porch.

"What are you doing?" Jules whispered harshly. "You can't go outside."

April stood and reached down for a pair of jeans. She shivered in the cool dark, feeling a wave of anxiety roll across her.

"I need to go talk to her," April said. "I won't be long."

"Off camera?" Jules said. "This is a terrible idea."

"I don't want Mom to see her," April whispered.

Jules continued to stare at the view of the empty front porch on the security app. The blue glow of the phone distorted Jules's features, making her look wide-eyed and terrified.

Whatever Marianne had to tell her, it had better be important.

"Stay here and watch," April said. "If I'm not back in a couple of minutes, call the police and wake Mom up."

April padded softly down the hallway, trying to be as quiet as possible so as not to wake Mom. She stopped by the shoe rack near the front door and slipped on a pair of sneakers. As she approached the door, sharp fear squeezed her chest.

She told herself it was just Marianne.

But what if it wasn't just Marianne? What if Jonathan was waiting by the end of the driveway, out of sight of the security cameras with an ether-soaked rag? Jules was right—this was a terrible idea. April wouldn't have considered meeting Marianne, but she was all out of good ideas.

She willed herself to move forward in the darkened hallway. The only light came from the small, face-height window in the door.

She reached the door and put her hand on the knob, knowing that she had to open it.

She had to walk down the driveway, past the Mexican plum tree, out of the line of sight of the security camera that faced the street.

Five minutes.

She'd give Marianne five minutes, no more.

April pulled the door open resolutely and stepped out onto the porch.

She froze.

Marianne was gone.

In the driveway, out of range of the security camera, stood a man dressed in black, wearing a black balaclava that covered his face and head.

Where was Marianne?

The sound of Jules running down the hall came from behind her, and her heart leaped with fear.

"Stay inside," April half hissed, half whispered through clenched teeth.

Jules ignored her.

She stepped through the doorway and looked toward the driveway and gasped.

"Where's Marianne?" Jules whispered.

At the sound of Jules's voice, the man in the ski mask whipped his head toward her.

He cocked his head quizzically, as though he hadn't imagined that Jules would be there and now he had to take her into account.

And then slowly, ever so slowly, he turned his gaze back toward April, as though to say *Look what you have to lose.*

April began to shake uncontrollably.

Blue and red flashes of light reflected in the puddles and damp pavement of the street. She turned her head toward the street to see a police car pulling up slowly in front of their house. Lights on, sirens off. Middle of the night. Mom had the app on her phone too, and she must have called the police.

189

"Do you think Marianne is okay?" Jules said. "I mean, that guy . . ."

"I don't know."

April turned back to the driveway. The man in the black ski mask was gone like he'd melted back into the shadows at the first sign of the police.

EIGHTEEN

WEDNESDAY

APRIL HAD STRANGE dreams—ambulances, fire trucks racing up to the compound to collect the bodies and take them to the bottom of the open-pit mine. Tiny figures cartwheeling into the pit, arms spread, ready to fly.

It didn't make any sense, but it felt so real. Ambulances winding down the long circular road into the bottom of the pit, ferrying the dead into another dimension, blood dripping down the sides of the wall . . .

She pulled herself awake with effort, fighting the image. Pulled on jeans and a T-shirt and made her way to the kitchen. Mom and Jules were sitting around the butcher-block island, eating yogurt.

"How can you sleep through all the sirens?" Jules said.

"Sirens? Where?"

"Sounds like they were headed to the big ditch," Mom said. "That bridge could have finally collapsed. They should have fixed it years ago."

Zach lived on the other side of the bridge. He rode his bike over it every day.

April left the kitchen, grabbed her shoes, and rushed out of the house. She ran to the edge of the street, fast walked up the way to the art chapel on the top of the hill.

Dozens of emergency vehicles were clustered around the big ditch on both sides, blue and red lights flashing. Oddly festive. Even from a distance and with the cover of trees, she could see that the old bridge was still intact. The small figures of people were gathered around the edges of the ditch, all looking down.

Zach. She'd been so stupid. April and her family had security cams and a police department behind them. Zach lived with his mother and brother in the row of manufactured homes, so flimsy that she could have kicked his door down.

Any number of people could have seen her with Zach at the Coppermine bar, standing close, whispering secrets.

If she was being watched, so were her friends.

She ran back down the hill, heart pounding with adrenaline. She grabbed her keys from the hallway and ignored Jules's scattershot questions. She got in her car and drove the short distance to the big ditch and got as close as she could, considering the forming crowd. She parked down the street and walked to the bridge.

Police had barricaded the bridge with a patrol car. There were officers on both sides of the ditch attempting to tie police tape around the scruffy brush, pushing the gathering crowds back.

April threaded through the crowds and scanned the other side of the ditch.

She saw him. Zach.

Relief flooded her, guilt subsiding like an outgoing tide.

Zach was standing in his backyard, a short strip of grass that gave way to the side of a cliff. He was shirtless, shoeless, his hair ruffled like he'd just rolled out of bed. He saw her and gave his usual half salute.

She should have been embarrassed that she'd driven halfway across town braless, before coffee, just to see his face in the crowd.

It didn't matter that she'd given herself away.

He was alive. That was all that mattered.

She'd been so absorbed with finding Zach that she hadn't looked down, but now she did. Half a dozen police officers stood around what was clearly a body.

It was the body of a woman, blue jeans and a red shirt smeared dark brown. Face down but even without the face visible, April recognized her from the soft brown ponytail, the red golf-style shirt she'd mistaken for a Sonic uniform.

Marianne.

Someone had thrown Marianne off the bridge.

Maybe they thought she could fly. The thought came into her head unbidden, and April laughed in spite of herself.

Heads turned to her, eyes cut in her direction. They looked away when she tried to make eye contact. So many people knew about the fight at the Sonic, as though she would have killed Marianne over a latte.

Laughing at her corpse didn't help her case.

April thought about Marianne standing on the porch, begging to talk to her, and a sharp regret stabbed at her, followed quickly by numb disbelief. She'd imagined Marianne's desperation had been another ploy, a way of getting her foot in the door.

April never imagined that Marianne might really be in danger.

She could have kept this from happening.

Marianne was dead because of her.

Why leave her body for the whole town to find?

It felt like a message.

Marianne had been truly terrified. April could have opened the door and invited Marianne into the house, but she'd thought it was another trick.

If only she'd opened the door, Marianne would be alive now.

To the side, technicians struggled to put up a small white tent, presumably to shield the scene from view.

Across the big ditch, Zach pulled his phone out of his pocket.

194

Did you know her? he texted.

Yes. That's Marianne.

The one from the Sonic?

Everyone in town knew about the incident at the Sonic, apparently.

Yes. She showed up at my house last night.

April looked down at Marianne's splayed body, now only partially visible behind the small white tent.

Why?

She wanted to tell me something, but someone chased her off.

And killed her? Zach said.

April thought about the man in the ski mask.

He'd made eye contact.

And then he'd stared at Jules.

Probably.

The reality of the situation hit her. A murderer had stood in her driveway, just out of range of the security cameras, as though he'd known or at least paid attention to where the cameras were. Had he followed Marianne to her house, or was Marianne simply in the way?

Do you know who it is?

April thought for a moment. The man in the ski mask and the man in the black truck were probably the same person, but she had no idea who that was.

No.

She felt the desperate, irrational urge to get back to the house and to make sure Jules was okay.

I've got to go, April texted. **I need to check on my sister.**

She turned back toward her car.

See you at school, he texted. **April, be careful.**

When April returned to the house, Mom and Jules were both standing on the front porch, craning their necks toward the big ditch. Neighbors stood in yards looking in the direction of something they couldn't see, alerted by sirens.

"What happened?" Jules said.

"Was it the bridge?" Mom asked almost simultaneously.

April trudged onto the porch and dropped into one of the chairs. She had a snapshot memory of Marianne standing in the Sonic parking lot, holding a coffee, a beatific look of hopefulness on her face. Okay, creepy, but she hadn't wanted Marianne to die.

"There's a body in the ditch," April said softly.

"Who is it?" Mom asked.

"It's Marianne," April answered. "The girl who was here last night. Someone killed her."

Jules's eyes widened.

"I'm going to talk to the police and tell them what happened here last night," Mom said.

"Okay," April said reluctantly.

The police had to know, but she didn't want to talk to them about Marianne. Not three days before her birthday.

"I will leave you both out of it," Mom said. "I'll just tell them she was on our security camera last night."

"Tell them there was a man in a black ski mask here too," Jules blurted out.

Mom blanched, and April shot Jules a look. The last thing they needed was Mom spiraling into anxiety.

"Perhaps you both should stay home today," she said. "Until the police sort this out."

"No!" April and Jules said in unison.

She needed to see Zach. As horrible as Marianne's murder was, it showed that they were on the right path. Someone wanted to keep them from opening the portal enough to kill a member of the Deep Well cult.

"We'll both be safer at school," April said.

"I'll pick you up today," Mom said to Jules. It was a good idea under the circumstances. High school let out forty minutes later, and April didn't love the idea of Jules standing under the flagpole, waiting for her. Usually there was still a crowd, but not always.

"And, April, come home right after school," Mom said.

April nodded.

There was nowhere else to go. Not anymore.

"You killed her, didn't you?" a voice whispered very close to April's left ear. A gray shadow skittered past her peripheral vision. The image of Dr. Travers-Steenkampf flashed through her mind. Face down on the dining room table, fat purple tongue protruding.

Why did you let him kill me?

April wheeled around, reached out with her free hand, and grabbed a wrist.

Emma.

Noise echoed down the hall. Break between periods. "What did you say?" April demanded, lifting Emma's wrist in the air.

"What the fuck? Get off of me!" Emma twisted her wrist, trying to get away, but April was half a head taller and stronger. She tightened her grasp.

April remembered the red paint on her locker, the red paint on Emma's hand.

"You painted the seven-pointed star on my locker, didn't you?"

"I didn't!" Emma protested, trying to wriggle away.

April put on her best Bicycle Girl face. She'd long since perfected the look, a tilt of the head, a blank Wednesday Addams look of intensity that suggested she was mentally drawing incision lines on your abdomen.

"I know you're lying," April said. "Don't you know that I can read minds?"

Emma looked around the hall desperately and, to April's mind, guiltily.

"I swear it wasn't me!" she said.

"How would you like to be the sacrifice?" April said, giving it a flourish. "I can arrange for you—"

"Stop!"

She turned her head to see Jessica.

"You're tripping," Jessica said. "And you're going to let go of Emma right now."

April dropped Emma's wrist. She felt a hot rush of shame. "I'm sorry."

Jessica threw April a look of disgust.

"That's what they all say," Jessica said.

Emma stood back, rubbing her wrist.

"I hope they lock you away," Emma spat out.

Jessica walked Emma away, arm around her shoulder. April leaned against the bank of lockers, eyes closed, and waited for the noise to end. The clattering, scuffing sound of people leaving faded too slowly.

A hand landed on her shoulder, and she opened her eyes. Zach peered into her face, concerned.

"Are you okay?" he asked.

She shook her head. Hot tears came to her eyes.

He wrapped an arm around her, and she sank against him, not caring that they were in the middle of school, in the middle of the hall, in the late afternoon where anyone could see them together.

"I'm losing it," she murmured.

You killed her, didn't you? April wasn't sure whether she'd heard Emma at all. Maybe she'd had an auditory hallucination, an echo of a dream.

You killed her, didn't you?—and her first thought hadn't been about Marianne but of Dr. Travers-Steenkampf face down on the dining room table, the past and the present twisting together in a dark unfathomable knot of disappearance and death. And the more she unraveled, the more tangled things got.

They were all careening toward something horrible and there was no way to stop it.

Too late.

Certainly too late for Marianne.

Zach smoothed her hair with his hand. Around them, stares and whispers, but of the *he's-with-her-now? Really?* variety.

Normal stares.

April wasn't sure she understood normal, not anymore.

"Let's get the hell out of here," Zach said.

NINETEEN

THEY HEADED OUT to the parking lot. April opened the back hatch of her car. Flipping down the back seat for his bike was beginning to feel like a normal ritual. April allowed herself a moment to imagine a future where his bike spent a lot of time in the trunk of her car, permanent pedal marks in the carpet.

It wasn't often she allowed herself to think of a future at all. The future stalled and blurred around her upcoming birthday. It was either the end of everything, or the beginning.

"Where should we go?" April asked.

Some part of her wanted him to suggest they go to the park or a movie—anywhere but back home to dig into the bundle of papers. But she had to keep working. For all that she'd learned, she was still no closer to figuring out how to open the portal.

But she wanted to forget this day.

"Your house," he said. "It seems safer there. You have security cameras, right?"

"We do," she replied.

Her house didn't feel safe. It felt like a crime scene. It wasn't the sight of Marianne's broken body in the dry creek bed that haunted her. It was the image of Marianne on the security camera, eyes ghostly in the night vision.

"She was scared." April choked on the words, a hard lump forming at the back of her throat. Her eyes threatened to spill hot, angry tears. Angry at herself. If only she could go back and open that door faster.

"Marianne?" Zach asked.

"Yes."

April kept her hands on the wheel, eyes locked on the street in front of her. She thought about Emma whispering in her ear—if it truly had been Emma—that she'd killed Marianne. In a way, she'd been right.

"You couldn't have known," Zach said softly.

"I left a frightened woman on my porch," she said. "And then she was killed."

"A cultist who stalked you," Zach said.

April looked over at him, surprised. She'd never told him about the first caramel latte.

Everyone knew about the second latte, the one she'd hurled at Marianne in the parking lot of the Sonic.

"Grace told me," he said.

April tried to imagine how this had come up in conversation. Had he asked Grace about her? Usually when people asked Grace about her, it made April anxious, not that Grace gave up any secrets. The idea that Zach cared enough to ask Grace about her gave her a warm feeling.

She turned onto her street.

They'd left school during the last period, late enough that middle school had already let out. Mom's car was in the driveway, and behind it, Grace's car.

April parked on the street so as to not block her in.

"That's Grace's car," she said.

She was surprised to see the car in her driveway. They hadn't talked about getting back together for research. Grace had the book on torsion fields and Dr. Travers-Steenkampf's lab books, which should have been more than enough to keep her busy.

"I wondered why she wasn't in history," Zach said. "She's always there."

"You have classes with Grace?"

"Yes, I have AP classes," he said. "You think because I play football, I'm not smart?"

"I didn't say that," she said quickly. "It's just, classes with Grace—well, that's next level. She's at the college half the time anyway."

April remembered what Grace had said about Zach—*It's a decent brain.*

"True."

They found Grace in the dining room, papers scattered around her in a semicircle. *So much for the white-glove treatment*, April thought ruefully. It was uncharacteristically disorganized, and April felt a stab of annoyance. Grace had gone into her room without asking.

"Zach," Grace said, looking up briefly. "April."

"How did you get in?" April asked.

"Jules let me in." Grace returned her attention to the lab books in front of her. "Dr. Travers-Steenkampf mentioned your dad. I wanted to look at his notes."

"What have you found out?" Zach asked.

He slid into a chair across the table from Grace and sorted through the stack of papers. He found a newspaper clipping and laid it to the side.

"It's frustrating," Grace said. "I've assembled a lot from Dr. Travers-Steenkampf's notes, but I think maybe there's something in the bundle of papers I might have overlooked."

April picked up a lab book and riffled through. As she remembered, there were indecipherable printouts of data points, paragraphs of notes written in such dense technical language they might as well have been in Russian.

"Did she believe there was a portal at the compound?" Zach asked.

"I'm not sure," Grace said. "She was working on something energy field–related, but I don't think—"

"Why is this such a hard question?" April asked sharply. "Either she believed in the portal or she didn't."

It was too late for Grace's scientific equivocation. It was Wednesday. April's birthday was Saturday. She needed answers. There was no point in digging deeper into geophysics if it wasn't going to help bring her dad back.

"Dr. Travers-Steenkampf was a respected scientist," Grace snapped. "I don't think she would have been throwing around words like 'portal,' even if she had found one. Not unless she had conclusive proof."

Conclusive proof had never come, because Dr. Travers-Steenkampf had died first. April couldn't think about Dr. Travers-Steenkampf without seeing her, face down on the dining room table, tongue fat and purple, all the muscles of her face slack.

"For what it's worth, I don't think your dad was convinced there was a portal either," Zach said.

"Why do you say that?" April asked.

"It's just a feeling I get from his notes," he said. "He seemed—skeptical. Wary even."

April nodded. She'd gotten the same feeling, but she ascribed it to the mining project going off the rails. Mentions of sabotage and not trusting the turn they were taking.

"This is interesting," Zach said.

He slid a yellowed newspaper clipping across the table.

"'Seven Killed in Explosion at New Mexico Mine,'" April read the headline out loud.

"And this one," he said.

Freak Accident Causes Death of Five at Shuttered Mine.

She read the dateline at the top of the page. October 10, 1996.

October 10. Her birthday.

"Here's another one," Zach said.

He handed her a photocopy of an extremely old newspaper clipping. Grace pushed the lab notebooks aside and studied the paper.

"'Worker Riot at Copperton Mine Leaves Eleven Dead; Eight Injured.' October 10—that's your birthday," Grace said.

"They're all from my birthday," April said.

"Not all," Zach said. "This newspaper is from October 12, 1972."

"Close enough. Hey, wait a minute," Grace said excitedly, "1936, 1948, 1960. Twelve-year intervals . . ."

"Exactly," Zach said. "All the incidents are twelve years apart."

"Amazing," Grace said.

Zach leaned back in his chair, arms crossed, basking in a rare moment of admiration from Grace.

"April—it's not about you, or even about your birthday," Grace said. "It's just the date."

206

It wasn't her.

A series of incidents, all twelve years apart, happened on or around her birthday. Like everyone else who had been near the mine on October 10 during those twelve-year intervals, she'd been a victim of coincidence.

It was possible that the portal opened on a twelve-year cycle.

But if so, why did so much death and mayhem happen around the portal opening?

She'd been near the open-pit mine recently and she'd felt the pull, heard the voice inside her head. It was possible that proximity to the portal caused a psychological distortion and a tendency toward violence.

If it was a portal, other people would have gone through it.

"Were there any disappearances in these accidents?" she asked. "Someone who might have inadvertently gone through the portal, like my dad?"

"Hard to say," Zach replied. "I don't think they kept track of people as well back then. But this one says two bodies were never recovered."

He shifted through the now haphazard pile of papers and uncovered the wedding party picture of her dad on the beach.

April reached out for the picture.

She studied her dad's smiling face and felt a great weight lift. If Grace and Zach were right, the portal opened every twelve years on or near her birthday. It had happened at regular intervals for a hundred years.

Whoever had dug the very first mine had unearthed something. It meant that she wasn't responsible for her dad's disappearance.

April handed Zach the Polaroid. "That's my dad, on the day of my parents' wedding."

Zach looked at the picture. He pulled it closer to his face, studying it intensely. He inhaled sharply and Grace looked up.

"What is it?"

"Oh my god," Zach said. "I've seen this guy before."

"My dad?"

April was confused. Zach was also five when her dad disappeared. She stood up and peered over his shoulder at the picture.

"No, this guy, on the right," he said. "He was the guy who came into the Coppermine after you."

"In the black truck?" she asked.

Zach nodded.

"The black truck?" Grace said. "Why don't I know about this?"

"Someone has been following April," Zach said. "This guy. He's younger here, but I'm pretty sure it's him."

April stared at the photo as the pieces slotted into place. His name, written on the back of the picture in black Sharpie—Dan.

The only person named Dan on the death map—Dan Turnbridge—had left before the massacre.

Or during.

Dan Turnbridge, the man who'd chased her through town. A man who'd attended her parents' wedding and was enough of a friend to stroll barefoot on a beach with her dad had left the compound that day.

She reached for her dad's notebook, looking for something that had bothered her for a while. It didn't take her long to find it.

I don't trust the Turn.

She'd wondered why Dad had capitalized "the Turn." It seemed odd for a drilling direction. Now she knew.

Turn was short for Turnbridge. Someone who had come with Dad from the Gulf Coast to the drill site in New Mexico.

Only, something had gone terribly wrong. She knew from her dad's notebook that the work had been difficult and plagued with problems even before the suspected sabotage. It seemed as though a lot of the workers thought the site was cursed.

April thought about the bumper sticker on the back of the black truck, the Bible verse—sins of the father, and the devil. April knew firsthand what proximity to the open pit could do to your mind.

Maybe Dan Turnbridge also heard the voice whispering in his ear.

Maybe he thought the voice was the devil.

It would make sense for Dan Turnbridge to have sabotaged the drill site if he really thought the devil was about to come through.

She turned the notebook around and showed it to Grace and Zach.

"'I don't trust the Turn'?" Zach said. "Turnbridge. Do you think he sabotaged the mud lubrication system?"

April nodded. "I think so."

"Why would he do that?" Grace asked indignantly. "Why sabotage a scientific research project?"

April pulled up the Bible verse John 8:44 on her phone and handed it to Grace. "This Bible verse is on a bumper sticker on the back of his truck."

Grace read the verse, frowning.

"Oh, damn," she said. "But if he was dead set on keeping the portal closed, wouldn't he go after the cultists too?"

"He killed Marianne," Zach said. "Who else could it be?"

Marianne. April felt a stab of regret. He'd been waiting outside her house when Marianne had shown up. She was the reason Marianne was dead.

The memory of that moment hit her like a punch to the gut. Dan Turnbridge had seen Jules before, outside the middle school, but this was different. The way he'd looked at Jules this time was a direct threat.

Was that really the same Dan Turnbridge who had laughed with her father on a beach, come to kill?

Zach laid a hand on her arm.

"Are you okay?" he asked.

April nodded, but she felt far from okay.

"You said Jules let you in, right?"

Suddenly, she was desperate to know exactly where Jules was.

"She's in her room, listening to a podcast," Grace said. "I'm going to call the police. They need to know about this guy."

Grace picked up her phone and began dialing.

Zach stood up.

"I wish I didn't have to go," he said reluctantly, "but I've got to get to work."

"Let me get your bike out of my car," April said.

She grabbed her keys and they walked out the front door together. It was later than she imagined, scuttling clouds, the sky already descending into early evening gloom.

She stepped past the spot on the porch where Marianne had pleaded with her the previous night. Where she'd stood when she'd seen the man in the black ski mask.

The man in the ski mask—Dan Turnbridge. She was sure of it now.

They reached her car and she opened the trunk.

"Be careful, okay?" Zach said.

April nodded. She had been careful for so long. That wasn't about to change.

"Don't worry, I'm not leaving the house tonight," she said.

She shivered. Arms bare, in a T-shirt. The near-dusk day had grown cold. Normally she loved the crisp cool of fall, the

211

end of the rainy season, but now it felt ominous. Dan Turnbridge had seen Zach, first on the night he'd chased her back from Aunt Silvia's cabin and later in the Coppermine bar, where Zach worked. She felt a mixed rush of fear and guilt at the thought that she'd exposed Zach.

"You be careful too, okay?" she said. "He's seen you."

Zach smiled.

"I'm just the guy who makes the sandwiches," he said. "Practically invisible."

She felt her lips quiver and he leaned his forehead against hers.

"I'll be fine," he said.

He looped a leg over his bicycle and rode away.

TWENTY

WHEN APRIL RETURNED to the dining room, Grace was bent over a book of lab printouts, a frown of concentration on her face.

"I called an anonymous tip line and gave them Dan Turnbridge's name as Marianne's possible killer," Grace said. "I told them about the truck and the bumper sticker."

April felt a swell of gratitude and relief. "Thanks," she said. Hopefully, the police would pick him up soon.

She thought of the man who'd shown up at her school with ether, duct tape, and rope in the trunk of his car. Even though the police eventually ended up letting the guy go, at least he spent a couple of days in lockup. But this was different. There had been a murder, and the police had to be taking it more seriously.

It was possible Dan Turnbridge *was* the man from her elementary school. The idea that a man who had once been one of her dad's closest friends had pursued her for a decade filled her with a sick dread.

"Are you angry with me?" Grace asked.

April looked up, startled. She noticed, for the first time, that Grace had dark circles under her eyes, and the gray UC Davis shirt she was wearing looked slept in. April had never seen Grace look this miserable before. She realized that Aunt Silvia's papers were not just torturing her. They were wreaking havoc on Grace's mental health as well.

"Why would I be angry with you?" April asked softly.

"Because I'm useless here," Grace said savagely. It reminded April that no one was as harsh a critic of Grace as Grace.

"Wow, you couldn't figure out a scientist's entire life's work in the space of one week, based on an incomplete set of notes?" April said. "You should be sorry."

Grace snorted.

"I've missed you, April."

April wanted to say *I've been right here all the time*. But had she? Even before Aunt Silvia gave her the notes, she'd been closed off, mentally manning the barricades against her own coming apocalypse. Shutting everything and everybody out.

Shutting out the one person who'd willingly jumped down this particular rabbit hole with her.

"I've missed you too, Grace," she said.

* * *

April woke to the sound of a small scratching noise coming from her closet.

A glimmer of light came from under the closet door. It moved in the dim reflection of the hallway, like a tiny eye. As April watched, the glimmer rolled slowly out from the gap under the closet door. A pool of dark liquid moved, spreading out like a creeping shadow, thick and slow.

Something was in her closet. She'd moved the stack of notebooks and papers to her closet after that first night. There was no reason to try and hide the papers from Jules anymore.

Without taking her eyes off the closet door, April reached over slowly, so slowly, for the light switch on her bedroom lamp. She hit the lampshade, adjusted her hand down, searching for the switch. She found it and flipped the light on.

The dark puddle disappeared in the glare of the light. Maybe it had been a shadow. She was seeing things. Or she dreamed it, her dreams bleeding into wakefulness.

She crept out of bed and stood by the closet door, willing herself to open it.

Nothing is in my closet. Nothing is in my closet. Nothing is in my closet. . . .

April reached over and pulled the door open sharply.

She peered into the bottom of the closet, looking for the source of the scratching sound. There was nothing. But the bundle of papers was different somehow. The death map was on top, where she'd left it, but the tape had come loose on one side, as if someone had refolded it in a hurry.

April got a trash bag from the kitchen and some strapping tape she found in the workroom off to one side of the garage. The death map was fragile, too fragile to wrap up tightly, and she set it aside. It was strangely beautiful, and it was Aunt Silvia's artwork. Some part of her couldn't stand to see it destroyed.

She put everything else—the lab notebooks, mining reports, and photocopies of government documents—in the trash bag. She pulled the drawstring of the trash bag tight, folded it over, and then wrapped the entire bundle in clear strapping tape over and over, until the whole thing was one seamless, heavy lump of tape.

TWENTY-ONE

THURSDAY

APRIL DIDN'T SAY anything to Jules about the bundle of papers until they were in the car on the way to school.

"If you want to look at the papers, just ask. You don't need to break into my room and mess with my stuff," she said.

"But it wasn't me."

Jules's voice had none of the usual outsize wounded quality she had when she lied about something they both knew she'd done. If anything, she seemed baffled. Jules was telling the truth.

"You expect me to believe that Mom got up in the middle of the night and rummaged through my closet?"

"What if it's not Mom?" Jules said, her voice edged with

panic. "What if the man with the black ski mask came into our house last night?"

If that had happened, we'd be dead, April thought.

Dan Turnbridge would have killed them both.

"No one can get into the house without triggering the alert," April said. "We're safe."

April wondered if someone could have snuck into the house. They would have had to disable all the cameras. It didn't seem possible.

They pulled into the drop-off loop in front of Jules's school. April scanned the loop and the nearby street for the black truck. If Dan Turnbridge did show up, she'd call 911. She spotted the school security guard by the flagpole. If she laid on the horn, he'd come running to help.

Probably.

April thought about the dark puddle leaking from her closet—a puddle of foul liquid that wasn't there when she turned on the light. She might have dreamed that, but she didn't think so. Dreams and memories were bleeding together. She thought of the foul liquid under Dr. Travers-Steenkampf's slack head, that dark tongue protruding from between her lips . . .

"April?" Jules asked in a small voice. "Are you okay?"

April shook her head to clear the image of the dead woman in the dining room.

"I'm fine," she said.

Jules studied her.

"I don't think you are."

April gave Jules what she hoped was a reassuring smile. From the skeptical look on Jules's face she imagined she was coming up short.

"A couple of days, and this will all be over," April said. "Everything will go back to normal."

"Normal," Jules echoed. "What if we could prove that you really aren't the Bicycle Girl once and for all? Wouldn't that be better than normal?"

Jules had a faraway look in her eyes.

April laughed bitterly. If only it were that easy.

"How would we do that?"

"I have an idea," Jules said.

"Tell me later," April said. "Be careful today, okay? Stay safe."

Hopefully, Dan Turnbridge was in police custody by now, but they couldn't rely on that.

"Fine," Jules said in a voice that told April it wasn't fine. Not at all.

Jules grabbed her backpack and her purse and left the car without looking back.

"I'm going to make this right," April whispered.

Two more days. Mom was as sick as she'd ever been, Jules was angry, and April was no closer to discovering the truth than she'd been when Aunt Silvia first called her.

* * *

219

April didn't want to go to school. The clock was ticking and school felt like an enormous waste of time. She only had today and tomorrow to figure out how to open the portal before the cultists descended.

Marianne had suggested going out to the compound together. She'd said she knew the words to the ritual, but now Marianne was dead. There was only one other person who would know the ritual to open the portal.

Aunt Silvia.

April pulled out of the parking lot, but instead of heading toward school, she took the winding road up the mountain to Aunt Silvia's cabin. It was a big risk to go out to the cabin by herself, but she only had two days left to figure it all out.

She had to take the chance.

She drove up to the mountain with her phone by her side, ready to call 911 if someone followed her. When she crested the mountain, she lost cell reception, but fortunately no one had followed her.

She parked on the shoulder and made her way along the deer path through the underbrush to the cabin.

The moon door was standing wide open.

"Aunt Silvia?" she called.

No answer.

April was struck with a sudden cold wave of fear. Not the panicked adrenaline burst of being chased by the black truck. This fear was a slower, weightier thing.

She realized that Aunt Silvia had always been at a terrible

risk, as a woman, alone in an isolated area, but now the danger to her was enormous. April's birthday was two days away, and the whole valley was swarming with cultists and disaster tourists. They crowded the Coppermine bar and the coffee shop on Main Street, and the Morgan hotel was supposedly booked up. At least some of them must have ventured into the mountains.

"Aunt Silvia?" she yelled, more urgently this time.

April strode onto the porch and peered through the open door into the gloom of the cabin. One room, packed with a claustrophobic array of art supplies, furniture, and stacks of cardboard boxes, but no Aunt Silvia. She turned away, glad for the open air, and went around to the back of the cabin to Aunt Silvia's garden.

April looked past the small garden of dying pepper plants and late season squash to the empty cliffs above, like the top layer of skin had been pulled off the fabric of reality here, stripped as bare as the hillsides. She couldn't think straight. She'd come here to find answers, but this place stripped the questions from her mind and left her with new questions.

Where was Aunt Silvia?

She stepped back onto the porch, lost. She could still feel the enormous emptiness lurking just below, as though the ground could crumble beneath the tiny cabin, hurtling her down the side of the mountain toward the endless empty hole in the ground.

There was nowhere else to look.

She stood on the edge of the porch and looked down.

The open pit was so enormous that at first she didn't notice the tiny figure walking along the base of the stone wall. Small and wiry, wearing the misshapen straw cowboy hat she also wore in the garden, carrying what looked like a backpack.

Aunt Silvia.

It couldn't be anyone else.

What was she doing?

There had to be some reason that Aunt Silvia was down at the compound.

"Aunt Silvia!" she yelled, hands cupped around her mouth.

She was too far away for the sound to carry.

April ran back to her car along the deer trail. She drove toward the wall faster than she should have. The road curved and wound through pine forests before it hit the ridge.

When April cleared the ridge, she could still see Aunt Silvia, a dark shadow in a cowboy hat against the rock of the wall.

She had her eyes fixed on her aunt and took a curve too fast and hit gravel on the shoulder. The car skidded, antilock brakes shuddering as she managed to pull the car back onto the road.

When she crested the last rise before the straight line road to the wall, Aunt Silvia was still there, more visible now in her torn jeans and a work shirt so old it might once have been denim but was now bleached more sand colored than blue. How long had it taken Aunt Silvia to walk the distance between the cabin and the compound?

Aunt Silvia walked up to the end of the wall where it met the mountainside. The road curved and April kept her eyes on the drive in front of her. When she looked up again, Aunt Silvia was gone.

The wall loomed, obscuring the open-pit mine beyond its gates from view. The road came to an abrupt end, as if the wall had been dropped from the sky onto the highway.

April parked in front of the large iron gate and got out of the car, feeling exposed. Anyone driving over the mountain would see her, just as she'd seen Aunt Silvia.

She scanned the length of the wall and the barren land that surrounded the compound. There was no one in sight. She glanced back toward the road, but it was also empty.

She stood at the base of the wall and looked up. The wall seemed to stretch to the sky, and she remembered staring up at the wall, trying to imagine what was on the other side, filling in the blanks with a fairy-tale kingdom of manicured green lawns and delicate purple flowers that stretched on forever. She'd been on the other side of the wall then. Aunt Silvia had told her to look at the wall and imagine that a perfect world existed past the imposing iron gate.

April closed her eyes and the memory drifted away.

She needed to find Aunt Silvia.

The wall wasn't straight. It bowed out slightly, and she walked along the wall, seeing only a short distance ahead. It wasn't until she was twenty yards away from the end of the wall that she saw what was invisible from the road. It looked like the wall met a solid mountainside, but there was a triangular gap between the wall and a giant boulder next to the side of the mountain. It was a small gap, just big enough to crawl through at the bottom. It was the only place that April could begin to imagine Aunt Silvia had gone.

She squatted down and shined the light from her phone into the hole. The light was swallowed by an unnatural, inky blackness. April felt a sudden wave of fear so strong she worried she would hurl in the dust. If she crawled into this small dark cave and got stuck, who would even know?

"Aunt Silvia?" she called into the small space.

Her voice echoed strangely, suggesting the space opened into a larger area.

No response. No Aunt Silvia.

April.

April stiffened.

The voice. The sound was small but so clear, April knew she couldn't have imagined it.

She'd come this far.

Her dad was waiting.

She had to go in.

April turned the flashlight on her phone on and stuck the phone in her bra, with the light facing out. She crawled through the gap to a short space that ended against a rock wall. It didn't look like a way in. The passage narrowed slightly, tight enough that if she reached a dead end, there wouldn't be enough room to turn around. The idea of crawling backward in the dark made her heart pound in her chest.

When she hit the far wall, she held her phone out. The passage made a right-angle turn and widened into a man-made, rectangular tunnel just tall enough to stand in. She crawled through, glad to be able to stand, and flashed her phone light around.

There was a cache of empty beer cans in a widened spot in the tunnel, which suggested that more than one group of people had partied up here.

"Aunt Silvia?" she called.

No answer. Aunt Silvia had gone through. She was waiting on the other side.

There was no other place she could be.

The tunnel extended deeper into the mountain. April didn't know much about the mining process, and she wondered if the tunnel was left from an earlier mine, or if King had built this tunnel for his own purposes.

At the end of the tunnel was daylight, and a door-shaped hole in the wall. Surrounding the door were piles of loose rock and mortar. The light from the doorway was so bright it temporarily blinded her.

As her eyes adjusted to the light, she could see that the edges of the door were scorched from what must have been a fireball from the explosion.

You know what to do.

She suppressed a sudden, frantic urge to turn around.

To run back the way she came.

No.

She was here for a reason.

She was here to bring her dad back.

April was yards away from the portal and from the possibility of seeing her father again. She stood at the doorway, aware of an unnatural rasping sound in the close space of the tunnel. It took her a moment to realize that it was her breath, short, anxious gasps echoing strangely in the small space.

She stepped through the door into the sunlight, into the compound for the first time in almost twelve years. Immediately she looked back at the doorway, seized with an irrational worry that the tunnel would close behind her and leave her stranded inside the compound.

There were black scorch marks around the edge of the tunnel, as though the tunnel had been closed off and someone had dynamited it open.

She turned back. It took a full five seconds to make sense of what she saw, a twisted wreckage of rusted and unrecognizable metal, and thick slabs of red-painted steel walls blackened from an explosion. The borehole tower loomed above, the open pit beyond.

She stood in the midst of a blast pattern that had sprayed giant slabs of metal and left a starburst of char on the side of the mountain. When her father wrote that the mud lubrication pump had been sabotaged, she imagined a pump the size of a washer-dryer combination, not a shipping container. Dan Turnbridge had taken no chances when he blew up the mud agitator.

April knew there had been an explosion.

She didn't remember it.

Even now.

What she remembered of the explosion was the aftermath. The tunnel had been filled with smoke and it had scared her. They'd stepped over a leg, a thigh bone protruding from tattered flesh. Aunt Silvia had squeezed her hand and told her not to look at it. To look up at the wall.

They'd crept along the wall, looking for the way out. Aunt Silvia holding tight to her hand, instructing her not to look down. And when her eyes had naturally gone down to the ground, as she stepped over the wreckage of machinery, of bone and blood, Aunt Silvia had tugged firmly on her hand.

"Look up at the wall," Aunt Silvia had said. "Imagine the world on the other side."

They'd made their way back through the tunnel, crawled on hands and knees through the smaller passage to emerge in an expanse as dusty and desolate as the land behind the wall. There had been no beautiful world on the other side, no soft carpet of green grass and purple flowers, no magical kingdom.

There'd been only an endless walk across the desert floor, up to the mountains, to Silvia's cabin. Her feet had hurt terribly by the end, and April had complained. They left behind a still-smoldering wasteland and endless loss.

And now, she was back.

You know what to do.

The voice was stronger now. It echoed across that terrible expanse; it filled the corners of her mind, blotting out everything else. She looked past the wreckage, up to the height of the bore tower and felt that strange dizzy sensation she'd last had on the porch of Aunt Silvia's cabin. That distortion of time and space, the feeling that she could fall and fall, and never land—and in the end, wasn't that same as flying?

What was it Aunt Silvia had said? *You feel it too, don't you?* She did.

April understood, suddenly and with absolute clarity, what the voice meant. What Aunt Silvia had been trying to tell her.

All the mining reports, the quantum mechanics it might take Grace a lifetime to parse. All of this was nothing. It was one thing to understand the mechanics of flying, and another to stand on the edge of an abyss and let go.

Time to fly.

The bundle Aunt Silvia had given her was not an instruction manual. It was an invitation.

Time to fly.

The walls of reality were thinning near the portal. She was so close.

She could change—everything.

Her heart hammered in her chest with a mixture of exhilaration and terror at the thought of opening the portal once again.

All she had to do was to walk to the edge of the pit, as she'd done so many times in her dreams.

She knew what to do, but the fear was so strong that her feet betrayed her.

Walk to the edge.

Look down.

Listen to the voice.

She forced her trembling legs to take a step forward, and then another one. She wasn't a five-year-old on a bicycle anymore. This time, she would stand on the edge of the open pit and demand the voice of the portal to give her father back.

Her foot slipped on gravel and the sound echoed against the mountainside and came back as laughter.

The laughter of a small child.

April stood still, listening.

"Kiki," she whispered.

You know what to do.

The voice, so familiar it was as though it had never left her.

Images of death and destruction crowded her mind, thigh bone sticking out of leg meat, a broken man in the pit. Dr. Travers-Steenkampf face down on the dining room table.

It wanted more.

A sacrifice.

Time to fly.

Step to the edge, all the way to the edge, arms outstretched, perfect swan dive into oblivion.

Time to fly.

"No!" April shouted, the sound of her own voice startling her out of stillness.

She plunged back through the door to the tunnel in an animal panic, into the cover of the darkness, careened into a wall before she found the smaller passageway and crawled, hands and knees bumping and scraping, to the other side of the wall. She ran along the base of the wall to her car and drove away without looking back.

TWENTY-TWO

IT WASN'T UNTIL she cleared the ridge and drove past the deer trail to the small cabin that April realized she had left Aunt Silvia behind at the compound. She accelerated past the trail, unwilling to even consider going back. Once she was over the mountaintop, and the open-pit mine disappeared from her rearview mirror, she slowed the car back to within the speed limit.

Standing at the door to the compound had unlocked dozens of terrible memories of death and destruction. Aunt Silvia had found her in the big house, standing over Dr. Travers-Steenkampf's body. And then they had hidden in a closet, Aunt Silvia holding her close, Silvia's hand held loosely over April's mouth to keep her from crying out. But it wasn't a closet, because there were giant cans on the floor and she'd accidentally kicked one. It made a terrible noise and Aunt Silvia had been afraid they would be found by the people with guns.

They'd waited for so long before they finally left the big house, eating Popsicles from the freezer to keep from getting thirsty. But most of all, she'd been bored and cranky, and she'd wanted her mom, and she hadn't understood any of it.

Until Aunt Silvia cracked open the door and they tiptoed out to the patio. *Mouse quiet*, Aunt Silvia had said. And then when it was clear all was quiet, they'd left the patio and had walked down the road to the field of death and destruction.

April gripped the wheel tightly to keep her hands from shaking from the memory of her escape from the compound, hand in hand with Aunt Silvia. They had threaded their way through the long-smoldering ruins of the mud pump and all the dismembered corpses, Aunt Silvia warning her not to look.

But she had looked.

She couldn't help it.

She and Aunt Silvia had been at the compound the day of the massacre. And now she understood finally why the death map existed and why it was so accurate. Aunt Silvia had seen the aftermath firsthand.

And April had been there for all of it.

Mom had told her that the two of them had left the compound together, before the massacre.

Mom had lied, as she had about so many things.

April drove past the national forest and made her way back to town, turning on University Avenue near the college.

It took her a moment to realize that she was being followed. She took a right turn into a neighborhood, another right turn and another, made a loop before turning back onto University Avenue to confirm that it wasn't her imagination.

The surprise wasn't that she was being followed but who was following her. She looked up to see the acid-green Jeep in her rearview mirror. She recognized it instantly as the car she'd seen Marianne in at the Sonic. At the wheel, the blond man in mirrored sunglasses. Jonathan, Marianne's boyfriend.

At least it wasn't Dan Turnbridge.

Jonathan followed her at a distance, never getting too close. At a stoplight, she ran through a yellow and he stopped for the red. She thought she'd lost him, but he reappeared behind her as she turned toward school.

She considered leaving her car in the drop-off loop of school and running for the front door. She hated the idea of arriving at school sweaty and frantic, being chased by someone who would disappear the moment the first phone came out to record a video of her.

April realized she wasn't afraid of Jonathan.

She was angry.

He'd come here with Marianne to hound and torment her, and now Marianne was dead. That was as much his fault as it was hers. That acid-green Jeep stood out. If Dan Turnbridge had followed April to the Sonic on Friday, he would have seen her talking to Marianne.

That had signed Marianne's death warrant.

She wanted to convince Jonathan to go back to wherever he'd come from. Marianne was dead. He had no business here, and she just wanted him to leave her alone.

April drove to the Sonic, the place where she'd first seen his car. The Sonic was open, but it wasn't lunch yet and there were only a few cars in the bays. The central picnic table was unoccupied. Perfect. It would be hard to get more public than that.

She didn't have her picture hat, but the oversize sunglasses were in her purse, and she put those on before leaving the car.

She sat on the cement bench at the round picnic table and waited. She watched as his car circled the Sonic before he turned, then parked behind the building and out of her line of view. If he was trying to be unobtrusive, it was a lost cause.

Kara roller-skated over to April. Red Sonic shirt, red plastic tray tucked under one arm.

"That's the guy who was here that day," she said. "He was here with that girl who died."

April didn't have to ask what day. Kara had been on shift when April had slapped the latte out of Marianne's hand.

"He was her boyfriend," April replied. "He's been following me. I don't really trust him, but I need to talk to him."

Kara's eyes widened. She glanced over her shoulder, as Jonathan cleared the side of the building.

She swirled closer on her skates and lowered her voice.

"You don't think he killed her, do you?" she stage-whispered.

"I don't think so," April said.

Kara looked dubious.

"He's coming this way," she said. "Sure you don't want me to call somebody?"

"I think I'll be okay," April replied.

"Give me a nod if you need help," Kara said quietly before skating away.

April was touched. She'd come to the Sonic because it was public. She hadn't expected help.

Jonathan slid onto the bench opposite her. His mirrored aviator glasses and his shaggy hair, beach blond at the tips, brown at the roots, gave him a casual surf boy look totally at odds with his mournful expression.

"I'm Jonathan," he said in an unexpectedly gravelly voice. He sounded hoarse, like he'd been crying. "I'm a friend of Marianne's."

She noted the present tense. Did he not know that Marianne was dead? But of course he did. His eyes said as much.

"I know who you are," she said.

"Marianne told you about me?" he asked hopefully.

"What do you want, Jonathan?"

"We need to talk about the Deep Well," he said.

235

She stiffened, thinking of that moment in the doorway, remembering the disembodied chunks of flesh, the horrible smell of sulfur and smoke and meat. She hardly wanted to think about the open-pit mine, much less talk about it with a cultist's boyfriend. Ex-boyfriend.

Ex-cultist.

It had been a mistake to stop here. She didn't have anything to say to him.

"Oh?" she replied. "And what do we need to talk about?"

He leaned forward and put a hand on the table.

"It's about Marianne," he said urgently. "I want her back."

"Back?" she echoed, surprised. This was not at all what she'd expected.

She'd seen Marianne's broken body in the ditch. There was no coming back for Marianne.

"You can bring her back," he said. "You're the only one who can."

He craned his head toward the mountains and the open-pit mine beyond. What was he thinking? Her dad had gone through the portal, but Marianne was lying on a slab in the morgue or a funeral home. It wasn't the same thing.

"Marianne isn't missing, she's dead," April said savagely. "I saw her myself."

Jonathan flinched visibly. He lowered his head, and when he spoke his voice was soft, barely a whisper.

"Please," he said. "If you perform the ritual, and bring the king back, he will know what to do. I know he will save Marianne."

He reached out, grabbed for her arm.

April wrenched away from him, horrified. She and Grace and Zach had focused so much on the engineering and science behind the portal that she'd almost forgotten about the cultists' beliefs. That King would return with the secret to immortality.

She disengaged from the bench and stood over him. Kara skated over the moment April stood up, picking up on her distress.

"Please, I just want Marianne back," Jonathan said. His voice was a hoarse sob, and tears that he'd been holding back began to flow.

April glanced over at Kara, who had her phone in hand, ready to make a call to the police.

"I'm going to leave now," April said firmly. "And you're going to stay here until I'm gone. Got it?"

"Thanks," she mouthed as she walked past Kara on the way to her car.

April drove home from the Sonic, half expecting to find a police car parked in front of her house, officers waiting to ask her difficult questions about Marianne. She was relieved when she turned onto her street to find the driveway empty except for Mom's car.

She had a strong urge to go straight to her room and collapse in a pile. Fire off a couple of texts to Grace on the way to face-planting.

April was so tired. And really, there was nothing left to research, no more answers to be had from Aunt Silvia's collection of lab books and journals.

She'd had her chance to open the portal, and she'd run instead.

She'd failed.

April opened the side door to the kitchen to find her mom sitting at the table. Mom was fully dressed in navy pants and a white linen shirt, a dark red sweater draped jauntily across her shoulder. Makeup and jewelry.

"Are you going somewhere?" April asked, confused. She couldn't remember the last time Mom had left the house for anything other than doctor's appointments and taking Jules to and from school.

"The police were here," Mom said quickly, angrily. "I thought you agreed not to go out to Aunt Silvia's cabin."

"How did you know?" she said, but instantly the answer came to her. Phone tracker. And it only made sense that Mom would track her movements, considering that someone had once come to her school, hoping to shove her into the trunk of his car.

"Well, for starters, I got the call from school," Mom said. "April, why would you go out there? You know it's dangerous right now."

Right now was as close to mentioning the whole birth-day apocalypse nightmare as Mom ever got. Seeing Mom had shaken the questions out of April's mind, but *right now* brought them all back.

"I wanted to find out why you've always lied to me about that day," April said.

Mom stiffened. She didn't bother to deny it.

"What did you find out?"

April considered for a moment.

"Everything," April said softly.

"Silvia told you?" Mom said indignantly.

"No," April said. "I remembered."

Mom turned a sickly ashen color. Her lip quivered slightly, and a dim background alarm rang in the back of April's brain, but it was too late. The truth was out.

"You left me behind," April said.

"I did. I'm sorry, April."

Mom dropped her head.

April waited. She waited for so long, she imagined this might be the end of the conversation. That Mom would climb the stairs and go back to bed, as she often did when things got tough.

April hated herself for thinking this.

"How did you not know where I was?" April asked. "I mean, I was five. Did you just let me wander around . . . ?"

"You were supposed to be with Aunt Silvia," Mom pro-tested. "You have to understand, I was pregnant, and so sick at the time. Aunt Silvia would serve lunch at the mess hall and then take you up to King's house when she brought him food. You loved it up there."

Aunt Silvia, King, the gardener all on the patio. There was a reason the patio stuck in her memory. She'd been up to the big house every day with Aunt Silvia.

Only, Aunt Silvia hadn't been with her that day.

"But you left," April said. "And you didn't know where I was."

"When the explosion happened, your dad told me to leave, for Jules's sake." Mom said. "He promised me that he would find you."

Dad had gone looking for her at the house. She was the reason Dad and King Steenkampf were together at the house when something happened. A loud noise, a flash of light, and her dad and King Steenkampf had disappeared.

The one part of her memory that was still missing.

April had wandered the big house, alone, until she found Dr. Travers-Steenkampf's body in the dining room.

And then Aunt Silvia found her.

"Are you going to tell Jules about this?" Mom asked.

April looked up. Mom had a look of congealed misery and guilt on her face.

April had been deep diving into her own tortured memories of that day, but she imagined that day had to have been just as bad, if not worse, for Mom.

240

Mom must have truly believed that Dad would find her and bring her out. And when the minutes and then hours ticked by, Mom had to have thought that all three of them were dead. April, Dad, Aunt Silvia, her whole family lost behind the wall.

She would tell Jules everything eventually. There had been too many lies and half-truths, and when Dad was back it wouldn't matter anyway.

When she figured out how to get Dad back.

"Not now," April replied.

Mom relaxed visibly, then she did the thing she always did when anyone got too close to an uncomfortable truth. She changed the subject.

"I'm going to go get Jules," Mom said. "I'd like to be there before school lets out. Do you want to come with me?"

April nodded. It was the one thing she and Mom could agree on. They'd both be happier with Jules safe at home.

TWENTY-THREE

JULES WAS ANNOYED to be picked up early from school.

"I had plans with Luna," she said.

"We have to stay close to the house for the next few days," Mom said. "And then things will go back to normal."

"Normal," Jules repeated bitterly.

There was no such thing as normal now.

Back home, Mom retreated into her office to have a phone conversation in hushed tones.

April went to her room to be alone.

In the late afternoon, April fell into a deep and dreamless sleep. It was a relief not to dream. When she woke up, it was dark and quiet in the house. It felt like the middle of the night, but it was only 8:37.

Jules's light was on. As April padded down the hallway, the light in Jules's room went out. As though April was the enemy.

Tomorrow was the last day before her birthday, the only chance she'd have to go back to the compound before the cultists arrived.

Everything was guiding her back to the compound again.

She needed to talk to Zach.

He was at work. CHAR closed at nine, so she had just enough time to put on a different shirt and some makeup before going to the Coppermine bar.

Do you need a ride home? April texted Zach. **We need to talk.**

Come get me, he texted back.

She looked up the address of the police station on her phone and programmed it into navigation, just in case she saw a black truck in her rearview mirror. She wasn't going to risk another run-in with Dan Turnbridge.

Twenty minutes later she parked her car outside the Coppermine and crunched through the gravel.

Zach came through with trash bags headed for the dumpster.

"Hey, April."

"Hey."

She stood in the parking lot, conscious of her too sexy boots and low-cut blouse. It tugged at her, a hard feeling in the pit of her stomach. She was the Bicycle Girl with a grand and terrible destiny. How could one boy make her feel this way?

"I'm almost done," he said. "I just have to lock up."

He turned off the lights and locked the door to the food truck, and they put his bike into the trunk of the car. They took off toward his house. It wasn't much of a drive. Ten minutes tops and she'd be alone again.

"I went to the compound today," she said.

"I thought you weren't going to go by yourself." There was an edge of annoyance in his voice, or maybe it was concern.

"I know, I know," she replied. "I shouldn't have gone by myself. But I need to go back. Tomorrow."

Tomorrow was the last day before her birthday. The last time to go out there without risking running into a bunch of cultists—or worse. The cultists dragging in some poor unsuspecting girl—and she knew it would be a girl, because it's always a girl—they planned to sacrifice.

"I'll go with you," he said.

She felt a wave of relief.

They lapsed into silence, the kind of hush where the blink of a turn signal filled the air with unspoken meaning. There was so much more that she wanted to say. She wanted to tell him about Jonathan. She realized she'd never told him about the voice, or about her suspicions that she had to make the ultimate sacrifice to open the portal.

"Hey, do you want to go somewhere and talk?" he said.

"Sure. Do you still have that broken-down couch across the street?"

Suddenly April was flush with nostalgia for his neighborhood, the haunted bridge, the broken-down couch, and impromptu bike ramps. If she really could open a time vortex, maybe she would send them all back there, to thirteen. BH—before *Hellhole!*

Zach laughed in the gloom.

"That thing? It fell apart and Mr. Wallace had the city haul it off. Took them years to get to it."

"What about chapel hill?"

At the end of the historic district was a tall, narrow hill. At the top was a tiny brick chapel. From there, you could see in all directions, the town on one side, the desert on the other, all ringed by mountains, a distant blue to the south.

"I live right by there," April added, in case he thought she had ideas. It was a place for ideas.

"I remember," he said, with a sly smile.

They turned onto the main street in the neighborhood and parked the car in the side lot, halfway up the hill. They walked the rest of the way to the chapel and sat on the bench in front.

She'd come up here to tell Zach about standing at the door to the compound and remembering the dark and terrible past. About hearing that voice.

But now that they were here the strangeness of the day faded away, and she found herself unwilling to think about anything serious. The town below looked lovely, not a place for black trucks and hidden cultists. Here, at the highest point in town, they could see anyone coming from any direction.

Here, with Zach, she felt safe.

She wasn't used to feeling this way.

"I've never been up here with someone," April said. "And you?"

Zach shot her a sidelong glance, a look that told April he knew exactly why people came up here.

"We used to ride our bikes up to the top of the hill and rocket down the concrete footpath," he said, avoiding the subject. "If my friends and I did that more than three times in a row, your neighbors would call the cops, and we'd get a talking-to. For our own good, of course."

April laughed.

"You didn't answer my question."

"I thought you didn't like awkward questions," he said.

They looked out over the town. The chapel had always been her favorite place, her refuge when she was younger. When the thick stillness of the house got to be too much. Across the valley, lights of houses and cars twinkled in the night air.

Her big two-story cream-colored house towered over a neighborhood of low adobe and ranch houses.

246

"I used to come up here to think, but the truth is, I came up here to not think," April said. "Just to be."

"What were you trying not to think about?" he asked.

She remembered being thirteen. How she would come up to the chapel and look over the whole town. It would seem simultaneously peaceful and distant, like a postcard so old that all the people in the picture were long dead. She'd fantasized about a future world where no one would remember her.

She didn't want to tell him the other reason she often walked to the top of the hill. She came to contemplate flying. That feeling that if she stretched her arms and fell in a perfect swan dive, everything would come to an end.

"Oh, you know, Bicycle Girl stuff."

"You always seemed so calm," he said. "Like you were unaffected by the whole Bicycle Girl thing. But now—"

"Now I'm a mess?" April said quickly.

He laughed.

"Not what I meant."

She looked over at Zach.

"Can I ask you something?" she said.

He nodded.

"When I showed you the death map, you never doubted me. Even when I told you about the portal. Why?"

Zach sighed.

"I don't even remember my dad," he said. "He was gone

before my brother was born. But my uncle, he was always there for me. He was solid."

"That's the way I felt about my dad," she said.

"I could never explain the feeling I had that he was still alive," Zach said. "Until you brought me the map."

April couldn't help but think of Jonathan, mourning Marianne.

Looking for magic.

But she and Zach were different. There had never been any trace of her dad, King Steenkampf, or his uncle, and there should have been.

Her dad was out there, waiting. She knew it in her heart.

"So you went out to the compound today," he said. "What happened?"

April looked out over the town. The night had turned cold, and everything seemed a little more ominous than it had before.

"Aunt Silvia went in through a hidden tunnel at the end of the wall. I went in after her, but once I was inside, I lost my nerve."

She thought back to the moment she'd stood at the doorway to the compound, hearing that voice in her ear, goading her to put an end to it all. She didn't want to go back, but she had to. And it terrified her.

Zach wrapped an arm around her shoulder and pulled her close. She leaned into him, feeling his broad chest against her shoulder, feeling less afraid.

"I'm sorry," he said softly.

"I had the chance to bring them back today and I failed," she said, her voice trembling. "When I go back, I don't know if I can . . ."

"April, you can't do this alone."

"Well, you say that. But isn't this my problem to solve?"

"No," he murmured. His lips were close enough to her hair that she could feel the warmth of his breath. "What happened up there the day of the massacre wasn't your fault, any more than it's mine. We both lost someone. That's all."

A soft breeze stirred the trees in the distance. He ran his fingers down her arm, sending a thrill along her skin.

"Are you sure?" she said. "You didn't try to end the world."

"Neither did you."

She looked up at him, his dark eyes liquid in the gloom.

"April, you're the toughest person I've ever known," he said. "I don't know how this is going to work, but I know we'll figure it out together."

She felt a hard knot in her stomach loosen, one that she hadn't even been aware of until that moment.

When she allowed herself to imagine a future beyond her seventeenth birthday, she envisioned herself somewhere else, pretending to be someone else. Waiting for that inevitable moment when new friends recognized her as the Bicycle Girl.

Cover—blown.

It had been unthinkable that someone could know her whole creepypasta sordid history and feel anything but fear or contempt for her. She was the punch line to a thousand jokes. She was the thing small children feared under their beds at night.

But Zach knew everything about her, what she'd done, and how much she'd lost. He knew that the day of the massacre had left a giant crater in her psyche and her soul, because it left him the same way too.

They were together.

And that was everything.

He kissed her softly, his lips barely touching hers. She leaned into a deeper kiss, as his arm slid around her waist.

They kissed like they were alone together, adrift in a world of ghosts, and the only thing holding back the darkness was this.

She wanted to stay here forever, with his arms wrapped around her, to forget tomorrow, and her birthday, and the day after that.

To be with Zach.

To forgive, and to be forgiven.

To be anything but alone.

"We should probably go soon," he whispered. "We have a lot to do tomorrow."

Too soon. Maybe this was the last bit of happiness April could wring out of the world. Tomorrow, they would go to the compound.

Tomorrow, they would bring her dad and his uncle back or die trying.

They stood and walked down the trail to the parking lot together. His hand found hers and they laced fingers.

He got his bike out of the trunk.

"Do you want me to drop you off?" she asked.

"I'll be fine," he said, looping a leg over his bike. "I'll see you tomorrow, okay?"

She grabbed the handlebars of his bike, straddled the tire, and leaned in for one last kiss. Freed from holding the bike, he threaded fingers through her hair. His other hand wrapped around her waist and pulled her close, handlebars pinned between the two of them. When she finally pulled away and released the handlebars, he struggled to grab the bike, his usual athletic reflexes failing him.

She laughed softly.

"You were going?" she said in a low, throaty voice.

"Was I?"

Instead of walking toward her car, she turned and walked back up to the chapel at the top of the hill. She watched him ride down her street, past her house, until he rounded the corner and disappeared from sight.

TWENTY-FOUR

FRIDAY

APRIL SLEPT FITFULLY and woke up late. Jules was already gone. In the kitchen, April noted the untouched cup of coffee cooling on the butcher block, the small carton of Scandinavian yogurt missing two bites, no more. Anger fought a war with long-term worry about her mother getting enough to eat. Not taking care of herself.

Worry won out.

It didn't matter. Soon, she would bring her dad back. Soon, everything would be different, and all Mom's lies would recede into the past.

If April didn't return, she didn't want to leave Mom with a fight as her last memory.

It was Friday.

The day she would go to the compound.

April drank the cold cup of coffee. Zach had volunteered to go with her to the compound, and Zach was at school, so that was where she needed to go.

She drove to school and headed to the office to make excuses for being late. Normally, a confrontation with the office staff would be cause for anxiety, but in her current state of mind, the whole business of school had an air of surreality.

The woman at the front desk took one look at April and decided that her excuse that her mom was sick and April had woken up late was deeply plausible.

"Are you sure you're well enough to be here?" the office worker who filled out her slip asked. "You don't look well."

"Where else am I going to go?" April said. "The apocalypse isn't until tomorrow."

April craned her head slowly in the direction of the mountain and the abandoned mine beyond and giggled. It struck her as funny that she was still here at school, when nothing really mattered anymore.

No one in the office laughed.

Today, she was going to open the portal.

Today, she'd get her dad back. Whatever that took.

No more running in fear. She'd go through that dark tunnel, step into the compound, and demand that the voice return her dad.

"Don't worry. When the time comes, you'll be spared," April said to no one in particular.

She imagined a *Hellhole!*-style volcano of demons erupting from the pit, spilling over the small town.

The school counselor emerged from her office like a slightly lazy watchdog, alerted to possible danger by a scent of decomposition in the air. She was a stocky middle-aged woman dressed all in brown, with an oversize pile of keys and badges swinging from a bloodred lanyard around her neck. She looked like she could hold her own in a fight. Mrs. C., they called her, short for her name or short for counselor. No one really knew.

As Mrs. C. stepped forward, everyone else faded back, glad to leave April to her. April scanned the office workers and gauged their responses. Some were genuinely afraid; others, head down, pretended to ignore April and her whole situation.

April was used to this, but not quite at this level. Soon she would pull her dad and King Steenkampf out of the void, and then what? How would the world react to the arrival of King Steenkampf, missing billionaire, from an alternate dimension? And April, the one who brought him back?

And her dad?

She had to remind herself that she was doing this to bring her dad back, because the thought of going back out to the compound filled her with dread. She couldn't shake the feeling that she was on the edge of something terrible.

Mrs. C. composed her weary watchdog face into a look of compassionate concern. It was a good performance. Convincing.

"I'm here if you need to talk, April," she said.

April gave a thought about what it would be like to tell her troubles to an actual competent adult. Someone with a broad, open face. Serious, with no secrets.

She wouldn't believe anything April told her.

Mrs. C. couldn't help her now.

"Maybe I'll come in after my birthday," April said.

She giggled again. Inappropriately. She couldn't help it.

She couldn't imagine a time after her birthday.

April had inadvertently opened a portal a decade ago and had dragged her dad and Zach's uncle through. But it hadn't been her idea. King Steenkampf was the reason her father was there at the portal.

Would anyone make him suffer for that?

Probably not. He was rich, and he'd find some way to capitalize on "his" discovery.

It didn't matter. April would bring her dad back. That was all that mattered.

Her phone buzzed in her pocket.

April noted Mrs. C.'s deep frown of disapproval as she pulled the phone from her pocket.

The text was from Luna. April's heart sank before she even read the full message.

Okay, so I don't want to get Jules in trouble.

April had received several *I don't want to get Jules in trouble, but . . .* texts from Luna over the past couple of years. Luna was the best possible friend for someone like Jules. They were loyal, but had an infallible sense of when Jules was about to plunge over a cliff.

Jules left school with someone she met online.

A hammer blow of fear struck her squarely in the chest. Jules, off with someone she'd met online. Why would Jules do something like this?

"Is everything all right, April?" Mrs. C. asked.

April looked up from her phone.

"My mom needs me," she said quickly. "It's an emergency."

April was prepared to fight her way out of the office, but to her relief, Mrs. C. simply nodded.

"Come by my office when you get back to school," she said in a gentle tone that nevertheless implied that a visit to her office wasn't optional.

April left and walked out the front door of the school.

How long ago? she texted Luna.

Just now. She told me not to tell you until later. She's going to be mad that I told you.

No, you did the right thing, April texted.

A thousand different questions flooded her mind, but there was only one question that really mattered.

Where were they going?

256

April already knew, but she didn't want to be right.

She looked toward the mountain.

They went out to the mine, Luna texted.

Why???

Why did Jules have to go out there on this of all days?

What could have possessed her to go to the most dangerous place in the world at the worst possible time?

She wanted to prove that the portal is a hoax before your birthday.

April wanted to scream that it wasn't a hoax. Yell at Luna in all capital letters. But it wasn't Luna's fault—it was hers. She should have kept Jules at home.

She should have told Jules the truth.

Thanks, Luna.

April shoved her phone back in her pocket. She thought about trying to find Zach, but she had no idea what class he was in.

There was no time.

April should have seen the signs. Jules had been planning this for a while. And now she was on her way out to the compound with god knows who.

April ran to her car and headed toward the mountain. It was only when she reached the first stoplight that she texted Grace.

Going out to the compound. Jules is out there. Find Zach and bring him with you.

257

The light changed and she roared away, hoping to catch Jules and whoever had lured her out to the compound before something terrible happened. She had the feeling that somehow everything had already been set in motion.

Today was the day.

TWENTY-FIVE

JULES

In June 2018, a HorrorTuber posted a video of a supposed portal in the Allegheny Mountains. The HorrorTuber did not disclose the exact location for "security reasons."

In the shaky handheld video, three people with flashlights entered a narrow tunnel on the side of a mountain. The sides of the tunnel were littered with strange graffiti, arcane spells, and a repeated image in chalk of a small human figure splayed in the center of concentric circles. The circles surrounded a heptagram star, seven points, with an arrow at the top, pointing down.

There had been videos of this supposed portal

location before, but this was the first time the chalk drawing had been seen. The video went viral, and suddenly the seven-pointed star was everywhere, including badly done versions on school lockers in Sharpie.

There were dozens of videos explaining the meaning of the graffiti, some of them outlandish and amateurish, others well researched.

The figure in the heptagram was believed to be the entity who wanted to come through the portal, or a man who had been sucked into a portal.

The heptagram star was alternately explained as a Christian protection against evil, a sign that law enforcement was involved in the highly secretive group known as "the Seven," or that fans of the band Tool were trying to open the portal.

In August 2018, urban explorer and YouTube personality Marcos Gil unearthed a 2003 shaky cam horror movie entitled *Tuberculum*, about mortuary tunnels underneath a 1930s tuberculosis sanatorium. No one ever admitted to doctoring the video, but Gil showed that the symbol was added postproduction to the existing movie.

After Gil debunked the video, the Allegheny portal entered the realm of creepypasta and urban legend. Many paranormal researchers believe that the crude and easily debunked *Tuberculum* hoax was engineered to hide the existence of the real portal from the general public.

> From *The Secrets of the Seven*
> by Marjorie T. Gortner

WHEN SHE WAS in fifth grade, her then-friend Zoe dared Jules to watch the Allegheny portal video. In the video, three college students explore a cave on the side of a mountain in West Virginia, when they come across the mark of the Seven. They laugh it off at first, but then they realize that they've stumbled across a portal. The three students are doomed, and the Seven hunt them down until they're all dead.

Jules watched in terror, unable to look away.

"Just like your sister," Zoe said. "She found a portal, right?"

After that, the Seven haunted her dreams. She hated the idea of the Seven looking for her sister, but for Jules it was almost worse to imagine that there were portals everywhere. She'd always planned to leave Copperton one day. In her fantasy, she imagined Aunt Silvia deciding that it was stupid to live in a dusty cabin all by herself. April would stop being so creepy all the time, and they would all move to someplace cool with palm trees and beaches, like Los Angeles.

But if there were portals everywhere, it meant no place was safe, not even Los Angeles, and they might as well stay in Copperton because they were all doomed.

Jules had been convinced everything would end on April's seventeenth birthday, when the Seven would come for April. Then, months ago, Jules had stumbled across a video by a guy named Kos on YouTube.

His name was actually Marcos Gil, but he went by Kos. Kos went through the Seven video point by point, explaining why it was a hoax. The scene of the girl being killed underneath the sign of the Seven was from a movie. The mark of the Seven wasn't even in that movie. The original film had some dumb goat head thing.

After that, Jules subscribed to Kos's YouTube channel and watched all his videos debunking urban myths.

Kos went into a lot of abandoned buildings and underground sites with his friend Trev, who was kind of a clown and liked to skateboard over everything, even though he sometimes ate it on hidden stuff. Kos just smiled at him and shook his head. That happened every episode.

Kos's younger sister, Kayla, started coming with them, and she was really something. She liked to skateboard too, and she had her hair short, bleached, and dyed pink and purple.

Jules so wanted to meet her. She wanted to be like Kayla. Brave, smart, and funny.

She watched Kayla's TikToks all the time. Kayla scrambled over walls and barriers at a gym where she was learning parkour. She also had lots of videos of Trev falling off his skateboard.

Kos, Trev, and Kayla had so much fun, and they were never scared at any of the places they went. They all lived in Las Vegas. They went into the tunnels of Las Vegas all the time, which should have been creepy, but really it was just sad.

Kos talked about homelessness and the housing shortage.

"People are just people," Kayla said. "You talk to them, and you understand their stories."

Trev said, "Just once, I'd like to find a really haunted place."

Kos and Kayla rolled their eyes at that.

They believed that no places were haunted.

No places were evil.

There were no such things as portals.

Kos and Kayla made her feel okay about things for the first time in a long while.

Kayla had a comment box where you could suggest new places to explore, and Jules sent her a message.

I live near a mine that's supposed to be haunted. Ojo de Cristo. You should come here and debunk it.

That was months ago.

Now Kayla was coming here, and they were going out to the mine together.

"You're not really going, are you?" Luna whispered across the aisle in English class.

"Kayla is coming all the way from Las Vegas," Jules whispered back. "I can't not go, can I?"

"I still think this is a dumb idea, Jules," Luna said.

Jules regretted telling Luna the plan because they hadn't shut up about it since. The way Jules saw it, she really didn't have a choice. April was losing it big-time, and now she was acting like she was going to go out there on her birthday with the cultists and perform a demonic ritual to raise their dad from the dead.

Like she'd never seen a zombie movie.

The cultists were dangerous.

Everyone said they were planning human sacrifice, which sounded hard to believe, but still. Even if nothing that weird happened with the cultists, someone would take a video, and April would never be able to leave the whole Bicycle Girl thing behind.

Jules had to save April from herself.

"What about after school?" Luna whispered. "So you don't get in trouble."

From the front of the class, the teacher scowled. They were supposed to be working on a paper, in silence. But everyone was on their phones. Even the teacher was on her phone.

"Kayla said it was too close to sunset," Jules whispered. "The light won't be good. No, it has to be now."

"Shhhhh," the teacher hissed.

Luna pulled out their phone and began typing furiously. Jules put her phone on silent and waited.

What if Kayla murders you? What if she chops you up into a thousand pieces and leaves you in the desert? they texted.

In some ways, Luna was the bravest person in the world. But they were super cautious in other ways, always worried about murdery stuff.

Kayla is famous, Jules texted back. **Famous people don't do crimes.**

Luna rolled their eyes.

Being famous means you get away with it. Don't go.

Poor Luna. Jules could see real worry. It was sweet. But Kayla was cool, and more to the point, she had a lot of followers. Kayla promised that she would post whatever they recorded at the mine tomorrow, on April's birthday, so that the whole world would see once and for all that there was nothing at the compound but a giant hole, some ruined machinery, and a bunch of rocks.

Kayla was convinced that posting on April's actual birthday would make the video go viral.

If I don't text you by three, you can call my sister.

Luna looked slightly relieved. But not all the way. Jules set a reminder on her phone to call Luna to tell them everything was okay.

265

The bell rang for lunch. Jules had a whole story made up in case she got stopped on the way out, but no one stopped her because there was a fight in the hall next to the cafeteria, and the security guard ran by her to break it up. She couldn't have planned a better diversion.

She walked to the convenience store next to the high school, which was where she had agreed to meet Kayla. Jules had lied to Kayla and told her that she was April. She worried that Kayla would be mad. But by the time she got here, it would be too late to back out. After a nine-hour drive? Kayla would want to see the compound anyway.

One side of the building was a liquor store, so Jules couldn't stand there. She waited by the side that faced the high school, hoping no one would notice her.

It wasn't too long before a new bright red pickup rolled alongside the building where she was standing. The tinted passenger-side window rolled down, and the driver leaned over.

"April?" he asked.

It wasn't Kayla. It was Trev. Goofy, skateboard-riding Trev. Wearing dark sunglasses and a backward baseball cap, shaggy dark blond hair sticking out of the back. Jules looked around, thinking that maybe Kayla was in a different car or truck. Maybe they had a lot of equipment to carry and one car wasn't enough.

No other trucks came.

He was alone.

A wave of crushing disappointment swept over her. She

hadn't realized how excited she'd been to meet Kayla until Trev turned up in her place. It would be different if Kos had shown up, but Trev?

Trev squinted at her.

"You're not April, are you?"

"I'm Jules," she said. "I'm the one who sent a message."

"Jules?" he said blankly. His eyes roamed the parking lot, the liquor store, and came to rest on the high school.

"I'm April's sister," she said. "Where is Kayla?"

Trev ignored the question.

"You don't look seventeen," he said.

"Neither do you."

Kayla was seventeen or eighteen. She'd seen dozens of videos with Trev, usually him skateboarding, laughing like a kid; but now, seeing him up close, she realized that he was a lot older. Like almost thirty, riding around on a skateboard acting like he was fourteen. It was strange.

"Okay, then," Trev said. "I guess this was a mistake."

Jules could see he was about to roll up the window and drive away, and she would lose her ride out to the compound. She wasn't thrilled that Trev had shown up instead of Kayla, but Trev had a following.

She had to think about April. This was her only chance to get out to the compound and show the world that it was all a hoax.

"Wait, wait, wait . . ." she said. "I thought we were going to go out to the compound together."

"And I thought you were April," he said.

He started to roll up the window.

"You need me," she said, loud enough that someone going into the convenience store turned and stared.

He lowered the window.

"I know things you don't know."

"Ooh, so now you're going to tell me about all the spooky local legends? About the ghost of a woman at the haunted cabin in the—"

"That's not a ghost," Jules said. "That's my aunt Silvia."

Trev quirked an eyebrow. "Is that right?" he said.

Jules nodded. "I know where her cabin is," she said. "You won't find it without me."

Aunt Silvia's cabin was hidden from the road. Even the trail that led to her cabin wasn't easy to find.

She could see that he was thinking. He stared at her.

"Get in," he said.

Jules opened the door and pulled herself up. The truck, which was so pretty on the outside, was a mess inside. It was dank and smoky. There was lighting equipment in the back seat but also beer cans and fast-food wrappers on the floor.

Trev backed out of the parking lot and turned on the road toward the mountain. He seemed to know where he was going.

"So was it you all the time?" Jules asked. "Not Kayla?"

Jules replayed all the text exchanges in her mind, feeling

268

weird about it. She'd tried to remember if she'd said some personal things to "Kayla."

"Me, all the time," he said.

"So Kos and Kayla never saw my message?" she asked.

"They did," he said. "They weren't interested."

Kayla wasn't interested in her. That made her feel terrible. She tried to remind herself that this was all about April, but she had to know.

"Why not?"

"Kos and Kayla don't care about spooky shit, even if it does bring views. They're just interested in people."

Trev spit out the word *people* like it was *giant spiders* or *angry rats*. Jules thought about Kayla and Kos. Everywhere they went, they found people living in abandoned spaces, under difficult conditions. It made her wish she was traveling to the mine with them.

But maybe it was better to go with Trev after all. If he went looking for "spooky shit" and didn't find it, that would be proof enough for the whole world.

"If we're going to do this, I'm gonna need you to agree to a couple of things," Trev said. "Because you're a kid, I can't have you on camera. You can't even talk because you sound like a kid. But you can hold the phone and film me."

"Okay," Jules said.

That seemed easy enough. She'd had this stupid dream of being in Kos and Kayla's videos, of gaining a following of her own and becoming an urban explorer. She didn't feel the same way about being in Trev's videos.

"Sweet." He turned his head to watch the road.

After a few minutes of driving along silently, she pulled out her phone to text Luna, but it wouldn't send. She remembered this about being at Aunt Silvia's. Her phone didn't work. It was a strange feeling, being completely cut off. She tried not to panic. They would record the video and get out quickly, before Luna even had time to call April.

Nothing would go wrong.

They went over the top of the mountain and the wall and the mine came into view. Fifteen minutes later, the road dead-ended at the wall.

Jules and Trev got out of the truck and walked up to the wall.

She'd seen the wall from Aunt Silvia's cabin, but never up close. She had no idea how big it really was. It cast a permanent shadow, colder somehow at its base.

Jules shivered.

"How are we going to get over it?" she asked.

"I've got a plan," Trev said. "We'll try to find a breach. You'd be surprised how quickly things start to fall apart when they're abandoned."

"It looks pretty solid to me," Jules said.

"Stone walls are expensive," he said. "Sometimes people put up the front and finish the back with regular fencing. It's pretty easy to get over a hurricane fence, if you can climb. Can you climb?" Trev gave her a skeptical look, like he thought that just because she was a girl, she'd never climbed a fence before.

"Um—yes!" Jules replied. "How old are you, anyway?"

"Okay, rude," he said. "You never told me how old you are, either."

"Kayla climbs," Jules said.

Trev rolled his eyes.

There were boxes, climbing gear, rope, and duct tape in the back of Trev's truck. Jules remembered hearing about the man who tried to kidnap April. He had rope and ether and duct tape in his car when they found him.

Suddenly, she felt a little sick. She remembered what Luna said about being chopped up into a thousand pieces and left to rot in the desert sun.

Trev got out a big box from the back seat of the truck. He fiddled with something Jules realized was a drone.

"Why do you have duct tape in your truck?" Jules asked.

"A million reasons," he said. "Sometimes you have to duct-tape lights in place."

That sounded suspicious. He had light stands for that.

"You don't need any light," Jules said. "It's super bright out here."

"It's also good for people who ask too many questions," he said.

He was joking, Jules told herself. He was joking.

271

She backed away from the truck.

Trev looked up and noticed she was moving away.

"Come here," he said, sounding annoyed.

She hesitated.

"I'm not going to bite you, I just want you to record me."

He stepped closer and handed Jules his phone.

"Remember, don't talk."

Jules started a recording on his phone.

Trev stood with a hand on the wall and began talking about the deep borehole and how it was supposed to go all the way to Hell, and how you could hear the screaming of the damned if you got close. Jules was annoyed with all the talk of Hell. He was supposed to be helping her to debunk the idea that there was a portal to Hell at the compound. They'd agreed over text. But maybe this was just how he planned to start out. He would rope his viewers in with the legend, and then show them there was nothing there, just a hole in the ground.

Trev made a slashing motion across his neck, and Jules stopped recording.

"So, what do we do now?" Jules asked.

"We look for a way in," he said.

He asked for his phone back. He had an app for the drone camera.

"Hold this up so I can see it," he said.

Jules moved closer to him and held the phone out at arm's

272

length so he could operate the controls and also see what the drone camera was seeing.

The drone lifted in the air. Trev got it to hover above the wall before he settled it down to run alongside the top of the wall, about ten feet up.

"I'm looking for a place where the wall is broken or where it doesn't look like it would be so hard to get over," he said.

Jules could see what was on the camera, but Trev mostly watched the drone. The barbed wire top of the fence was falling apart in places, but otherwise, the wall looked solid.

Behind the wall, in the shadows, something moved.

It was a momentary gray streak, probably a rat or something. But it seemed bigger than a rat. The drone passed over—just a flash and it was gone.

Jules shivered. Was she seeing things now, like April?

Trev flew the drone to the very edge of the wall, where it ended in the side of a cliff cut into the mountain. He hovered over the spot.

"Did you see that?" he asked.

"See what?"

Trev flew the drone slower on their side of the wall. When the drone got to the end of the wall, it hovered near a big boulder propped against the sheer cliff face. Between the wall and the boulder was a space about three feet wide.

"I've never seen anything like this before," Trev said, steering the drone over the same spot. He carefully guided the drone inside the space. It was dark, so dark that the camera blacked out for a second until he guided the drone out of the gap.

"I think there's a tunnel there," Trev said.

He lifted the drone in the air again, over the top of the wall, and down on the other side where it disappeared from sight. Trev leaned close to the phone, flying from the image in the camera. They both saw it together.

A perfect rectangular hole in the side of the mountain.

"Hidden passage," Trev said. "I've heard rumors, but . . ."

"It's a door!" Jules blurted out. "It's a door into the side of a mountain."

They were really going into the compound. She hadn't fully believed until this instant.

"How cool is that?" Trev said.

They both laughed. They'd figured it out, together. They were going in, together.

It was an adventure.

TWENTY-SIX

JULES

JULES HAD TO crawl on her hands and knees through a gap in the rock. Trev told her to go first.

"You're smaller," he said.

Like that was a reason.

"What if I get stuck?" she asked.

"Then I'll pull you out by your feet," Trev said.

She looked to see if he was laughing but he wasn't.

"You're so brave," she said.

Jules didn't like crawling in the dark. She turned on the flashlight on her phone, held it in her left hand, and tried to crawl through without putting her phone hand down. The walls of the small tunnel brushed her back and made her think of spiders. It was the desert. Was it too dry for spiders out here?

No spiders, she told herself.

No spiders, no spiders . . .

When she got to the end of the narrow tunnel, she stood and flashed the light around, looking for spiders. She was in a rectangular tunnel, maybe seven feet tall and three feet wide. There were no spiders as far as she could see.

Beer cans.

She leaned over the opening of the smaller tunnel.

"I'm through," she yelled.

She heard Trev grunt and imagined he was crawling through. She followed the tunnel forward, arm outstretched with the flashlight on. The tunnel took a turn and ended in a rectangular doorway, the light from outside blinding her for a second.

But only for a second.

The area around the door was covered in graffiti. Underneath all the spray paint was a layer of charcoal black, as though something had burned through the doorway.

"Whoa!" Trev said. He shined his flashlight across the scorch marks. "I knew there was an explosion but I didn't expect—this. You couldn't design a better set for a portal to Hell."

"It's not real," she said. "Portals aren't real. It's a hoax, just like the one Kos debunked."

"I know," Trev said sharply.

She was beginning to realize he didn't like talking about Kos.

"You were there!" she protested. "You know it's a hoax."

"Look, this is just window dressing," he said. "Stuff like this gets the views. You want people to see this, right?"

"I guess," Jules said.

Because he'd worked with Kos and Kayla, she'd assumed that Trev wanted to debunk the whole portal thing. But now he was acting like he wanted to make his own hoax video. She'd made a terrible mistake coming here with him. Still, when they got to the borehole and nothing happened, he'd have to acknowledge that the portal wasn't real.

Trev handed his phone to her.

She took the phone reluctantly.

"Try not to get the doorway in the shot. It's too bright."

He stood, pressed against the wall of the tunnel.

"Whoa, check this out," he said to the camera, pointing to the scorch marks on the wall.

"I'm about to enter the Ojo de Cristo mine, where, twelve years ago, noted industrialist King Steenkampf supposedly drilled a hole to Hell before disappearing off the face of the earth."

A shadow crossed the bright light of the doorway. It was gone so quickly that Jules wondered if she had imagined it.

Her heart sped like she'd just run a mile.

"What was that?" Trev turned quickly, but the shadow was gone.

Trev grabbed the phone and played the video back. She leaned over his phone. There was nothing on it.

"What the fuck?"

Trev lunged through the door and Jules followed him.

"Where is he?" he said.

They stood at the edge of a bunch of destroyed machinery. There was no one there. No place where anyone could have gone.

Jules shivered in the sunlight, feeling a sudden wave of nausea. Was that really a ghost?

"I don't think that was a real person," Jules said. "It didn't show up on the video."

"Where are you hiding?" Trev yelled.

He ran toward a piece of wreckage, the only place big enough for someone to hide. She followed him.

She had a bad feeling about being here. They were standing at the spot of the explosion, probably standing in the exact place where people had died. And Trev was running around like Scooby-Doo looking for people in masks.

He turned to her.

"How did you do that?" he demanded.

"I didn't do anything!" Jules protested.

Trev peered at her suspiciously.

"C'mon," he said. "Let's get to the open pit first. Then we'll finish at the borehole."

They walked out to the gravel road that led to the open-pit mine, past a tall narrow building. The air smelled wrong, dusty and sharp. It smelled like blood, the metallic smell of fresh blood from a cut.

"What's that smell?" she asked.

"It smells like metal, right?" Trev said. "But it's all over. See where the hill is green? It's copper."

Jules was surprised how long it took to walk to the edge of the open pit. From Aunt Silvia's cabin, the open-pit mine looked deep and forbidding, but nowhere as big as it was on foot. They must have walked for twenty minutes. Jules was silent, thinking about the shadow in the doorway. Trev would probably make a big deal about the shadow. People would still think the mine was haunted, but there wasn't anything Jules could do about that.

Maybe it was haunted. It hadn't even occurred to her that there really could be a ghost or something.

She didn't like being here. It felt wrong. She wanted to leave. She couldn't shake the terrible feeling that something bad was about to happen, but wasn't that the way with all spooky places? She'd seen enough stupid haunting videos to know that if you shook the camera and ran around screaming, people would assume the place was haunted.

The worst thing here was Trev. She didn't know him, and the more time she spent with him, the less she liked him.

But she'd come this far, and she had to stick it out.

For April's sake.

The open-pit mine was just a hole in the ground.

There wouldn't be anything there. Trev would upload his video on April's birthday, and then the whole world would know that there wasn't a portal. It was probably for the best that Trev asked Jules to stay off camera, because the kind of weirdos who drove by the house and took videos were always mistaking her for April.

But that shadow in the doorway? It was strange. As they got closer and closer to the open-pit mine, Jules realized her heart was pounding with fear. She didn't want to look over the edge. What if there really was something down there?

April thought the portal was real. It was easy enough to convince herself that April was wrong, back home in the safety of their kitchen. But out here, things were different.

They moved close to the edge of the pit, but Trev hung back. He was panting, from more than just the walk. He held the phone out to her.

"Can you go up a little closer and take a panoramic shot? I'll do a voice-over later."

She grabbed the phone with an outstretched hand and backed away.

"You're not going to . . . ?" she began, but then stopped.

If he planned to push her into the pit, he wasn't exactly going to tell her. What if he really was a secret cultist? If you trusted the internet, that was what happened that day. Someone got pushed into the open-pit mine and the portal opened.

She moved farther away and looked back at Trev. He was frozen, and Jules wondered if he was afraid of heights. That was a reassuring thought. If you were afraid of heights, you probably wouldn't want to step right up to the edge just to push someone else in.

She took his phone, but just to be safe she walked a little farther away from him before creeping close enough to the edge of the pit to get the panoramic view.

Jules had never been to the mine. It was so much bigger than she had imagined, like standing on the edge of a sky-scraper without any railing and looking down at the earth below.

There was water at the bottom of the mine, a blue pool from the rain. It was unexpectedly beautiful.

A soft breeze lifted her hair and she heard a murmur, like a voice. But maybe it was just the wind.

She kicked gravel into the pit and it seemed to fall away forever, bouncing and echoing, making strange noises.

"What the fuck was that?" Trev asked.

"It's just rocks," she said.

She turned. Trev wasn't looking at her; he was looking back toward the tall, skinny house.

"There was someone there," he said.

She stepped away from the edge.

"I was recording the mine, like you asked," she said. "I wasn't looking. Here."

She held out the phone, but didn't move any closer to him. They both backed away from the pit, as though

281

something might reach out from beneath and try to pull them both in.

There was a sound like a whisper from the bottom of the pit.

A girl's voice.

Jules turned back to the trail, back to the door in the mountain, running, like she was being chased.

She was on the trail first, but Trev caught up to her quickly. "Stop!" he yelled.

She stopped and turned back, panting.

He looked just as terrified as she was, and for a moment she wondered if all her sense of impending doom wasn't about him.

It was this place.

Maybe they could leave together, before anything horrible happened. Maybe he would admit he was just as scared as she was.

"Did you hear the voice too?" she asked.

"Get ahold of yourself," he said sharply. "You said it yourself, it's just rocks. Everything echoes around here."

She decided she hated him at that moment, more than she'd ever hated anyone. Why couldn't he just admit he was as scared as she was?

Unless . . . ?

Another possibility crossed her mind. He wasn't scared, because *he* was the thing to be frightened of. She looked around for a stick or a rock, anything she could use as a weapon. There was nothing.

"Let's just go to the borehole, take a video, and get out of here," he said.

"Yes," she said mechanically. "Let's go to the borehole."

Best to play along with him—for now.

They walked the twenty minutes back to the bore house in silence, and rounded the side of the building. It was dark inside, the only light coming from the big open sliding door.

Trev stood out in front, with the darkness of the door behind him.

Jules centered the camera on his face with the building in the background, like he asked.

"Behind me is the drill house for the deep borehole," he began. "In there is where people heard the mysterious screams from the depths of Hell. If you believe the stories, people who heard the screams went mad and attacked each other. A lot of people died, and it's all because of what's in that building, over there."

He made a slashing move across his throat, meaning for her to stop.

"You haven't said anything about how it's not real," Jules said. "How April didn't have anything to do with it."

"I'll get to it," Trev said.

They both hesitated outside the bore house.

"You scared?" he asked.

283

"No," Jules spit out. Of course she was afraid, but she wasn't going to admit that to him.

"Good," he replied. "Don't worry about it. People like to think there are ghosts everywhere. I've been in a thousand haunted places, but, trust me, there is never anything there. It's all bullshit."

"As long as you tell everyone that," Jules said. "So they all know that my sister isn't the Bicycle Girl."

Trev pursed his mouth into a tight line and nodded.

They walked through the open metal door. The door let in a bright rectangle of light. April had told her the borehole was disappointing, but Jules thought it would be more exciting than this. In the middle of the room was a hole the size of a large dinner plate with a piece of pipe sticking out of it. That was it. The pipe went all the way to the top of the building and disappeared into the gloom. There were windows covered with years of dust along the side of the building, but not at the top. It was dark. There were banks of dials and panels and what looked like a forest of pipes. That was kind of creepy. Someone could hide back there and you would never know it.

Steep metal stairs zigzagged up to the top and disappeared into the darkness.

Trev wandered into the room, looking at things on the walls, touching the pipe sticking out of the hole in the ground.

"Not much to look at, is it?" he said.

Trev set the phone on record and handed it to Jules. She stood in the rectangle of light by the door, not wanting to go any farther in. It was creepy.

"Come on," he said impatiently.

"I'm not going up those stairs," she said.

"So don't." Trev shrugged. "They're probably not safe anyway."

Jules looked around the bore house. She didn't like it here. Even though she knew there was no portal to Hell, she had the worst feeling in the world about this place. Like something bad was going to happen.

She pushed record on his phone and moved out of the light.

"This is the borehole," Trev began. "The one to the center of the earth. Supposedly, when they breached the earth's crust, they heard screaming. Someone on a catwalk up there fell and died instantly. You can still see the bloodstains."

Trev pointed toward the top of the building, and Jules followed his line with the phone. Jules had to admit, the site of the pipe disappearing into darkness was creepy.

"Is that true?" she asked. "Did someone really fall?"

"Shhh . . ." he hissed. "Remember, you're not supposed to talk on camera."

She didn't know if the story of a worker falling to their death was true, but it gave her a shiver. There were dark stains on the floor. Maybe it was blood, or maybe it was oil or something.

Trev crouched down near the borehole and held the pipe with one hand.

"And this is the hole to Hell. It's so small and yet so powerful. If we lean closer and listen, you just might hear the voices of the damned, screaming in eternal torment."

Jules had had it with the spooky stuff.

"I thought you were going to prove the portal was a fake," she said.

"Don't talk," Trev said.

"No." Jules raised her voice. The camera was still running. "You lied to me. You told me that you were going to prove April wasn't the Bicycle Girl."

"And you told me you were April. Listen, kid, no one cares about the truth. They want to see murders and ghosts. That shit gets the views."

Trev stood up and held his hand out.

"Give me the phone," he said.

"No."

She backed away toward the entrance. Near her foot was an abandoned wrench. She picked it up and held it out, keeping the phone behind her back.

"Oh, so you're going to hit me with that?" Trev said.

"I'm going to post this so everyone can see you're a fake," she said.

There was a soft noise like a sigh or a breath and the clunk of the pipe.

286

Trev turned toward the wall of pipes.

"What the hell was that?" he said.

Trev had told her not to talk, but now Jules couldn't have formed words if she had to. She went perfectly still. In horror movies, it's always the noisy, crazy guy like Trev who gets it first. Jules had never understood that until this instant, when there was someone nearby, watching them from the shadows.

"Who's there?" Trev yelled. His voice echoed up the tower, against the wall of pipes. No one answered.

"Turn that thing off," he said angrily.

The wrench hung at her side. Trev reached out and took the phone from her hand, turned it off, and shoved it in his pocket. He grabbed her by the elbows and shook her.

"Who is with you?" he said.

"No one."

She had the wrench but couldn't move her arm. She could have hit him when his back was turned. Now it was too late.

"I saw someone in the shadows. You looked right at them."

"But I didn't," Jules protested. Her voice came out as a harsh croak. She was trying not to cry.

Kill him, a voice whispered.

She hadn't seen anyone.

A scream came from behind them in the dark shadows of the building, along with a blur of motion. Trev let go of her arms and tried to turn, but the figure was already on him. Only her swing of dark hair was familiar.

Aunt Silvia.

She jumped on Trev's back and wrapped her arms around his throat.

Trev staggered back. Jules heard a deep pong as they hit the pipe, a noise that seemed to come from under the ground, all the way deep down. They fell back, fell together on the floor. There were creaks and groans of metal, and Jules ran out of the doorway as the drilling pipe tilted and gave way, showering the floor of the drill house with sections of pipe in a violent series of clanging noises. A huge cloud of dust rose up from the floor and pushed out the door, covering her with dust. Jules spat out dust, coughed out dust, and stood there frozen, waiting.

The cloud settled. Aunt Silvia was under a pile of pipes. Her head had hit the floor and stayed in a muddy pool of blood mingling with the dust.

Kill him.

Trev sat up, coughing from the dust, moaning a little bit. He'd hurt Aunt Silvia. He wanted to kill her, and Jules knew he would, if he got back up on his feet. It was too late to talk, too late to leave.

Kill him, before he kills you.

Jules gripped the wrench, took a few steps forward into the drill house, and swung.

TWENTY-SEVEN
APRIL

Thompson-Moore, the director of *Hellhole!*, has achieved an astonishing feat. He's taken one of the most intriguing creepypastas in recent memory, based on a truly terrifying real-life event, and turned it into a one hundred minute snoozefest. **** Spoilers ahead***** One imagines Thompson-Moore planned the end as a twist on the final girl trope, an old twist that's received better treatment elsewhere. By the time older sister Kendall throws herself into the pit—for no apparent reason—it was a relief.

—Critic review from Rotten Tomatoes

APRIL DROVE TO the compound, the thirty minutes it took to get there an eternity. There was traffic on the road behind her; but it was a sunny fall day, almost the weekend, and she imagined people were heading into the national forest. As she rounded the top of the mountain, she didn't notice anyone behind her on the road. The open mine and the stone wall came into view, a bright red truck parked at the base of the wall.

Red truck. April didn't know what car she'd expected to see. She was glad it was not Jonathan's acid-green Jeep or, worse, Dan Turnbridge's black truck.

Who was Jules with? April had been so busy trying to keep Jules firewalled from the papers, she'd forgotten that Jules was relentless. She'd wanted to know what was going on, and April had put her off.

In her desire to keep Jules away from the more horrible details of the massacre, April had made her easy prey for someone who would satisfy her curiosity.

Unless . . . ?

Duct tape, rope, ether . . .

No. Jules had gone along willingly. She'd told Luna where she was going.

Jules wasn't the sacrifice. She couldn't be.

April remembered that Aunt Silvia had gone into the compound with a backpack, as though she planned to stay for a while. Chances were, Aunt Silvia was still in the compound. April hoped Aunt Silvia would look out for Jules.

At the spot where the road ended at the wall, April parked behind the red truck. April pulled her Mace out of her backpack and crept up to the driver's side window, half expecting to find Jules and some random cultist in the cab behind the tinted windows. Waiting for her. Every muscle in her body tightened, ready to throw open the driver's side door.

They were gone. She tucked the Mace in her pocket and ran along the base of the wall toward the tunnel. She crawled through the triangular gap between the wall and a giant boulder next to the side of the mountain. She made her way through the square door to the tunnel.

It had been so hard to go into the compound before. Now, nothing would stop her. She stood at the rectangular door of the tunnel, blinking in the bright sunlight. Jonathan, or whoever had brought Jules here, would let her go.

She would make them.

April wished for a gun.

"Jules!" she yelled, her voice echoing strangely against the mountainside.

No answer, but a feral yell came from the direction of the bore house tower and a hollow, metallic sound of pipes shifting. April ran to the bore house as a clatter of noise echoed. A billowing cloud of smokelike dust came through the open door.

"Jules!" she yelled again.

April held her breath as the dust settled around the coughing figure of Jules, holding a bloody wrench. Jules dropped it in the dust with a thud and lunged toward April, grabbing her in a tight hug.

"Aunt Silvia," Jules said, between raspy coughs. "She's under there."

April blinked away dust and pulled gently out of Jules's grasp.

"Under where?"

For a moment April imagined Aunt Silvia had fallen into the borehole, plummeting down an endless shaft, through to the portal below. But the borehole was too small. The words didn't make sense.

Jules tugged on her arm impatiently.

"Under there!"

Inside was dark, and at first April only saw a chaotic pile of what looked like pipes through a thick haze of dust that hung in the air. The dust cleared to reveal the crumpled figure of a man on the floor and a hand emerging from a jumble of pipes.

The hand moved.

A wet spluttering noise echoed from within, a familiar sound of disaster.

292

Blood in the mouth, crawling, muscle and bone moving . . .

"Aunt Silvia?" April said tentatively.

April crept slowly through the open double doors, T-shirt over her mouth to keep the dust out of her lungs. She was afraid. She'd heard that spluttering death rattle before.

Muscle and bone, crawling toward oblivion, a mouthful of blood. The past and the present blurred.

Here she was again, the wet rattle of impending death.

April followed the hand down through the pipes to eyes shining bright in a dust-covered face, like a buried miner reaching to light through a small gap in a mountain of stone. Aunt Silvia, buried alive.

No. They would get her out. Make their way through the small tunnel, drive Aunt Silvia to the hospital in the valley below. They would save her.

"April?" Aunt Silvia said. Her voice was so like Mom's, but with an edge of grit as though years in the sun and copper dust had honed all softness away.

"I'm here," April said.

April stepped as close to the pile of pipes as she dared. Jules touched April's shoulder lightly and her hand stayed there.

April understood. She had an irrational fear that Jules might slip into the dust and gloom and vanish altogether. It was this place. The walls between dimensions, already thinned, were growing weaker by the second.

They needed to stay together or risk losing each other forever.

April directed the flashlight on her phone through the smoky haze of dust and the tangle of pipes. Aunt Silvia, completely covered in dust and pipe, her face barely visible underneath. The flashlight caught the shine and bright red of blood around her mouth.

"We're going to get you out of there," April said.

"How?" Jules asked in a small voice.

April turned to Jules. She was covered in dust, arms clutched tightly around herself, shivering.

"Help me move these pipes," April said.

April picked up the end of what she thought was the top pipe and the whole pile shifted like a giant game of pick-up sticks they could only lose. Aunt Silvia groaned in pain. Jules whimpered.

"Fuck," April whispered.

They needed help. The fire department would have a saw that could cut through pipe. They would be able to cut Aunt Silvia out.

She stepped back, pulled out her phone, and dialed 911. Nothing happened.

"Jules, my phone isn't working. See if you can find a signal and call 911."

"Okay," Jules murmured, but she didn't move. Jules, wide-eyed, looking not good.

"Walk around until you find reception," April said, as much to hear her own voice as to calm Jules. "But don't go far. I don't want to lose you."

"Okay," Jules said, shaking. April worried that she'd gone into shock.

"Grace and Zach are on their way," she said. "See if you can find them. Call them."

That seemed to shake Jules out of a trance. "Grace," Jules echoed. "I'll find Grace."

Jules pulled out her phone and walked away from the bore house, away from the wall, toward the all-encompassing open pit.

April had no idea if what she'd said was true or not. She'd sent a text to the two of them, but never received any response. She'd lost reception. And even if they did show up, they wouldn't know how to get in.

Time to fly, the voice whispered.

She watched as Jules disappeared from view. "Not my sister," she whispered. "Not ever."

Grace had to have called the police. She would do that even if she knew that April hadn't wanted to involve the police. April longed to hear the wail of sirens in the distance. To know that help was on the way. Or a helicopter ready to airlift Aunt Silvia to the hospital. She didn't want to face the blood and chaos in the bore house, the impossible tangle of pipe that held Aunt Silvia down.

The man on the floor, covered with dust, was looking quite dead.

Who was he?

April was alone. It was better that Jules was out in the open air, trying to find a signal.

She put her phone away and stepped close to the pile of pipes, careful not to shift anything. Aunt Silvia's breath came in short, ragged spurts. April reached across and gently touched her hand.

"I won't leave you," April said.

Aunt Silvia laced fingers with April, her hand soft and almost lifeless.

"April?" Aunt Silvia whispered.

April leaned closer.

"He's lost," Aunt Silvia murmured. "You have to bring him back."

April didn't know if Aunt Silvia was talking about her dad, King Steenkampf, or Zach's uncle, but it didn't matter.

"I will," April said.

Aunt Silvia spasmed, her hand grabbing on tightly to April's, three tugs like a fish on a line that suddenly breaks free and swims away.

Her hand went slack when she died.

There was nothing more April could do. She let go of Aunt Silvia's hand and stood, aware of the tang of dust in her

296

mouth, the thick silence of the room. The smell of blood and copper and dust.

April stepped out of the bore house and stood in the too bright sunlight, a strange weightless feeling, a spinning inertia. She should go find Jules. Leave her dream of opening the portal, of finding her dad, behind in the dust with the dead. She knew that now.

She'd already lost too much.

Time to fly.

"Shut up," she murmured to the voice.

April pressed the palms of her hands into her eyes, hard enough to see a flash of light behind the eyes.

"April?"

The voice was far away, and loud.

A man's voice echoed across the artificial canyon of the open-pit mine.

"Amy, she's over here!"

"Are you sure, David?" a woman asked.

April turned her head in time to see a man emerge from the dark rectangle of the tunnel doorway, the stock of the rifle slung across his back visible in the distance. Followed by another woman and a man, a stream of people emerging from the mountain, carrying weapons. Six in all, two women and four men. Making their way past the ruins of the mud lubrication pump heading toward the bore house.

The Deep Well cultists.

She'd been so stupid.

She'd followed Jules and the cultists had followed her.

This was what the voice wanted, what it had always wanted: April and the cultists together. There were so many moving parts to make this happen. Had the voice whispered sweetly to the man on the floor of the bore house? Asked him to bring Jules here?

Regret was a bowling ball in the center of her chest. She wanted to run, but she knew they would just pursue her; and once she cleared the side of the bore house, there was nothing but open air. Nowhere to hide.

Ahead was the edge of the open-pit mine. A wide asphalt drive stretched around the open pit, cracked now and pitted. To the left, the road extended across the vast distance, ending in a large windowless building, modern, covered in what looked like corrugated tin. April knew this building had been Dr. Travers-Steenkampf's lab. Even farther beyond was what looked like old, long-disused mine buildings and equipment.

Jules couldn't have gone to the left. If she had, she would be visible on the road from the bore house.

To the right, behind the bore house was a collection of low buildings. The largest of these was the mess hall where Aunt Silvia had once ruled the kitchen, connected to a barracks for short-term workers. The road followed the outer edge of the open-pit mine and ran around the skirt of the mountain, a slope that hadn't been mined, covered in low brush and pine trees. April couldn't see past the stand of pines, but she knew from memory that beyond the trees around the curve was a group of workers' bungalows and, behind them, higher in the rift between two mountains, was the big house that belonged to King Steenkampf.

Even though she couldn't see it, she knew exactly where the house her family had lived in was; and in this strange moment, waiting for the cultists to cover the distance, she realized that they'd left furniture, toys, her beloved *Kiki's Delivery Service* DVD behind, and it would all still be there, dust covered, untouched.

Jules had to have gone to the right, and hopefully she'd gone around the side of the mountain to the workers' bungalows, and the industrial entrance beyond.

April longed to peek around the edge of the bore house to see where Jules had gone, but she didn't dare.

Had Jules heard the woman yell April's name?

Did she know that they were in a new, more urgent kind of trouble?

Hopefully Jules had headed to higher ground, threading through the trees to stay out of sight.

April longed to yell out a warning, but that would only let the cultists know she wasn't alone. Jules was smart. For once, April had to trust that Jules would think on her feet.

299

And maybe, just maybe, Jules had gotten her phone to work.

Too late for April.

The cultists were yards away now.

Not too late for Jules. Whatever happened, she would keep Jules safe.

TWENTY-EIGHT

JULES

AT FIRST, JULES walked out toward the open-pit mine, trying her phone over and over. When that didn't work, she ran along the road, stopped, and tried it again. Nothing. The battery on her phone was low. She'd used it as a flashlight for too long in the tunnel.

And then, she just ran. The road rounded the mountain and curved toward what looked like a bunch of little houses in the distance. Houses meant people, but of course these houses were empty.

As Jules got closer to the little houses, she could see a much bigger house through the trees. It was higher than the rest, set back from the road. If she went higher, she was more likely to get a signal, but part of her just wanted to run as far away from the bore house as she could.

She turned around, looking toward the bore house and April, but she couldn't see past the turn in the road.

There was blood on her left shoe. It could have been her blood, or it could have been Aunt Silvia's blood. Jules wondered if she would even know if she was hurt. There was no reason for her to be hurt, but she was numb all over and the blood . . .

What if it was Trev's blood?

She didn't want to think about Trev.

The world was painfully bright and crisp, the gravel underneath her feet making too much noise, echoing across the empty space.

How could this be happening?

How could any of this be happening?

April.

She'd left April behind.

What if Trev got up and attacked April?

No. She'd killed him, just like the voice told her to.

This was crazy. She'd never meant to hurt anyone.

She'd done exactly what April had asked her to do. She was trying to get help for Aunt Silvia.

But it didn't make her feel any better.

She'd been glad to leave April with Aunt Silvia, because the sight of the blood pooling around Aunt Silvia's mouth was bad. She and April hadn't been able to move the pipes without hurting Aunt Silvia.

She was running away. She didn't want to stay with Aunt Silvia and listen to her horrible whistling, gurgling breath.

She didn't want to see Aunt Silvia die.

No.

She had to get help.

But this was a terrible place, not a place to be alone.

And she'd left April alone.

If only 911 worked.

She thought she heard a woman's voice echo across the open-pit mine. It sounded like she'd said "April," but Jules couldn't be sure. And maybe it was just the voice again, playing tricks on her.

Jules stopped on the road. She couldn't see anything.

Then it was eerily quiet, the only sound her breath, coming in short, angry spurts.

She tried to slow her breathing, to listen. She hesitated. Maybe she should go back and find April.

If only she hadn't left the wrench behind at the bore house. If she still had the wrench, she could defend herself against anyone.

Like Trev.

Don't think about it, she told herself. *Don't think about Trev. You didn't mean to kill him.*

She'd made it past the small houses and walked up the

steep road to the edge of a stand of trees. She was close to the big house now.

She walked past an old golf cart on a large, cracked asphalt driveway. The house was hidden behind overgrown bushes. She ducked through the underbrush and stepped onto a broad stone patio.

The doors to the house were thrown wide open, like an invitation to be swallowed whole. There were lights on in the house, which was super creepy; but at the same time, if there were lights, maybe there was internet. She looked down at her phone. For the first time there was a single wavering bar, a tiny bit of reception. She pushed 911 and held her phone over her head, hoping that the call would go through. Even if the call faded before she got a chance to talk. Didn't the police go anywhere there was a 911 call? She'd heard that somewhere.

Behind the house, the ground sloped up sharply. Jules was sure that if she climbed high enough she could get a call through. The house was long and the patio ended in a lot of scrubby brush that she had to crawl through.

She rounded the side of the house and froze. Tucked out of view of the main house, behind a wall of bushes was an acid-green Jeep.

She recognized it instantly.

Marianne's car.

Maybe it just looked like Marianne's car, but that would be too much of a coincidence.

And Marianne was dead so why would her car be here . . . ?

Jules's breath caught in her throat with the sudden shock of recognition. Marianne hadn't been driving the car the day they saw her at the Sonic. There was someone else with her, a tall blond guy.

This was his car.

He was here.

Jules looked around frantically. Ahead, past the car, was a long flat backyard that ended with boulders she thought she could climb. To get to the hill and cell reception, she'd have to walk across that long yard. If he was inside, he'd see her.

She could run, and if he was somewhere in the house, maybe he wouldn't see her. She'd get back on the main road around the open-pit mine. You couldn't see much of the road from behind the wall of overgrown bushes and brush. It was just a short walk across the patio, until she reached the spot where she'd crawled through.

She turned and peered around the corner of the house. The patio was empty. She couldn't see anything through the open doors of the house.

She shoved her phone in her pocket, stepped onto the patio, and scooted, a quiet fast-walk more than a run.

"Hello, Jules," a voice called from the doorway.

She stopped and turned.

The tall man stepped through the double doors, his blond hair dusty in the sun. He was wearing hiking boots and shorts, thick socks rolled up over the edge of his boots like he'd planned on a good day of hiking. He looked like a camp counselor from an old slasher movie, the one who tells everyone it will be fine and then gets stabbed first.

"Who are you?" she asked. Her voice was small, wavering.

"I'm Jonathan," he said. "I'm a friend of Marianne's."

"But Marianne's dead," Jules said.

"I know," Jonathan said. For a moment, he looked so sad that she felt sorry for him. He bowed his head as though Marianne's name had been mentioned in a church service, but when he looked up his eyes had a strange gleam.

"I can get her back," he said. "This can all be undone."

"How?" she asked.

She wished she hadn't asked.

"You can help me," he said.

He took a step closer, and she crouched instinctively, her legs wanting to send her into flight. She knew better. Jonathan looked fast, quick enough to catch her if she lunged through the brush back toward the road and the open pit beyond. It was better to stay here. She didn't want to go anywhere near the edge of the open-pit mine.

Jonathan laughed.

"Where is April?" he mumbled.

Jules thought about what to say. She didn't want Jonathan to know that April was here. She didn't want him to go looking for her sister. But at the same time, she felt like she should keep him talking.

"I don't know," she said.

"She's got to be here somewhere, right? It has to go through her. April has to say the words."

"What words?" Jules asked.

"Yes," Jonathan said slowly. "Of course. You're right."

His voice got so low, she couldn't hear what he said next, but it didn't matter. He wasn't talking to her anymore. He was talking to himself.

No. He wasn't talking to himself. He was answering questions he hadn't asked.

He was talking to the voice.

Kill him, the voice whispered in her ear.

"How?" she answered.

Kill him before he kills you.

Jonathan was going to kill her. Her stomach flopped. She heard a whimpering sound. It was her own voice, she realized. She was crying softly.

She glanced around the patio, looking for an abandoned tool, even a rock. Nothing.

If the voice was going to tell her to do things, it had to give her power. It had to give her a weapon.

Where was April? Even if April had made it past the bore house, she wouldn't know about Jonathan. The acid-green Jeep was hidden behind the house.

The sound of a car engine came from beyond the line of trees and brush. There had to be someone else, someone who would help her. April had said Grace was coming to help.

Jules turned and ran but she hadn't made it ten steps when Jonathan grabbed her, his arm around her shoulders. She bit his arm, and he clubbed her sharply across the head. Her vision went gray and her legs went slack.

She came to as they cleared the brush near a small house, her eyes turned toward the expanse of open sky. She struggled to get her feet under her, and as she did her head turned toward the road.

They were on the road, near the open pit.

Kill him!

The voice in her head wouldn't shut up. It just kept saying the same thing over and over.

"Do something!" she said to the voice. "Help me!"

She fought violently, arms, knees, teeth, anything to stop him from throwing her into the open-pit mine on the other side of the road, but it was only a matter of time before she lost the battle.

TWENTY-NINE
APRIL

THE CULTISTS WERE a pack of dogs. April knew that if she turned her back to run, or showed her fear, they would be on her in an instant. If there was ever a time to pull out her frosty Bicycle Girl calm, it was now. She'd pretended to be this person her entire life to keep the curious at arm's length. Now she had to play it for real.

She thought of Jules, wandering around the pit, looking for a cell connection. It strengthened her. Whatever happened, she would keep them away from Jules. Give Jules time to hide.

At the front of the pack was a woman, the obvious leader. Tall and slightly stocky, with soccer mom looks, her brown ponytail brushing against the stock of the assault rifle. One of the men had called her Amy. April took a gamble and decided that she was realamy7070.

"Hello, Amy," April said. She worked to keep her voice low and even.

The woman stopped, her eyes widening in surprise, and maybe even a little fear. She straightened, smiled, and walked forward, her military stance softening into meeting-an-old-friend-at-the-coffee-shop casual.

You and I, we're not friends, April thought.

"April, you're here!" Amy said cheerily.

"Of course." April folded her arms across her chest.

Was Amy really going to try and pretend that this was a chance meeting at the edge of the portal? They'd followed her here.

Time to fly.

April let out a short bitter bark of a laugh. The voice was greedy—and loud. The sight of Jules, standing in the dust, a bloody wrench in her hand, had pushed the voice from her mind. When she watched Aunt Silvia die, it quieted into a reverential whisper.

But now it was yelling into her brain.

Was it trying to suggest that she throw Amy into the pit instead?

"Go ahead and scan the perimeter," Amy said.

The men and the woman with Amy spread out, guns drawn. April swallowed past a tight lump in her throat as a man with what looked like a hunting rifle walked to the edge of the bore house and disappeared around the side, heading toward the open pit.

Please hide, Jules. Don't come out, no matter what you see.

A man with a pistol walked around April and Amy, eyes averted. He walked into the bore house.

"You came armed, I see," April said.

"Oh, that's not for you, hon," Amy said apologetically.

"No?"

Amy leaned forward.

"You know what happened to Marianne?" she whispered like she was passing on some juicy school gossip about the latest popular pairing. April couldn't believe she was standing here, talking to Amy like they were old friends. But it was eating up time. Time for Jules to hide.

"No," April said. "What happened to her?"

Time to fly.

"She was killed."

"Oh my god," April said, hoping she sounded sincere. "Do you know who did it?"

Amy shook her head tightly. "No. There are zealots everywhere who want to stop our glorious movement. It had to be one of them."

Our glorious movement. April suppressed a shudder.

"There was a man in a black truck who's been chasing me. It could have been him."

Amy's eyes widened. "Thank god he didn't get to you! Without you, none of this would have been possible."

April wanted to keep the conversation going for as long as possible to give Jules more time to get away. She scanned the group and realized that Jonathan wasn't with them. She hadn't given him much thought.

"Where's Jonathan?" she asked.

Amy bowed her head.

"Poor Jonathan," she said. "He's taken Marianne's death quite hard. I had to pull him from the team. Unstable."

"Oh," April said.

The man who had gone around the corner of the bore house to scan the perimeter returned. April exhaled in relief. If he'd seen Jules, he would have said something.

"I'm sorry, but it had to be done," Amy said, evidently mistaking April's short utterance for disapproval. "You know as well as I do that when the portal opens and the king returns, we all will—"

"Amy?" One of the men called from inside the bore house.

Amy turned. With all attention on the bore house, April surveyed the group. One other woman besides Amy and four men. Only Amy and one of the men had assault rifles, but that was enough. The man with the pistol returned from the bore house.

"It's Silvia," he said.

He was older and looked vaguely familiar. He said Silvia's

name with genuine regret, even grief. Maybe he'd been here at the compound before.

Amy walked to the open double doors of the bore house and April followed her. She wished that she had a sheet to cover Aunt Silvia's hand, sticking through the field of pipes in a loose fist. She'd seen that hand in the exact position holding a charcoal pencil or paintbrush.

Never again.

The cultists clustered around the man on the floor. Face down, curled on his side as though sleeping, the only sign of injury was the pool of blood underneath his head. It was easier to look at him.

"Who's the man?" Amy asked, glancing at the crumpled form on the floor.

"I don't know," April said.

The question took her by surprise. Whoever he was, he'd taken twelve-year-old Jules into the compound a day before April's birthday and exposed her to incredible danger. It was hard to feel sorry for him.

"You don't recognize him?"

April shook her head.

"He's not with us," Amy said.

"What happened?" the older man asked.

April was pretty certain that Jules had killed him. She'd had a bloody wrench in her hand. She hadn't asked Jules who the man was, or why she'd come here with him. It seemed like he'd struggled with Aunt Silvia, and they'd both ended up dead. She couldn't feel sorry about him.

Jules was alive, and the man on the floor of the bore house was dead.

"You killed him," Amy said.

Amy gave her an appreciative look, as though pleased that April had taken the initiative to solve the common problem.

April shrugged.

The man next to Amy nodded. He looked at April adoringly, and she wondered what he saw in her eyes.

April's lips moved; words came out, but they were not her words.

"Time to fly."

The voice curled around the words as though tasting them. The voice from below, in her mouth.

"'Time to fly.'"

She understood. Someone had to fly. It had never been her, and it damn sure wasn't going to be Jules.

All heads turned toward April. In their faces were awe, even fear. Amy unconsciously took a step away from her.

April looked down to the dead man at her feet.

"You're right," Amy said. "He is the one."

It was all so simple.

Yesterday, April had stood on the threshold of the compound, and the voice had demanded a blood sacrifice. She'd wanted to believe that she could bring her dad back some

314

other way. She'd planned to ask—nicely. And if that didn't work, to demand that the voice give her father back. But in her heart, she'd known that a sacrifice was required.

Someone would have to fly.

It hadn't occurred to her that a dead man could fly. The man on the ground, whoever he was, had killed Aunt Silvia. And then Jules had killed him which only seemed—fair.

Amy turned to the group and raised her voice to a shout.

"We have our sacrifice!"

April exhaled in relief.

Jules was not the sacrifice.

It had never been Jules.

The Deep Well had spoken.

THIRTY

JULES

JULES DUG HER heels into the gravel, trying to slow the march toward the edge. She picked up her right leg and tried to mule kick Jonathan, but he saw it coming and swerved back. She leaned forward. He lost his balance and they both fell with a painful thud. The shock of gravel grinding into her face cut through everything, even the fear.

Kill him, the voice said.

One arm was pinned underneath her. There was a sound of running feet pounding through the gravel, and Jules turned her head to look, feeling gravel scrape painfully against her face.

Zach was running full speed toward them.

Jonathan struggled to disentangle himself, but Jules was

on top of one of his arms, and he'd barely managed to get to his knees before Zach tackled him.

Zach and Jonathan wrestled on the ground as Jules got to her feet and brushed the hard gravel off her cheek.

Kill him.

A weapon. She needed a weapon. She searched for anything she could use. In the road, the gravel was small and pounded down by years of large trucks, but the road was edged by a long pile of gravel and dirt and large rocks. She ran across the road and searched the pile until she found the perfect stone. It was a triangular slab that fit into her hand and had a sharp point, like a stone ax-head.

Kill him.

She ran back. Zach and Jonathan were rolling on the ground, inching closer to the edge of the pit, fighting, kicking up dust. They were like a cartoon blur of movement—arms, legs, and a dust cloud—and she was scared to get too close, and also scared she'd end up hitting Zach by mistake. But that shaggy blond hair was a good target. She waited until the blond hair rolled back on top and she brought the rock down with an arcing swing.

Jonathan made a terrible low wail.

Zach rolled back on top. He pulled Jonathan up by the shoulders and slammed him back down hard on the ground. The back of Jonathan's head hit the ground with a dull thud. And then Zach did it again, and again.

Zach stood unsteadily. He leaned over, looking like he was about to throw up in the gravel.

"Are you okay?" Jules asked.

Zach doubled over, hands on his knees, and nodded. Jules wondered if he was agreeing with her, or if he was just trying to shake off the dizziness.

Jules looked to Jonathan on the ground, groaning and clutching his head. She wondered how badly hurt he was. She wondered if she shouldn't kill him, just to be sure. She still had the rock in her hand, and she lifted it experimentally.

"Don't," Zach said sharply.

She dropped the rock.

"How did you even get here?" Jules asked.

"Grace found the back way in," he said. "Someone had already cut through the padlock at the gate. It was open."

April had told her Grace and Zach were coming to rescue them. She'd forgotten about Grace.

"Grace? Where is she?"

"Back by the entrance," Zach said. "The road was bad, and she worried that her car would get stuck."

Zach looked down to Jonathan on the ground. Jonathan had stopped moaning and was looking more and more like he wasn't going to get back up.

"Come on," Zach said. "We have to call someone for him."

They fast-walked along the road in the opposite direction of the bore house.

They walked for what seemed like a long time. Everything was so huge—the road, the open pit. It was too much to take in. Why had she ever thought to come out here? She'd expected to come out, take a few videos of the dusty, disappointing landscape and the small, unimpressive borehole. The last thing she expected to find was real horror.

And the voice.

Trev was dead, because she'd hit him with the wrench.

Jonathan might be dead? But he'd tried to kill her. He deserved to die.

The voice had told her to kill them both.

She realized she was shaking, her teeth clattering like she was cold, but it wasn't that cold out. She tried to make herself stop shaking just to prove to Zach that she was fine, but she couldn't.

Zach pulled off his jacket, which was very dusty, and wrapped it around her shoulders. It was big and warm, like a tent. She pulled the edges of the jacket together with her hands, letting the arms flop free, and leaned into Zach. He put an arm around her shoulder, and she felt a little bit better.

"Who was that guy anyway?" Zach said. "And why did he want to—I mean why was he trying to . . . ?"

Jules realized that Zach didn't want to say *Why did he want to kill you?* The reality of the situation hit her like a wave, and she started shaking again. Jonathan had tried to kill her.

"That was Jonathan, Marianne's boyfriend," she said. "He

thought that if he threw me into the mine, it would make Marianne come back."

"Are you serious?" he said.

Zach dropped his arm.

He looked back over his shoulder, but they'd walked so far along the curve of the mountain that Jonathan was out of the line of sight. Zach had a look on his face that made Jules think that he was considering going back to finish Jonathan off.

They rounded more of the mountain, and there was Grace, walking along the road.

Jules shrugged out of the jacket and ran toward Grace. She barreled into her, almost knocking her off her feet with a hug. Jules didn't care.

Everything had been crazy, and April was not herself, but Grace was always Grace. Grace could make sense of anything.

Grace pulled back from the hug. She held Jules at arm's length and peered into her face.

"You look a little ashen," Grace said.

She laid a hand on the side of Jules's face.

"Clammy," she pronounced.

Grace looked past her to Zach.

"I'm worried she might be in shock," she said.

"I'm okay." Jules had been feeling shaky, but just seeing Grace made her feel better.

320

"Where's April?" Grace asked.

That's when Jules remembered Aunt Silvia's hand, sticking up through the jumble of pipes, the blood around her mouth. She shuddered and wondered if she would ever stop shaking.

"Aunt Silvia is hurt," she said quickly. "April is with her at the bore house. I think it's pretty bad."

Grace and Zach exchanged glances.

Grace pulled out her phone.

"Still no cell reception," she said.

"I'll go back for April," Zach said. "Get to a place where you can call 911. Hopefully they can get through the road. We'll meet you back here."

Zach turned and jogged down the road.

"Be careful," Grace yelled. Zach lifted his arm but didn't turn around.

They watched him go before heading to the car. In the distance there was a small booth with an oversize pole that held a tattered flag that must have once been red and an American flag. Grace's car was near the booth, on the other side of a tall chain-link fence topped with a swirl of barbed wire. Jules thought it was strange to have such a big fence surrounding the mine, as though someone was going to break in and steal rocks.

But the mine was dangerous. The fence wasn't there to keep the rocks in but to keep people out.

"So what happened?" Grace asked.

Jules told her the story, starting with Trev showing up at her school to pick her up. She realized that she was talking and talking, but wherever she started in the story, it all circled back to Aunt Silvia, trapped under the pile of pipes, her hand sticking out from underneath.

She didn't tell Grace about the wrench. In her story, the pipes fell and killed both Aunt Silvia and Trev.

Instead of turning the car left toward town, Grace backed out and turned to the right.

"Where are you going?" Jules asked.

"It would take us too long to get around the mountain to decent cell reception," Grace replied, keeping her eyes glued to the climbing road. "This way, we'll reach the top of the mountain in a few minutes and get a call to 911 out. As soon as we've made the call, we'll go back."

Grace was so smart. Jules admired the way she thought things through. If she had been Grace, she probably would have figured out she was talking to Trev, not Kayla. She wouldn't have been fooled.

Grace would have debunked the whole portal thing with so much less drama.

Except . . .

There was the voice. The voice had wormed its way inside Jules's head. The voice told her to pick up a wrench and told her to hit Trev. The voice had shown her the best rock alongside the road to hit Jonathan with. Heavy, with a pointed end.

And as they left the compound, Jules slowly felt the voice inside her head fade away, like a radio losing signal.

She thought back to the day at the Sonic when April had slapped the drink out of Marianne's hand. Everyone had looked at April like she was some crazy drama princess, and Jules had been super embarrassed. Marianne seemed like a nice person and not a cultist with a terrible boyfriend who would end up trying to kill Jules.

She'd had no idea what April had been up against.

She'd been wrong about so many things.

She hoped she'd get a chance to tell April she was sorry.

"Grace?" Jules asked in a small voice.

Grace turned her head momentarily to look at her.

"What?

"Do you think there really is a portal?"

She hoped that Grace would laugh. Tell her that she was being ridiculous. That there was no such thing as a portal to another dimension.

Grace paused for a long time. Too long.

"I don't know," she said finally.

THIRTY-ONE
APRIL

THE FOUR MEN reached down and picked up the man on the floor. The dead man was athletic and wiry and didn't look like he weighed much. He was maybe thirty, with shaggy dark blond hair. He wore ripped jeans and high-tops, a well-worn T-shirt with a band name she didn't recognize. The two women stepped aside as they carried him slowly out of the bore house and around the corner, leading in one direction only.

To the open pit.

April fell in step beside Amy, behind the men carrying the sacrifice.

Time to fly.

A Kiki giggle came from the pit.

This had always been the plan. And the one person in her life who'd never been touched by all the wrongness of this place, the one person she'd hoped to keep away from here, had been tricked by the voice into killing.

Jules had given them the necessary sacrifice.

Wherever Jules was, April hoped she wasn't watching. It wasn't her fault. This was always destined.

"I want him back," she whispered. She'd done everything the voice had asked for.

Beside her, Amy nodded in solemn agreement.

She imagined Amy thought she was asking the voice for the return of King Steenkampf. Let King return—she didn't care—as long as her dad was released from the alternate dimension where he was trapped. Time to open the door and release them both.

Around the bore house, the open pit and the rest of the compound came into view. Across the open pit, a building glinted in the sunlight. Dr. Travers-Steenkampf's old lab, covered in corrugated tin.

To the right, the road curved around the edge of the mountain, obscuring the bungalows where she'd lived. Behind the bungalows was King Steenkampf's house, a house she remembered better than her own.

Jules was nowhere to be seen.

Good. Jules must have gone in the direction of the

bungalows. The fire department or an ambulance couldn't possibly make it here until the ceremony was over. The timing didn't matter now anyway. Aunt Silvia was dead.

A shadow passed overhead, and April looked up to see a buzzard circling lazily. Waiting for a feast. A small white cloud drifted across the sun, moving slowly, like it had nowhere to be. The sides of the cliff above the mine were ribboned with green rock and red, copper and iron, cut deep into the side of the mountain.

A beautiful day for a sacrifice.

The four men set the body parallel to the edge and stepped away.

All in place, waiting.

With a start, April realized they expected her to push him in.

Time to fly.

He was already dead. It didn't matter.

April took a step forward, suddenly fearful that if she leaned over to push him in, Amy would come up behind her and throw her in as well. As if sensing this fear, Amy moved alongside her and smiled encouragingly.

The man moaned and tried to lift his head. His eyes darted around the group frantically. April took a step back in horror.

He wasn't dead. She'd thought he was dead.

He lifted an arm toward her, beseeching. His arm wavered in the air like a frond blowing in a breeze, brushing up

326

against Amy's leg and grabbing hold of her jeans with surprising strength.

Amy pushed him away as she fell off-balance.

The man rolled over the edge of the pit and out of sight.

A split second later, a dull thud echoed across the pit.

April leaned over the edge. Where he'd landed, a cloud of dust arose and lingered. When the cloud settled, it covered him with a fine layer of dust, an archaeological ruin, as though he'd been there for months or years, not seconds. Carved out of stone, carved into the stone. Even at a distance, it was impossible to miss the strange angle of his arm, the upturned elbow. His head twisted, his place on the death map secured.

She'd directed the cultists to bring this stranger to the open pit and throw him in. She'd thought he was dead, an easy sacrifice.

She'd killed a man.

Someone gasped.

A cloud rolled away from the sun, and a stab of golden light came from the bottom of the open-pit mine. April looked past the body to the bottom of the pit. There was a pool of water in the bottom of the mine left over from the recent rains, shallow and strangely turquoise. It reflected the sunlight, throwing golden rays, shimmering, a series of circles within circles, as the portal began to open from within, from underneath the water.

It was just like the movie.

April laughed. Who would have thought that real life would turn out like a dumb movie with a 27 percent rating on Rotten Tomatoes? The portal under a lake.

Only it wasn't like the movie. There was no water volcano spewing demons. It wasn't terrifying and overblown; it was subtle and golden and beautiful.

More beautiful than April could have imagined.

"It's wonderful!" Amy said, her eyes were wide and filled with stars.

The other woman fell to her knees at the edge of the cliff and began to chant. One by one, the cultists knelt, eyes trained to the portal below, chanting a strange litany in a mix of English and some other language April didn't recognize.

And then she did.

Torsion fields and rotational vectors, garbled phrases from the book *Supergravity and Akimov's Torsion Fields*, by G. Scripps Gardiner. She wished that she had read past the first page, to find the incantations inside, the prayers for life within the eternal suspension of time in a weightless floating dimension without pain or suffering.

The king, the cook, the gardener, like characters from an old nursery rhyme, chosen by the voice to open a portal to another dimension. On the subreddit, people talked about the king and the cook, but only rarely the gardener. They talked about the importance of the book, but never about the author of the book.

The gardener—G. Scripps Gardiner.

Why hadn't she seen this before?

She remembered Gardiner, a tall, stern man in heavy boots who was always on the patio with King. In her five-year-old's imagination, the gardener was someone who trimmed bushes and planted flowers, not the mastermind of a plan to open a portal to another dimension.

The cultists continued their chants.

April had been waiting her whole life to understand why and how a series of events that had happened when she was five collided to shape an inescapable destiny that had nothing to do with her. That had made her the Bicycle Girl.

The king, the cook, the gardener, the girl. That had been her name.

The voice laughed.

April wasn't having it.

"Where is my father?" April whispered.

She was here, a day ahead of schedule. She'd brought a blood sacrifice and the cultists to open the portal.

April looked down to the bottom of the open-pit mine, but the lovely golden shimmer was gone, replaced by a smooth pool of water, rock surface visible underneath. April felt a wave of dark depression.

Nothing happened.

No. It couldn't be over. She'd done everything the voice had asked for. The voice was supposed to answer to her.

"Where is my father?" she demanded of the voice.

329

You know.

It was a quiet voice, a voice inside her head.

You know. You've always known.

The house.

All she had to do was take the path she'd discovered at the age of five. She had to follow the pink stones on the patio. The pink stones led into the house and pointed the direction down the hallway, to the place where she'd seen the flash of light and had heard the noise.

To the room in the back of the house where King and her father had disappeared from the face of the earth.

Everything important had happened at that house.

All her answers were there.

April walked slowly toward the house, the chants of the cultists still ringing in her ears. She glanced back at the group on their knees around the edge of the open-pit mine. Eyes closed, murmuring in unison in an expectant trance, still waiting for the king to appear. No one noticed April leave. Her part of the ritual was over.

April took the gravel road around the curve in the mountain. There was a strange lump in the road beside the pit. As she continued walking and the bungalows drew near, the lump formed into a body.

She moved even closer, and April recognized the shaggy blond hair on a long frame. Jonathan.

Jonathan had to come to the compound to get Marianne back. Now he was dead.

April glanced back over her shoulder toward the direction of the bore house, but she couldn't see around the side of the mountain. Amy and her group had followed April in through the tunnel. They couldn't have killed him.

Jules. She'd run this way. April shuddered at the thought of Jules meeting up with Jonathan, but whatever had happened here, Jules had come out on top. "Good for you," April murmured.

Jules must have made it to the main house. She would catch up with Jules. They would find Dad together.

The voice giggled with barely suppressed glee.

April walked up the cracked asphalt drive to the Steenkampfs' house, past dusty workers' bungalows with a few cacti and mostly dead shrubs. April and her family had lived in the biggest bungalow, the one with the shaded front deck where April had played in the warmth of the early afternoon while Mom and Aunt Silvia drank tamarind soda and talked during the short break between lunch and dinner prep in the mess hall.

She tried not to look at the house as she went by.

Aunt Silvia was gone. April had hoped that someday Aunt Silvia would come down from her cabin in the mountains and Mom would welcome her back. That was never happening. That version of her family had died in the bore house.

She walked to the end of the asphalt, past a dusty golf cart, vinyl seats cracked in the sun.

Dr. Travers-Steenkampf's cart.

The shrubs and bushes surrounding the patio of the big house were overgrown and lush from water funneled down the cleft of the mountain during recent rains. Something skittered under a bush and out of sight when she stepped on the patio. She didn't see it, but she heard it frantically running away as she approached.

April threaded her way to the front door on the pink stones. She half expected the gardener to pop through the hedges, to lead her into the house like a monk escorting an important guest into the inner sanctum. Knowing glances, quiet solemnity.

But Gardiner was dead.

He'd been part of the inner circle, along with Aunt Silvia and King. April remembered them all standing around on the patio, talking about the voice. They'd all heard the voice, and that made them special.

G. Scripps Gardiner had leaned over to peer into her face, to ask her . . . April couldn't remember what he'd asked. She couldn't remember what he'd said. Gardiner had frightened her. All his talk of torsion fields and blood sacrifices, his strange litany of prayers. He'd always looked at her like she was a particularly interesting rat in a cage.

"Someday you'll fly," Gardiner had whispered.

But King had other ideas.

The day of the massacre, Gardiner had come for her.

That was the day Gardiner sealed his fate.

King had killed him.

She didn't remember his death, but she remembered his boots sticking out from under the hedge where he died.

G. Scripps Gardiner.

"I think we're going to sit this one out, sugar," King had said.

He had a gun in his hand. She remembered that now.

She hadn't wanted to go into the house with King on that day.

But now April had a reason to go in.

The sacrifice had been made. The portal had opened again.

Her dad was there, in the house with King. She knew it in her bones.

The double front doors to the house were wide open.

April walked in, along with a gust of wind that carried dust across the tiled floor.

"Hello?" she called.

She listened for an answer. None came. That didn't mean they weren't here. The house felt alive, as though it had been waiting for her.

There was something strange about the house and it took April a second to realize what it was. The lights were on. There was a bank of solar panels behind the house. They were still working after all this time.

The doors opened into a long hallway. To the right was the kitchen and the dining room. April walked toward the dining room, feeling a mounting fear. There was a thick, weighty quality to the silence of the house, an expectation.

She crept toward the dining room, knowing that the secretary and the maid had left while they could, before everything started happening.

She didn't want to see Dr. Travers-Steenkampf face down on the long dining table, not moving, her tongue sticking out from between her teeth. Eyes half open, strangely glittering and unmoving.

She forced herself to walk into the dining room.

Dr. Travers-Steenkampf wasn't there. Of course not. She'd died at this table years ago.

This was where Aunt Silvia had found April on the day of the massacre. She remembered now, the moment when Aunt Silvia arrived in the dining room, looking frantic.

We have to hide.

They'd gone down the hallway into the kitchen, where Aunt Silvia worked.

"Dad?" April called.

Her voice echoed in the corridor, followed by a strange squeak, like a tennis shoe on the concrete floors. She resisted an urge to run away.

"Hello?" she called. "King?"

She'd always known in her heart that she would be back here one day.

When April and her mom had fled, they lived first in

334

hotels, then in a tiny apartment, a glorified motel with a cracked pool and a tacked-on kitchenette, and then finally, once the Steenkampf estate settled Mom's lawsuit, in the big two-story adobe house with too many rooms that they never entered. That house had a long and storied history that had nothing to do with them. April felt like they were squatters.

Her home was here, with her dad.

Maybe when she found Dad, they could finally leave and start a life elsewhere.

Again, a squeak.

The noise had come from the other wing of the house and April walked in that direction. The hall made a ninety-degree turn past a warren of bedrooms and sitting rooms, and a library filled with dusty-looking books. The hall turned again, and at the end of it was a large study. The room had an oversize desk of smooth, burnished wood. Most of the other rooms had windows and stone or adobe walls, but this room was windowless and paneled in honey-colored wood.

One of the panels was slightly offset from the rest of the wall. April walked over, put her hand on it, and pushed. It sank in and then popped out. A panel swung open a crack and a light went on. The panel was heavy and gimbaled but moved surprisingly smoothly. It turned out to be a hidden bar, dark golden liquid in bottles, crystal tumblers lined up, sparkling in the warm glow of under-shelf lighting.

It felt like a clue in an escape room.

April searched the drawers of the bar but found only silver ice tongs and spoons, other bar tools. She turned all the bottles over, wondering if there were messages written on the bottoms. Nothing.

There are times in any game when you realize that you are on the right track. You push a panel; a door swings open unexpectedly. The door doesn't reveal any immediate clues, but it does tell you what you need to know.

April looked at the edge of the door to the bar. A section of wood paneling an inch wide hung out past the edge of the bar. She closed the bar with a soft click. The paneled edge of the bar pulled flush with the rest of the wall, leaving not so much as a playing card's gap between the wall and the door. It was completely invisible.

She clicked it again and the door swung open, lights on.

If the door to the bar hadn't been slightly open, April never would have found it. But then again, maybe she would have. It felt horribly familiar.

There were more hidden doors in this room. It was just a matter of finding them. April had known how to open the bar. She was five the last time she was here. How would she know how to open the bar—unless there was another door just like that one?

She remembered closing another similar door with a soft click, marveling at how the door disappeared into the wall.

She searched the length of the wall, pushing against unyielding paneling until finally, on the opposite side of the room, she pushed and felt a telltale give. A door cracked open. April pulled it all the way open and was faced with what looked like a door-size safe. It was gunmetal gray, thick and imposing, like something you'd see in a bank. Maybe this was where King Steenkampf had kept all his money. Except, not. He was rich and had holdings all over the world.

This was something else.

Whatever secrets were behind this door, he'd meant for April, and her alone.

THIRTY-TWO
APRIL

NEXT TO THE door was a thumbprint plate, and for a moment April worried that she wouldn't be able to get in. She held her right thumb up to the pad and heard the thick sound of metal bolts coming free. King had expected her.

Whatever was behind this door was the answer to everything. This was the key to finding her dad.

April hesitated. She remembered being in this study with King and Dad, the two men talking about business while she swiveled in the bucket chair, trying to go around in circles. Dad had cleared his throat, which April took to be a warning to stop doing whatever she was doing.

She didn't remember much about Dad. His face was blank

in most of her memories. When she finally saw him again, would she even recognize him?

Her hand on the wooden panel in front of the vault door left a print in a seamless layer of dust. No one had opened the door for a very long time. She doubted Aunt Silvia had even known about it.

April opened the heavy door and cabinet side lights came on, as though it were another bar. She swung the door open, and the first thing she saw were guns. Rows and rows of guns in a honey wood cabinet on the wall, backlit with the same glamorous lighting that made his old scotch glow like amber. Rows and rows of guns, assault rifles, barrel rounds, even more places where guns had clearly been and were now missing.

Sleek silver pistols shining like jewels behind glass. So eye-catching that April missed the rest of the room for a heartbeat. A small cot against one wall. On the opposite wall on a low couch was a figure dressed in cowboy boots and pin-pressed khakis, a straw cowboy hat drooped over the face.

King Steenkampf. She recognized the hat.

In his desiccated hand was a pistol. His index finger still tightly gripped to the trigger even though his hand looked on the verge of falling apart, as though his will to keep shooting persisted after his death.

At the end of the cot, one of those expensive kinds of dolls, dressed in colonial clothing. A doll-size butter churn by her side. And next to the doll, a tiny pink pearlized object April remembered intimately.

Her gun.

April didn't want to look down. Because she knew. Maybe she'd always known. It had been easier to think that her dad and King had stepped through a portal where time and distance wouldn't matter. That he would return to her as the dad she remembered, the dad she'd had at the age of five. She'd wanted to believe in the impossible because the truth had been too hard to face.

Her dad was gone. He was on the floor, a crumpled pile of clothing around a mostly mummified skeleton. Beneath him, a circle of dried blood. April didn't recognize him, because there wasn't enough to recognize in the clothing, the work boots that could have belonged to anyone, the remains of short black hair on the skeleton.

But it was him. On his left hand, the wedding ring her mom had given him. Mom's ring was a slim white gold band with a single diamond, but his was thick stainless steel with meshed gears that turned. April had loved that ring. Sometimes her dad would take it off and let her play with the gears, rolling the outer edge of the ring, watching the tiny gears spin. Why did she remember her dad this way, things he wore or his hand reaching out to grab her, laughing as she ran past the couch where he pretended to be asleep?

But never his face. So little to remember.

So little left of the man on the floor. The man who had been her father.

She remembered now, how it had started. Hopscotching across the patio that day, trying to touch only the pink stones. And then Gardiner had shown up on the patio. He'd always scared her.

Always talking of the sacrifice to come.

He'd pulled her to the edge of the patio, toward the open pit.

Time to fly.

There was a terrible loud noise, and Gardiner let go of her wrist. He fell in the bushes, his boots sticking out.

At the end of the path of pink stones, at the open double doors, King waited for her. He still had the gun in his hand. April knew that King had shot Gardiner because he was mean and wanted to hurt her.

There been a loud boom in the distance, followed by a popping noise like fireworks. She didn't know at the time, but it was gunfire.

"We need to go," King had said.

"Where's Aunt Silvia?" she'd asked.

"Silvia will find us later," he had said.

They'd walked through the open doors to the house, down the hallway, past the dining room where Dr. Travers-Steenkampf sat, her head down on the table, like she was taking a nap.

"I just wanted her to come with us," King had said sadly. "I didn't mean to hurt her."

There had been a bottle on the table and a knocked over glass, spilling a clear liquid on the table. It had smelled like the doctor's office. Like rubbing alcohol.

Vodka, maybe.

Oh god, April thought. King Steenkampf had drugged his wife's drink, hoping to drag her into the room. Instead, he'd killed her. He must have gotten the dosage wrong.

April looked around the room. She'd gone with King Steenkampf willingly to the room with all the toys and the dolls. It had been an exciting adventure, a game of hide-and-seek. They waited for Aunt Silvia, waiting for all the wonderful things the voice had promised her, once the bad things were over.

Her dad was the enemy. He didn't understand about the voice. Not like King. Not like Aunt Silvia.

King could have closed the door and locked them both in, but he hadn't. He leaned back on the couch, gun in hand.

What had he been waiting for? Was Aunt Silvia really supposed to have joined them? She would never know now. Another secret Aunt Silvia took with her.

She didn't remember the moment her dad showed up. Dad's face was always a blank in her memories. It was too much to remember his face, but she remembered his voice. He'd been so angry.

"Bob, this isn't you," Dad had said.

Everyone called him King except Dad. Dad called him Bob. She remembered that too.

Dad had pushed her roughly out the door. She'd remembered that much in an odd way, all these years. Dad pushing her roughly aside, and how it scared her, and more than that: It made her angry. The missing piece in her memory was the gun in King Steenkampf's hand pointed at her dad.

But she did know what happened next. After Dad had pushed her out of the secret room and sent her tumbling to the floor.

She'd stood up.

She'd closed the outer door to the room.

King could have left. But he'd stayed and he'd died. That was a mystery that might never be solved. Why had he died? He'd been sick and it was possible that the strain of the moment had been too much for him.

No one else had known about the room. King had said it was their little secret. Once April closed the outer door, she'd made sure that no one would ever find them. The existence of the room was a secret she'd locked deep in her brain— until now.

April knelt down beside the crumpled form of her father. He'd fallen on his side, and she touched his sleeve gently, afraid that he would crumble into dust under her hand. There was so little of him left.

343

"I'm sorry," she said.

Her voice was a dull knife cutting through the thick silence. Why had she trusted King over her dad? It didn't make any sense.

But it did.

It was the voice.

Even as a child, April had known that King was sick. He'd come to the compound seeking immortality, a trip through a mythical portal to escape his illness. He'd wished to stay here forever.

He would stay here, in this place, forever.

Dead, with a gun in his hand.

The gun he'd used to kill her father.

April thought about the shimmering golden light at the bottom of the open-pit mine. The collected water, a stunning tropical turquoise, no doubt from the copper in the rocks. A cloud had rolled away from the sun at just the right moment, sunlight hitting the pool at the perfect angle, creating an explosion of light. Maybe the falling dead man had made ripples in the pool, circles within circles that made her believe the portal was opening. Or maybe it was a hallucination brought on by the lying voice in her head.

A trick of the light.

A trick of longing.

Time to fly, the voice whispered.

April had killed a man over a lie. Aunt Silvia was dead, and

Jules was wandering around the compound alone because of her. Everything had gone wrong because of her.

Time to fly.

April had closed the door on her father, shut the door on her memory. He was dead because of her. And wouldn't it be a perfect moment of symmetry if she ended it all here, by finally stepping out over the edge once and for all? She was the Bicycle Girl, after all.

Time to fly.

"No." April's voice was muffled in the small space. But loud enough for her to realize she was talking out loud to the voice inside her head.

She was no longer a five-year-old, wishing to fly like Kiki.

The voice had no real power. It was all evil intention, a bad spirit whispering in her ear, telling her to want the one thing she could never have. To fight for it, to kill for it.

To die for it.

To die.

The voice wanted her to die.

Time to fly.

April stood up.

The voice stilled. Her mind grew quieter than she could have ever imagined possible. She would never again stand in front of the chapel on the hill at the end of her street, arms outstretched, longing for the dramatic end to everything. Longing for that one perfect moment when she would fly.

And plummet.

The voice told her to fly.

The voice never told her she wouldn't fall.

THIRTY-THREE
APRIL

"APRIL?" ZACH CALLED out, his voice echoing down the hallway.

A great wave of relief swept over her. But it was more than relief, it felt like being pulled back from the brink of something terrible and inescapable. She stepped out of the room for fear that the evil thing here would close the door and she'd be trapped.

It didn't work that way. The voice told her that she needed to be punished. It couldn't punish her. She could only close the door on herself.

"In here," she yelled.

Zach rounded the corner of the office, panting slightly,

like he'd run a great distance. He took a few quick steps into the room and wrapped his arms around her.

She nestled her head in the crook of his neck. Every muscle and tendon relaxed, as though she'd carried a great weight a long distance and had just handed it over to someone with broader shoulders.

"I was so worried about you," he murmured. "Grace too."

She pulled away from him suddenly.

"I don't know where Jules is," she said quickly. "I sent her to make a call, but she didn't come back."

"She's with Grace," Zach said. "She's safe."

Jules, safe. It seemed like an eternity since she'd sent Jules to call 911. So much had happened. The body in the road.

"I saw Jonathan," she said. "I thought Jules had . . ."

"We killed him together," Zach said grimly. "Why are you here?"

She gestured toward the open door.

Zach peered into the room.

"Fuck!" He jumped away from the door.

He'd seen a cowboy, hat slung low over his face, pistol pointed in his direction. Murderous cowboy, first thought. Dead cowboy was the second thought.

"Who is he?"

"King Steenkampf," she said. "And that's my dad."

She was glad Zach was here, glad to have someone else to witness this terrible tableau.

"King shot your dad?" he said.

"He did," April replied.

Zach walked over and picked a pen up off Steenkampf's desk. He walked back to the secret room, past her father to King Steenkampf on the couch. He used the pen to lift the brim of Steenkampf's hat. Smart. He didn't want to leave fingerprints. April's were all over the place.

She was curious to see if there was anything of the man she recognized. His face had stayed in April's memory, more clearly than the face of her own father. The dry desert air and the seal of the room had mummified them both. His eyes were closed and his lips pulled back from his teeth in a strange snarl of a smile.

"How did he die?" Zach asked.

"Broken heart?" April laughed bitterly. "I left him."

Zach looked toward the cot and the tiny pink gun with recognition. Under the bed were children's board games, still in shrink wrap: Candy Land and Sorry! There were balls and mermaid-themed Lego sets. Everything brand-new and unopened. Everything you might need to entertain a five-year-old. She hadn't noticed that before, but she saw all this now through Zach's eyes.

"He was a monster," he said.

"I suppose he was," April said.

"My uncle isn't here?"

April shook her head. The scene inside the room had been

349

so overwhelming, she'd forgotten all about Zach's uncle David.

One of the cultists out there was named David. She'd heard them call his name.

"I thought he'd be with my dad," she said. "I don't know what . . ."

"April?" Amy's voice came through the door. She was outside on the patio, near enough to be heard through the open doors.

They both froze.

"April, where are you?" Amy's voice was closer now, a few yards away from the front door. It was only a matter of time before they were found.

"Who is that?" Zach whispered.

"Cultist," she mouthed.

His eyes grew wide.

Amy and the others had guns. They were dangerous. They'd come ready to kill to open the portal, only there was no portal.

"We need to hide," she whispered.

Aunt Silvia had worked at the mess hall, but she'd also cooked for the people here in the house. April remembered the back hallway that led to the left wing of the house, the housekeeper's bedroom, and the kitchen and pantry beyond.

Aunt Silvia had brought her into the kitchen while she cooked dinner for the residents of the house. April remembered the giant pantry and shelves of industrial-size cans. A giant can of food at her feet as they hid. She'd kicked a can accidentally and made a noise.

A full day of anxiety and boredom hiding in the pantry, Aunt Silvia telling her to be quiet. Long-forgotten memories cascaded, a deluge of useless information flowing from her past. The cans of food were comically large. Without water, they'd eaten Popsicles to stay hydrated.

Or was that the mess hall? April had to take a chance on her faulty memory.

She motioned to Zach.

They ran silently through the gloomy, windowless back hall.

She and Zach crept past the back bedrooms to the kitchen.

"April?" Amy's voice had a lilting tone, the kind of voice you use to lure stray cats out of hiding. "Come on out, hon. We just want to know where the king is."

The king. She realized with horror that they'd left the door to the room open. The cultists would find King's corpse soon.

She wished with all her heart that she'd closed the door to the secret room—too late.

Zach grabbed her hand and squeezed.

At the far end of the kitchen was the pantry door.

April opened the door slowly, careful not to make any noise. She was greeted by a narrow closet, deep enough to hold racks of spices and jars of flour, sugar, and rice. Not the walk-in closet–size room she remembered.

"We can't hide in here," Zach whispered.

"I've been here before," she whispered back. "This isn't right."

She remembered a room, a chest freezer, metal shelves full of supplies. There was a pantry in the mess hall too. What if she was wrong and she and Aunt Silvia had gone to the mess hall instead?

A muted, unearthly wail came from the far side of the house, a man's voice.

"He's dead!"

The cultists had found the secret room.

There was a wild rush of yelling from King Steenkampf's office.

Amy must have stepped into the hall, because her voice was louder.

"Spread out," Amy said. All the *Here, kitty, kitty* sweetness was gone from her voice, replaced by a hoarse, murderous rage. "Find her."

"Fuck," Zach whispered. "They're going to kill us."

April remembered standing over Dr. Travers-Steenkampf's body in the dining room. The mess hall was behind the bore house, near the spot where Tyler Landry had been thrown into the pit the day of the massacre. To get to the mess hall pantry, she and Silvia would have had to wade through a firefight. The pantry where Aunt Silvia had hidden her had to be here, in this house.

"He's dead!" The crying man was still wailing, as though in shock.

"Shut up, Carl," someone said. "We just need to find her."

The door to the secret room had been gimbaled, and a simple push had popped it open. Maybe there was a hidden door here as well.

April pushed on the back wall of the pantry, and the wall swung open smoothly, revealing a room the size of a large walk-in closet. She and Zach walked through the door. She shut the outer door quietly and pushed the inner door back in place with a soft but unmistakable click.

"What was that?" a man's voice said, somewhere nearby.

"She's here," Amy said.

The next interchange was muffled as they moved away from what April assumed was the nearby staff dining room.

She and Zach crouched in the pantry, waiting. At her feet were the industrial-size cans of beans and jalapeños, the room unchanged from the last time she was here on the worst day of her life.

The voices that had receded in the distance suddenly came close.

"I think they're in the kitchen," a man said.

"He's dead," the crying man said. Carl. "How can he be dead? After all these years?"

353

"She killed him." Amy spit out the words percussively, loud enough to be heard through the door. "She must have. . . ."

Amy's next words were unintelligible through the two layers of the pantry door. April could only guess what she was telling the other cultists. Maybe the voice had told Amy that it could all be undone if they found April and sacrificed her.

It didn't make sense. None of this made sense.

April stifled a gasp as the outer door to the pantry was thrown open with a rattle of spice jars. A can fell to the floor.

Zach squeezed her hand.

"She's not here," the man said. His voice was alarmingly loud and close by.

"Keep looking," Amy replied. "King built this house with a lot of places to hide. I'm sure she's here."

"What does it matter?" the crying man said. "The king is dead."

"We can still open the portal," Amy said. "But we're going to have to . . ."

Amy lowered her voice and April lost the rest of the sentence.

April moved quietly to the back of the pantry and felt along the walls for another door or escape.

The clatter of pans and dishes hitting the floor echoed throughout the room, followed by pounding noises on the inside of cabinets. The man was looking for hidden compartments or doors. And then, the worst sound of all, spices, cans, and jars being pulled off the shelves on the inside of the pantry.

Zach stood and quietly braced his shoulder against the hidden door, hoping that if the man on the other side pushed the door in, it wouldn't give. April ran her hands along behind the shelves searching for what she knew wasn't there. No paneling in here, just smooth walls.

The man outside the pantry door swore effusively.

They were trapped.

The cabinet noises stopped. There was a moment of quiet.

"I know how to flush her out," Amy said.

An unintelligible murmur of voices came from the other side of the door, followed by running feet.

The sound of boots receded down the hall.

April didn't trust the deep silence on the other side of the door. What did "flush her out" mean?

"Do you think they're gone?" Zach whispered.

"I don't know," she whispered back. "We should wait a few minutes."

They waited for what seemed like an eternity.

April smelled smoke. It had an acrid, chemical edge and April realized with horror that one of the cultists must have searched the garage or the tool shed for a flammable liquid.

"We can't stay here," Zach whispered.

"They're going to shoot us if we come out," April said. There was a back exit that led to the firing range and a steep wall of rock beyond. They were boxed in.

"I'll take my chances," Zach said.

Zach picked up the industrial-size can of beans, held it over his head, and motioned for April to open the door. April put her hand on the doorknob, counted to three softly, and pulled the door in quickly.

A spice jar rolled toward them.

The kitchen was empty, the house silent except for a crackle of fire. A thick, bitter smoke rolled in from the direction of the big open living room in the back of the house. The back exit was out of the question. They'd have to go through the double front doors. April held her T-shirt over her mouth to block the smoke. Zach gripped the industrial-size can of beans. It wasn't much of a weapon against assault rifles, but it was all they had. April reached out and grabbed Zach's hand to guide him through the maze of corridors. She knew the layout of the house from dreams and memory.

When they reached the front door, a shot rang out, whizzing past them, hitting somewhere down the hall. As she'd feared, the cultists were on the patio, waiting to shoot them when they came out. They crouched low next to the door to avoid the smoke. She coughed and Zach squeezed her hand tightly.

She understood. Soon, they would be forced to make a run for it. Anything would be better than inhaling the smoke. He dropped the can of beans with a dull *thunk* and they stood.

"Ready?" he said.

She dropped her head to the center of his chest for a moment and he caressed the back of her head.

She couldn't believe it had come to this. To face death, finally, on the patio where it had all started and, worse, to have brought Zach with her.

At least Jules made it out.

There was the popcorn noise of gunfire in the distance followed by the sound of yelling.

"Amy!" someone yelled.

There was a much closer sound of gunfire.

The smoke was unbearable, and they ran hand in hand onto the patio. Amy was lying in a pool of blood, unmoving, at the edge of the patio. Cultists ringed the patio, but they were turned around, firing in the other direction. Bullets whizzed past, slapping against the adobe, and Zach pulled her hand in the direction of the long driveway.

The smoke was thicker now. The big house, long empty and untended, was burning. Gunfire sounded from the direction of the patio.

The wind shifted in their direction, sending billows of acrid smoke that burned their eyes and throats.

"We should run for the trees, while the smoke covers us," Zach said.

They ran for the pine trees that lined the road out of the compound. Behind them, the firefight continued. Zach and

April jogged down the road toward the industrial entrance. Smoke rose from a smaller fire outside the compound. The smoke from the larger house fire mushroomed into the sky. If fire trucks weren't on their way, they would be soon.

"Come on," Zach said.

He grabbed her arm and they continued running until they cleared the bend of the road, and the industrial entrance came into view. Grace's car sat alongside the gatehouse.

April doubled over and struggled to catch her breath. The muscles of her legs shook and threatened to give way.

She heard Jules before she saw her—a strange guttural cry, feet pounding along the gravel road. April straightened as Jules wrapped her arms around her in a bear hug.

"You're alive," Jules murmured into her hair.

"So are you," April said back.

She hadn't fully believed that Jules had made it out until that moment. This place had taken their dad. It had wanted Jules too.

But now they were free.

THIRTY-FOUR

JULES

THE RIDE BACK was strangely calming. Jules sat up front with Grace. They didn't talk, but every once in a while, Grace would cast a knowing glance in Jules's direction. She felt like Grace had understood her plan to debunk the Deep Well myth. It was scientific.

April and Zach sat in the back of Grace's car, holding hands, occasionally whispering together. They smelled of smoke, so Jules guessed they had been close to the fire. In the past few weeks, Jules had worried almost constantly about April. Seeing the two of them together, you would never have guessed that April had been moody and strange and obsessed with the compound.

Now that was over.

Jules had thought she wanted to debunk the whole Bicycle Girl urban legend to save April from all the mean people on the internet who tormented her. But now that she thought about it, what she really wanted to do was to save April from April. Having a nice new boyfriend didn't make everything okay for April, but it was a start.

She was almost sorry when they made it back to their neighborhood.

When they drove up to the house, people were standing in their yards, craning their heads toward the mountain in the distance. She turned her head back toward the mountain. A thick plume of fire rose in the distance.

Mom was waiting on the porch and hugged her tightly.

"You're home," she murmured in Jules's ear, not letting her go. It felt nice after all that had happened. "I was frantic after I got the notification that you'd left school."

Mom wasn't mad. That was a relief.

Mom had been crying. Her eyes were puffy, and there were streaks running down her cheeks. Jules felt bad. She'd been so worried about April, it hadn't occurred to her that Mom would be worried about her. It was the day before April's birthday.

Mom hugged April and then Grace.

"This is Zach," April said. "He helped us look for Jules."

"Nice to meet you," Mom said. "Thank you so very much."

360

April and Grace stood on the porch, looking serious. April looked at Zach and he nodded.

"Um, hey, Jules, I've never seen your pool," Zach said.

Random. And kind of weird.

"I'm sure Jules would like to show you," Mom said.

"Okay."

She had no idea why Zach wanted to see the pool so badly, but since he'd asked, she led him down the path, past the guest house toward the wrought iron fence in the back.

"Well, okay, here it is," Jules said.

The pool was overfilled due to the recent rains, and the normally bright turquoise water was a bit hazy. But the palmettos and the flower bushes were lush and green. Jules didn't normally spend a lot of time back here, but it was pretty.

Zach plopped down on a lounge chair and put his feet up. She brushed water off a nearby chair, sat down, and faced him.

"Why did you want to see the pool?" Jules asked.

"I didn't," Zach said. "I just think your sister wanted a moment alone with your mom, to tell her about your aunt."

Aunt Silvia. Her death was always there at the edge of her brain, a terrible image of a hand sticking through pipes. Jules was glad that Zach had brought her out here. She didn't want to be the one to tell Mom.

"Thanks," Jules said, and she meant it.

He nodded.

"How are you doing?" she asked.

She thought of Jonathan and the fight at the edge of the pit. It must have reminded him too, because he got a faraway look on his face.

"I've been better," he said.

"I'm sorry," she said. "I mean, thank you for, you know, saving me and all."

"You have blood on your shoe," Zach said, without looking away from the pool.

Jules looked down. She'd forgotten about the blood on her shoe. The accident in the bore house felt like a lifetime ago. Was that Aunt Silvia's blood? Trev's blood?

Jules whipped off her shoe and threw it.

It landed in the pool and drifted slowly toward the bottom, a pinkish trail like a puff of smoke coming off it as it descended.

"That's one way to solve a problem," Zach said.

"Do you think Mom noticed?" Jules asked, suddenly worried.

Zach looked over and frowned.

"I don't think she wanted to notice," he said.

Jules picked up a rock and threw it in the pool, aiming for the shoe. Zach did the same. The pool maintenance man was always complaining about the landscape rocks ending up in the pool. He said it was hard to scoop them up and somebody ended up having to go down after them. But, then again, somebody would have to go in after the shoe.

That somebody was Jules.

362

Her head hurt. Jules sighed, a sudden heavy feeling in her chest. She'd killed someone. Well, maybe two people. Except Jonathan had tried to kill her first, and she hadn't exactly killed him alone. Zach had helped.

"I feel like I did something terrible," she said.

"So do I," he said.

He picked up a quarter-size rock and stood. He carefully aimed the rock before throwing it into the center of the pool. It fell straight through the water and landed inside the shoe.

"Nice!" she said. "Perfect aim."

"Thank you." Zach took a small bow before sitting back down on the chaise.

"Maybe it wasn't you or me," he said. "Maybe we aren't fully responsible for that terrible thing."

He was talking about Jonathan. And she could tell he felt bad about Jonathan. She didn't, because Jonathan had tried to kill her. He'd tried to kill them both.

But Trev was a different story. Trev hadn't done anything to her, not really. He'd freaked out and acted weird, but then so had she. She wished more than anything that she could go back in time to that instant after the pipes collapsed when she picked up the wrench and swung. She'd told herself that it was self-defense, that if she didn't hit Trev he would attack her, but that wasn't true. He was dazed.

Why did she have to hit him?

It was the voice. She closed her eyes and remembered.

The tiny voice in the back of her brain that said *kill him*.

A gleeful, angry little voice that was super mad that Trev had lied and pretended to be Kayla. That felt he deserved to die for that alone.

Lightning lit up the sky, followed a few seconds later by a clap of thunder.

"You didn't hear a voice, did you?" Jules asked.

Zach stood, grabbed a handful of rocks, and pulled back his arm like he was going to violently fastball pitch a hundred scattered pebbles into the pool. But then he dropped the rocks back into the flower bed instead. He brushed off the few bits that had stuck to his hand.

"Maybe," he said. "Did you?"

She nodded. She didn't want to tell him that the voice wanted her to kill. It was embarrassing.

"What did the voice tell you?" she asked.

He hesitated before speaking. "It told me it could bring my uncle back," he said.

"Your uncle?"

"He was at the compound that day," Zach said. "His body was never found."

"Like my dad?" Jules said.

Zach got a strange look on his face. "I hope not," he replied.

Jules picked up another rock to throw into the pool, but it was smooth and had a nice shape, so she hung on to it.

April had been obsessed with getting Dad back, but that wasn't happening. April should have known that someone

364

who'd been gone for as long as Dad wasn't ever coming back. It wasn't logical. And Jonathan had wanted to throw Jules over a cliff just so he could get his girlfriend back which was—wild. Marianne was dead and there was nothing Jonathan or anyone could do about it.

And now the voice had told Zach pretty much the same thing.

"I think the voice is evil," Jules said. "They should put up something to keep people out of there."

Zach laughed.

"Like what, a bigger wall?" he said. "That wall is pretty huge."

"Maybe," she said.

Jules imagined a mile of barbed wire like the wall of thorns around Sleeping Beauty's castle. Something that would really keep people out.

"I think you would have gotten in anyway," he said. "And April. You're both stubborn."

"April went in because of me," Jules said.

As she said it, she realized it was true. April had followed her to the compound. It was all her fault. If she hadn't gone out to the compound, Aunt Silvia would still be alive. And Trev.

She would never forget that she'd killed Trev.

Zach stretched on the chaise and yawned as though talking had worn him out.

"Don't blame yourself," he said. "April was always going to go out to the compound. One way or another."

Jules slumped into the chair next to him. A drop of rain hit the pool and then another. She wondered what was going on in the house. She imagined the three of them in the kitchen, Mom and April huddled over the butcher-block island, talking. Grace making tea no one would drink. If it started raining for real, Jules would have to go inside too. Would Mom be crying over Aunt Silvia, or would she have retreated to her room? And April. April had wanted more than anything to bring Dad back from the dead, and instead there were more dead people out at the compound.

And then a terrible thought occurred to Jules. People had died at the compound the day before April's birthday, and now the whole world would think it was because of April. Jules had wanted to free April from the curse of being Bicycle Girl, and instead, she'd made it worse.

THIRTY-FIVE
APRIL

IT WASN'T AS hard to tell Mom about Aunt Silvia's death as April imagined it would be. Her mom greeted the news with a grim nod of the head.

"When I saw the smoke, I knew something had gone terribly wrong," she said. "Like last time."

Last time, when Dad had pushed her to leave the compound. The day of the massacre when she'd left her daughter, her husband, and her sister behind, not knowing if she would ever see any part of her family again. April added this to her growing list of regrets about this day. She'd forced Mom to relive the worst moments of her life.

"I'm sorry, Mom."

Mom put a hand on April's arm and gave her a small squeeze.

"You brought your sister home," she said. "And you, Grace. Thank you."

"Of course," Grace said into her cup of tea. "I'm glad Jules is safe."

Mom didn't seem to want to know the details of what had happened, which was merciful, considering.

"I've got to go soon," Grace said. "I should find my parents before they hear about this on the news."

This would be on the news. The reality of that hit April squarely in the chest. Not only the local news but the national news. The apocalypse came a day earlier than expected. Bicycle Girl on the scene.

"Let me walk you out," April said.

"We need to get our stories straight," Grace whispered while Mom was out of earshot. "For the police."

"The police," April echoed.

She realized that her car was still outside the wall of the compound. The police would have questions.

"I'm going with the cultists did it," Grace said. "You went out there, but when you realized that the cultists had followed you, you called me and I came and got you."

April nodded. It made sense.

"And Jules wasn't there," Grace added.

April felt a wave of gratitude for Grace, who had always looked out for Jules.

"Definitely not," April said, thinking of Jonathan and the man in the pit, whoever he was. "Jules was home playing video games. And Zach wasn't with us either."

"Zach," Grace murmured. She nodded in agreement. "Do you want me to give him a ride home?"

"No," April said too quickly. "I'll borrow Mom's car."

Grace smiled.

"Sure," she said.

April wasn't sure there was much to smile about in that department. She'd held Zach's hand at the double doors of the big house, convinced that they were going to die together in a hail of bullets. For her, it was just another day in the life of Bicycle Girl, but she wouldn't blame Zach if he never wanted to see her again.

They drove in silence. The occasional lightning flashes bathed the streets in a blue glow, throwing the streetlights into temporary darkness. April had the urge to turn the car in the opposite direction, to head to the top of chapel hill, lightning be damned. But that moment at the chapel with Zach was unreproducible. She would have to content herself with the memory of that one perfect kiss.

Zach leaned the seat back, his eyes closed, and April wondered if he was sleeping. She wanted to take a long and circuitous route to his house, just to keep him in the car for a few minutes longer. But that wasn't fair. Zach's mom had to have received the same robocall from school. He'd texted his mom to tell her he was okay, but still, she had to be worried.

He didn't speak until they were on the bridge near his house.

He turned his head and opened his eyes.

"Worst first date ever."

She laughed.

"Technically our second," she said, thinking of that night by the chapel, the stars and the kisses.

"Oh yeah, forgot about that," he said, smiling.

"You did?" she said. "I hadn't."

She turned the car down his street and parked in front of his house.

"So what now?" he asked.

She studied his profile in the strange blue-green light of the impending storm. Zach hadn't asked for any of this. Not the chaos and the violence, not being dragged into a world where the laws of human decency, and even the laws of physics, did not seem to apply.

He'd volunteered. He'd saved Jules from Jonathan, and that alone was enough for her to want to let him off the hook. No quip, no chaser. He could return to being the football hero, but she would always be the Bicycle Girl. If she'd ever thought she could escape that destiny, this day proved otherwise.

"No one needs to know that you were ever there," she

said. "Grace and I agreed we would tell everyone that I went into the compound alone, and Grace came to get me. End of story."

She sighed, thinking this might be the last time she and Zach would sit together in a car, in a quiet bubble, shielded from the rest of the world.

"So we go back to school and pretend none of this ever happened?" he asked. "You return to ignoring me?"

She wanted to protest that she'd never ignored him. She'd tried. It had never worked.

"Pretty much," she said. "If that's what you want."

"Oh—if it's what I want?"

Zach smiled, that same sly smile he'd given her in the school hallway outside the gym an eternity ago, and she had the feeling he was laughing at her.

"What?"

"Nothing," he said. "It just seems like you've got this all figured out."

Now, she *knew* he was laughing at her.

He turned his head toward her, suddenly serious.

"April, what makes you think I could forget this day, even if I wanted to?"

"But you want to forget?" she asked.

"Not all of it," he said.

He reached over and brushed a hair away from her cheek. His hand lingered on the side of her face and traced the curve of her cheekbone. She closed her eyes and leaned into his hand; and when he wrapped an arm around her shoulder, she nestled her head in the crook of his neck.

She'd stepped into a world of darkness, but she hadn't been alone.

And that made all the difference.

After a moment, he pulled away and kissed her softly. He opened the car door, got out, and stood with his hand draped over the door.

"I'll see you at school, Bicycle Girl," he said.

He shut the car door, and walked away, head bowed, looking as exhausted as she felt.

Those words had never sounded quite so sweet.

SATURDAY

The next afternoon, the Copperton chief of police held a press conference while the remains of the main house in the compound still smoldered in the rain. He told the local news that a shoot-out at Ojo de Cristo mine had led to an undisclosed number of casualties. About as vague as you could get it, but the news spread downtown through the coffee shop and the historic art deco hotel.

The afternoon of April's birthday, Zach texted to wish her a happy birthday. So did Grace. April had forgotten that it was her birthday. The day before at the compound felt like her real seventeenth birthday, her trial by fire.

Mom made dinner, roast vegetables and pasta with pesto. She'd ordered a tres leches cake from the bakery, April's favorite. It wasn't until Jules stuck a candle in it and began singing that April really thought about what the day meant.

Her seventeenth birthday was almost over. That would be a relief.

Her mom gave her a black Victorian pendant, like the kind of stuff April usually wore but real Whitby jet. It was beautiful, crafted in the 1900s to mourn a loved one. More appropriate today than Mom had imagined when she'd bought it.

April tied the black silk ribbon around her neck and held her phone out to take a selfie.

"I helped her pick it out," Jules said.

"When I bought it, I didn't think that . . ." Mom began.

Her eyes filled with tears for Aunt Silvia.

"It's perfect," April said. "Thank you."

April would never wear the pendant without thinking of Aunt Silvia, and Dad.

Over the next couple of days, news trickled in.

There were eight dead at the mine. One man in the open-pit mine died of injuries from a fall. Trev. The day after his body was discovered, Kos and his little sister, Kayla, posted a touching in memoriam video for Trev, complete with a montage of his best scenes from their show and some never-before-seen shots that made him seem less like a big goof and more like an underground scholar. It was tasteful. It was kind.

One man died on the service road into the mining compound. Jonathan Ray Schuyler died of an apparent concussion. Internet sleuths found a picture of him on the Facebook page of his fiancée, Marianne Mayweather, an estranged member of the Deep Well cult, who had died under mysterious circumstances days earlier. The engagement photo on her home page went viral, two pretty people in love, standing on a beach at sunset—so very dead.

Armchair detectives formed theories about what had happened to the two of them. Most people agreed that Jonathan first killed Marianne, and then was killed by vengeful members of her cult. Jonathan and Marianne had had a very noisy argument the day before she died.

April was glad to see the collective internet obsess over the deaths of Jonathan and Marianne. It took a little pressure off her.

One died in the bore house, crushed under a pile of pipes. Aunt Silvia. One person died of smoke inhalation in a Winnebago outside the wall when a Molotov cocktail was thrown in.

The other four died in a gunfight near the big house in the compound.

Three of the dead were familiar to April. One was Amy Klosterman. Carl Black, the cultist in the house who had cried when they discovered King Steenkampf's corpse.

One of the two others was Dan Turnbridge. He died of several gunshot wounds in a stand of trees a little distance away from the patio of the big house. He left behind a rambling fifteen-page manifesto, full of fire and brimstone, claiming that God had called him to fight the devil at the edge of the pit of Hell. He never mentioned April by name in his manifesto, and for that, she was grateful.

Law enforcement agents speculated that he'd followed the cultists into the compound, intent on stopping the ritual. He'd killed as many cultists as he could before they in turn shot and killed him.

There was a strange irony in knowing that Dan Turnbridge had distracted the cultists long enough for Zach and April to leave the burning house.

Two cultists had escaped on foot.

There was no one named David among the dead.

Fire investigators found that an accelerant had been used to set the house ablaze.

Later in the week, forensic investigators upped the death toll to nine as they found remains of bones in the smoldering wreckage of the main house. A few days later they determined that the bones were from two different bodies.

Ten dead.

Neither she nor Jules went to school. April's car was at the scene of the massacre, but no one questioned her. Grace told the police that she picked up April at the wall outside the compound before the new massacre began.

Somehow, no one questioned this story.

It wasn't until a few days later that everything changed in Copperton. The trickle of podcasters and disaster tourists turned into a full-fledged media assault. The *New York Times* sent a reporter. So did the major news networks. The historic Morgan hotel was booked full. The coffee shop on Main couldn't keep up with the demand for lattes, rented several new machines, and began serving coffee in the courtyard. Their high school made concessions for students who wanted to work at the coffee shops, the Sonic, the Mexican restaurants, and the food trucks at the Coppermine bar.

The joke was that you could get full credit for the alternative math class, "money and management," because you were managing to strip an army of reporters of their money. The tips were great.

The Coppermine bar was always full to the brim now with reporters eating dirty bird sandwiches and drinking bourbon.

Zach sent April pictures of the melee of reporters drinking in the yard, the rows and rows of sandwiches he made from noon to eleven every day without even taking orders, because he knew as soon as he made a sandwich, it would get eaten.

The day the New Mexico Bureau of Investigation released the news was the day that both Jules's middle school and April's high school casually suggested they homeschool for the foreseeable future.

It was the day that changed everything in Copperton.

It was the day that the police chief made public the news that a DNA test had identified one set of burned bones as belonging to missing billionaire oil and mining magnate Robert "King" Steenkampf IV.

I miss you, Zach texted, a week after April's birthday.

April and Jules had been hovering inside, dodging disaster tourists, waiting for it all to blow over.

I miss you too, April replied.

What have you been doing? he asked.

Playing video games with Jules, mostly. We ordered edible glitter and made a mirror glaze cake. Want to see?

Sure.

April sent Zach a picture of the mirror glaze cake. She was pretty proud of the cake. It was perfectly smooth, a glaze of dark blue and purple with edible glitter stars.

More to the point, it made Jules happy. April was all about Jules being happy. When Jules wasn't happy, April could see her thoughts close in, all light reflected inward.

That's cool, he texted. **I want to see you.**

Are you sure? April texted back. **This is not a great time to be associated with the Bicycle Girl.**

There were horror casters and disaster tourists camped out all over the neighborhood. They tried to be subtle about it, but they weren't. There was talk of the next movie about April's life going into preproduction. No script yet.

She wanted to give him every chance to escape.

She hoped he wouldn't.

I'm absolutely positive that I want to see you, he texted. **I've never been more certain of anything in my life.**

Meet me at the chapel after work, she texted.

Eleven? he replied.

At ten thirty, April laced up a pair of over-the-knee boots. She put on a scoop-necked burgundy dress and a full-length black duster and, of course, the beautiful Whitby jet pendant on the black silk ribbon that Mom and Jules had given her. Dark lipstick, dark glasses even though it was night outside.

That first day no one approached April on her slow stroll down the street and up the hill to the chapel. They were too surprised to see her outside, dressed like a teen witch from a nineties movie.

The questions started the next night.

Reporters quickly learned that April was not going to alter her stride or answer any questions. Years of being the

Bicycle Girl had taught her that silence is a great tool. Most people find silence deeply unnerving.

When CHAR changed closing hours from ten to eleven to rake in the extra money, Zach and April moved their meeting time to midnight to accommodate his work schedule.

That made the horror casters even happier, to see the Bicycle Girl stroll down the street at the stroke of midnight.

That first night, they didn't talk much. They kissed under the watchful eyes of the disaster tourists and reporters. They kissed and dreamed of the time when they could be truly alone.

Later, even kissing became tabloid fodder, the subject of telephoto lenses. By tacit agreement, they never discussed anything they wouldn't want overheard.

"What will you do when this is all over?" she asked. It was a week in, at the height of the public attention.

"This will be over?" he said.

"For you," April replied.

She'd made her peace with being the Bicycle Girl for now and forever. It bought Jules a chance for a different future. Jules did not exist in the public imagination. After all she'd been through, Jules deserved a fresh start. Mom was spending a lot of time looking at private schools in far-flung locations. They didn't need to be tied to Copperton anymore now that Aunt Silvia was gone. The thought of leaving seemed to breathe new life into Mom.

April didn't want to go. Strange as that seemed. She felt like she belonged to this place.

"Hard to imagine this will ever be over," Zach said.

He wrapped his hand around hers. Holding hands was hard to catch on camera, or to make a big deal about. *Bicycle Girl holds boyfriend's hand—news at eleven.* Already people were beginning to get bored of them. Zach just couldn't see that yet.

April had been here before. Just when you think no one will ever talk about or even think about anything but you—*you!!!!*—that's the moment it's all over.

"So what will you do?"

"I don't know," he said. "Do you know, someone paid our rent for the next three years? Mom wanted to claw that back, but it was anonymous."

April did know. People were doing outrageous things. A GoFundMe for Zach to buy him a full-size bike. Marriage proposals from conservative women who wanted to save his soul from the devil—from April.

"So you think you'll stick around school?" April said. "Now that you're famous?"

"I want to be around for baseball season," he said. "I'm still hoping for a scholarship."

Zach was as good at baseball as he was at football, and

April was secretly glad that football season was coming to an end. Zach's brain would be ready for baseball season, and he'd be in much less risk of a new concussion.

And as Grace said, it was a decent brain.

"What about you?" he asked.

"For me," April said in a deep Dracula-tinged voice, "there is no escape."

Zach laughed.

"You could leave," he said.

"What?" April said, laughing. "And leave this place where I'm so adored?"

She spread her free arm to encompass the view of the tiny downtown. Below, someone snapped a picture of her.

"Are you kidding?" he said. "You're worshipped here. I expect the chamber of commerce to put up a Bicycle Girl statue on Main Street with a plaque. You put this town on the map."

"Nice," April said. "They can sell murder cookies in the coffee shop. Bicycle Girl T-shirts."

"Like Roswell," he said.

"Just like Roswell."

Silence fell between them, a silence that had grown over the time since they left the compound. He never said it out loud, but she knew he wanted to go back. Everyone who had been at the compound the day of the first massacre was accounted for except one. Once King Steenkampf's body was discovered, the world at large moved on from the mystery. But there was one mystery that hadn't been solved.

What happened to Zach's uncle?

April thought about telling him that one of the cultists was named David. But too much had happened. His part in Jonathan's death weighed heavily on him, and she didn't want to add to that.

She wasn't sure that the cultist was even his uncle.

Zach had become more and more convinced that the answer was at the compound. His uncle had to be there somewhere. And though he wouldn't admit it to her, she knew that he was still holding out hope that his uncle had somehow slipped through the portal and would come back.

Investigators were still combing through the site. Renewed interest in Dr. Travers-Steenkampf's work led a team of quantum geophysicists to forensically pick apart every piece of data in the lab. The FBI was there, going over the site, and it was possible they would find evidence they had missed a dozen years ago. The compound was temporarily crawling with people, and that kept Zach from going out there on his own. But it was just a matter of time.

The voice wanted them all back.

"Promise me something," she said.

"Anything."

"Promise me that if you ever want to go back out there, you'll tell me first," she said.

She didn't want to go back out to the compound—ever again. Whatever was there was evil. She knew it for what it was. But she wasn't going to lose anyone else to the voice from the open-pit mine.

He leaned over and kissed her softly.

"I don't want to go anywhere without you," he said.

THIRTY-SIX
APRIL

THREE DAYS AFTER the most recent incident at the mine, the police called to say that she could come get her car. Federal investigators had been over it with a fine-tooth comb, looking for evidence. They didn't find anything, and apparently everyone bought the story that she'd come out to the compound to visit her aunt Silvia, been chased by murderous cultists, and hidden until Grace came around the back of the compound to get her. The rain that fell that night and well into her birthday helped to obscure any evidence to the contrary.

There was nothing to link her to Amy and the rest of the cultists.

Eight days after April's birthday a terrible thought hit her.

The r/truewell chat.

It was out there.

April was all over it.

Realamy7070, who had died in the gunfight, had mentioned her by name. April had replied.

Anyone who thought to trace Amy's browser history would find the thread.

They would find April.

The detectives could trace the cultists straight back to her if they hadn't done so already. She had no part in all the gun deaths.

But what about Trev?

April hadn't killed Trev, but she was as responsible for his death as anyone. The bigger worry was Jules. Jules had hit Trev with a wrench. Her fingerprints had to be all over that wrench.

There wasn't much that April could do now to mitigate the damage, but she had to look. If the detectives did find the thread, April would have to get her story straight. Whatever happened, she had to protect Jules.

She pulled up the thread, afraid to look.

By now, everyone knew about the deaths at the compound. The blurry body being pulled from the open door of the Winnebago, her car in the background was all over the internet. Someone had thoughtfully placed a circle around the license plate of her car, so that everyone would know April was there.

She was sure whoever was left on the r/truewell thread blamed her for this new massacre. Two cultists had escaped from the compound. A man and a woman, both no doubt harboring a murderous rage toward April. It was a stark reminder that this would never be over for her.

But then again, the two cultists who had escaped the compound left behind a trail of bodies. They had every reason to lie low—for now. One of them might even be Zach's uncle David.

She went to the thread.

A post disappeared.

And then another.

Years of posts vanished as April watched.

The only person who could do that was the thread moderator. TH3D33PW311.

Anyone reading would have mistaken realamy7070 for the moderator, since she'd led most of the discussions.

Realamy7070 was dead.

Amy had seemed like the leader of the cultists, but maybe she wasn't. One of the people who escaped the compound had to be the moderator.

The Deep Well—TH3D33PW311—was purging the thread. April supposed she should be grateful, but the sight of line after line of text disappearing filled her with a numb horror.

Who was making this happen?

But it was worse when it stopped suddenly.

She heard a breath near her left ear.

She looked down at her phone.

Hello April, typed in TH3D33PW311.

She scanned the room, her heart pounding. Jules lounged nearby on the couch, playing a video game, absorbed in an imminent attack on a snowbound fortress.

Her phone! Someone had hacked the camera. She'd never fixed that.

Too busy with the apocalypse.

She turned her phone off and shoved it in her purse.

"Can I borrow your phone for a minute?" April asked Jules in the most casual tone she could manage.

Jules was absorbed in the video game battle and gestured with her head toward her phone on the couch. Jules put the game on pause, unlocked the phone, and handed it to April without a word. Fortunately, Jules didn't ask why.

Jules didn't have the Reddit app installed, so April did that. While she waited for the app to load, she found a Band-Aid and placed the sticky sides over the front and back camera.

When April got back on the thread, *Hello April* was gone. More comments had disappeared.

And then it stopped. April sucked in a breath. She couldn't help it.

Jules looked up warily and went back to her game.

How is Jules? TH3D33PW311 posted. **Tell me, where did she leave the wrench?**

The message vanished an instant after it was posted. It was a message for her alone.

All the oxygen seemed to have left the room. They were in a spaceship running out of air, perilously close to being sucked into another dimension. They were being watched every day from all angles.

Someone who had witnessed everything that day knew that Jules had hit Trev with the wrench. What kind of person witnesses a stranger taking a twelve-year-old girl to a place as dangerous as the compound and doesn't intervene?

It had to be someone from the cult.

She'd seen all six of the cultists up close. Their murderous, rapt faces as Trev went into the pit. She wished she could forget.

But the cultists had arrived after Jules had swung the wrench at Trev. Any one of the cultists seeing the bloody wrench and Trev on the ground, away from the pile of pipes, would have put two and two together and assumed that April had hit Trev. April remembered the appreciative look Amy had given her when she spied a body on the ground.

Jules had gone by then. How did the cultists even know she was there?

Who told them that Jules had been the one to hit Trev on the head with the wrench?

April looked up at Jules. She was intently focused on her game, her eyes tracking motion on the screen. It made April happy to see Jules doing—something. More games, more ice cream, more fun. She understood now, why her mom had given her endless orange sodas and trips to the motel pool after the massacre. When the fun stopped, the darkness closed in. It was always there, waiting.

April suppressed a shiver. She reminded herself that it was easy to be this creepy from a distance. April had been a master of long-distance creepy.

But now, she was done with playing games.

What do you want?

No answer. TH3D33PW311, whoever they were, was continuing to purge the back threads. April grunted in frustration. Fighting with cultists was like fighting a ghost. The cult could go underground, reappear in twelve years with new members and new lies to tell. The only common denominator, the need for a sacrifice. And when they did show up again, would they return with the wrench?

If they planned to threaten Jules, they'd have to come through her first.

"What do you want?" April murmured.

Jules looked up from her game and frowned.

"Who are you talking to?" she asked.

389

"No one," April replied.

She tried to smile. Given the look on Jules's face, her smile was less than convincing.

"You should stay off the internet," Jules said before returning her eyes to her game.

April suppressed an eye roll. Jules, of all people, telling her to stay off the internet. Rich.

You know what I want.

The answer came from a voice, bright and childlike. So loud that April looked around the room to see where the voice had come from. She wanted to see if Jules had heard it too, but Jules continued with her game, unmoving. She hadn't heard it.

The voice came from inside her head.

April heard a small Kiki giggle in the back of her mind.

The voice had never really left her.

She knew what the voice wanted.

Pure chaos. Pure joy. It was all the voice had ever wanted from her. It was all it had ever wanted from anyone. It crawled inside your mind and offered you the thing you wanted most in the world, in exchange for confusion and death.

It wanted April back.

She knew that now.

And it would do anything, including use Jules, to bring her out to the compound again.

390

April stared at the phone screen as back posts disappeared into oblivion.

The last post.

Goodbye, April. For now.

And then, her name vanished like a puff of smoke in a breeze. Like the drifting sound of a voice from a well.

ACKNOWLEDGMENTS

I know there are authors out there who write a clean draft, but I'm not one of them. Every time I kill a subplot, my ADHD brain spits out three more. I need a good editor more than most.

Courtney Stevenson is not just a good editor, she is a great editor. She closed off a half dozen blind alleys and tied up all the loose ends in this novel with superhuman patience and good humor.

My agent, Jim McCarthy, encouraged me to make the leap into the genre I love most of all—horror. I am so lucky to have his continued support.

Thank you, Erika West and Danielle McClelland, for your amazing attention to detail. Thank you to Sam Wolfe Connelly, David L. DeWitt, and Joel Tippie for a book that gives me the chills just to look at—in the best possible way! Thanks to Matt Maguda, Michael D'Angelo, and Anna Ravenelle for their support.

I would never have finished a novel without Tahereh Safavi and the Ubergroup. Her unwavering commitment to helping other writers humbles me.

My appreciation to all the writers in the Ubergroup, especially the Monday night regulars. Thanks for listening.

Continued thanks to my husband, Henry, for putting up with me, and for all the coffee.